Memphis Belle

WARNER BROS. *Presents*

An ENIGMA PRODUCTION

"MEMPHIS BELLE"

MATTHEW MODINE   ERIC STOLTZ   SEAN ASTIN

HARRY CONNICK, JR.   REED EDWARD DIAMOND   TATE DONOVAN *and*

JOHN LITHGOW   D.B. SWEENEY   BILLY ZANE   COURTNEY GAINS   NEIL GUINTOLI

Music by GEORGE FENTON   *Written by* MONTE MERRICK

Produced by DAVID PUTTNAM *and* CATHERINE WYLER

Directed by MICHAEL CATON-JONES

K.H.

Р.Н.

MEMPHIS ★ BELLE

A Novel by Monte Merrick
Based on a Screenplay by Monte Merrick

BERKLEY BOOKS, NEW YORK

MEMPHIS BELLE

A Berkley Book / published by arrangement with Warner Bros., Inc.

PRINTING HISTORY
Berkley edition / October 1990

ISBN: 0-425-12313-8

A BERKLEY BOOK® TM 757,375
Berkley Books are published by The Berkley Publishing Group,
200 Madison Avenue, New York, New York 10016.
The name ''Berkley'' and the ''B'' logo
are trademarks belonging to Berkley Publishing Corporation.

PRINTED IN THE UNITED STATES OF AMERICA

10 9 8 7 6 5 4 3 2 1

MEMPHIS
⭐
BELLE

1

Shortly after lunch, at 1310 hours, Lieutenant Luke Sinclair took off his shirt and stretched out on the broad wing of a B-17 to get a suntan. It was overcast and damp, but Luke had an instinct about the sun. When his shirt came off, the sun always came out.

The crew looked up at the sky with anticipation. There would have been nothing exciting about sunshine back in the States on a spring day in the middle of May, but this was England, and for the past six months the English weather had been wind, fog, cloud and rain, rain, rain.

Sure enough, not long after Luke stripped to the waist and lay down for a little nap, the clouds miraculously rolled away and sunlight poured down bright and hot. It made everyone want to play. So the football came out of Jack's locker, Virge rounded up the other guys, and now they were on the thirty-yard line, the closest they'd been to a touchdown since the game began.

"Okay, Jack will hike to me. I'll pass to Danny. Danny,

1

get out as far as you can," Virge said. He had appointed himself team captain.

"Virge, I can't catch," Danny said. "Throw to somebody else."

"I'll send it right into your arms. Just open them up," Virge reassured him.

"Pass to me!" Rascal said excitedly. "I'll make the touchdown!" This was vintage Rascal. Although Rascal was only eighteen years old and five foot five and a half inches tall, he thought he could do anything. He could walk on water better than Jesus, tell jokes better than Bob Hope, and make love better than Clark Gable.

"Rascal, shut up," Virge said. "Okay, here's the play. I'll pass to Clay. Everybody else block. Break." They all clapped once and moved to the scrimmage line.

Virge was really taking the game seriously, but that didn't surprise anybody. Virge was a very serious young man, especially when he started talking about that crazy hamburger restaurant he wanted to open. Virgil Hoogesteger was nineteen with sandy, wavy hair that never quite stayed in place. When he got excited, his cheeks flushed bright pink.

He was the kind of guy who had been a shrimp all his life, until one day he woke up and discovered that he was six feet tall with broad shoulders. Maybe that's why he always looked slightly surprised. He came from Duluth, Minnesota, wherever that was. Nobody on the crew had ever been to Minnesota.

Virge hiked the ball into Clay Busby's broad, rough hands and the two teams charged at each other. It had started out as two-hand touch football, but of course that hadn't lasted very long. Now the two teams were tackling each other as hard as they could and trying to slam each other into the ground.

Clay faded back and looked for someone to pass to. He saw Rascal waving frantically, but before Clay could throw to him, the little guy was squashed into the ground by a hulking halfback. Nobody else was in the clear, so Clay started to run. For some reason he found himself singing "Puttin' on the Ritz" as he ran.

Songs just popped into Clay Busby's head. It was funny how most of the songs fit the situation. "Puttin' on the Ritz" didn't suit a football game much, but it was a good song, anyway. Clay learned to sing and play piano when he worked in his daddy's import-export business in New Orleans. Import-export was the genteel name for it. The crude name was whorehouse.

Clay hadn't even gotten to his favorite part of the song, the part about trying hard to look like Gary Cooper, when someone slammed into him and he was down on the forty-yard line. They had lost ten yards, but Clay didn't worry about it. Clay didn't worry about anything.

The most important lesson in life, Clay believed, was not to let anything bother you. Life went on whether you worried about it or not. Maybe it was being a farmer that made Clay so easygoing. His first daddy had the import-export business. His second daddy had a farm.

On the farm Clay learned that things are born and things die every day—it's no use getting excited about it. Your fate is in the cards and you don't shuffle the deck. You might as well sit back, have a smoke, and see what happens. Clay found himself humming "Life Is Just a Bowl of Cherries" as he jogged back to the huddle.

"Okay, Rascal, you're hiking to me," Virge said in his serious, team captain voice. He had taken a tumble during the last play and had a grass stain on his right cheek. It made him look even more like a kid. "I'll fake like I'm passing to Clay and they'll think we're doing the same play again. But I'll really pass to Jack or Eugene, whoever's in the clear."

"I'll be in the clear," Jack said confidently.

"So will I," said Eugene with just as much confidence.

"Okay, break," Virge said. They clapped once and got into position. Two scaffolds were set up at either end of the field as goalposts. The ground crews used the scaffolds to work on the planes. It was a ground crew they were playing, too—big, hulking brutes who were steelworkers or coal miners when there wasn't a war on.

"Thirty-six, twenty-four, thirty-six," Rascal called out, and hiked the ball to Virge. Virge jogged backward and looked for Jack and Eugene. There they were, side by side. Those guys were always together. They made Siamese twins look like pen pals.

"Jack, Gene!" Virge shouted, then sailed the ball to them. Later it was a matter of debate whether Jack bumped into Eugene or Eugene bumped into Jack. Regardless of whose fault it was, Jack and Eugene both jumped for the ball, crashed into each other, and fell to the ground swearing.

The ball sailed past them and right into Danny Daly's arms. Danny couldn't have been more surprised. He had never been much of an athlete. In high school he used to cut physical education classes and go off by himself to read. He didn't like any sport very much, but he really hated football. It was violent and stupid and didn't make sense. Now here he was, about to score a touchdown for his team.

"Go, Danny, go!" the team shouted. Danny ran toward the goalpost. Danny was twenty-one and had red hair. If there was a contest for the world's reddest hair, Danny would be in the finals. He would also be a contestant for the guy with the greatest number of freckles.

His heart was pounding in his chest. He knew one of those huge, sweaty ground-crew members was right on his tail. Danny ran a little faster. His team was counting on him and he didn't want to let them down. He didn't care about football but he cared about his crew.

He felt two strong arms grabbing him around the waist. He was a foot from the goal line. He flung himself up in the air, dragging his tackler along. Whatever happens, don't let go of the ball, Danny told himself. As he fell on

4

the grass with his opponent on top of him, Danny saw that he was over the goal line. He had done it—the first touchdown of his life.

He jumped to his feet, raised the ball in triumph, and shouted in exhilaration. He looked at his teammates, expecting them to be cheering and shouting his name.

They weren't. They were looking at a plane that had appeared right behind Danny's head. It was a giant, olive-drab B-17 bomber name *Doll Face*. Painted on the side of the nose was a pretty girl looking at herself in the mirror. Her enormous breasts were only partially covered by a lacy brassiere. Most of the planes had girls painted on their noses. Not a single one was flat-chested.

The plane roared overhead, so low that the prop wash ruffled Danny's hair. He noticed that the plane had one feathered prop. The propeller on Engine Four, the farthest engine on the right wing, wasn't turning. Danny and his crew had lost an engine on their last mission. Their plane was still in the shop. It was called *Memphis Belle*.

"Two! Three! Four!" Men were coming from all over the base on foot or bicycle and shouting out the number of planes in the air. The football game, which had seemed like a matter of life and death only a moment before, was forgotten. Danny, Virge, and the rest of the team ran toward the control tower.

"Eight, nine!"

"You counted that one twice!"

"I did not. Ten, eleven!"

The horizon was filling with planes. Some were grouped in twos or threes, others flew alone. They looked no bigger than sea gulls on the horizon, but as they got near they became huge.

"There's two more." Eugene pointed out above the trees.

"How many went out?"

"Twenty-one."

A red flare shot up into the sky. The flare meant there

5

was a wounded man aboard one of the planes, perhaps a dead man. An ambulance streaked across the field.

Men were gathering on the lawn below the boxy, two-story control tower. Others gathered on the second-floor balcony. Dogs barked. A siren wailed. More planes appeared in the sky. Five minutes ago the base had been so quiet, you could have heard a baseball fall into a mitt halfway across the field. Now it was bustling with activity.

Bassingbourn was in the middle of the countryside. There were sheep grazing on the other side of the barbed-wire fence and a church steeple could be seen in the distance. In this sleepy corner of East Anglia, sixty miles northeast of London, it was easy to forget the world was at war. Now, as a plane came down on the landing strip with half of its tail missing, you knew that there was a war out there—a scary one.

"Where did they go today?" Rascal asked.

"Saint-Nazaire," Danny answered. Danny had been to Saint-Nazaire twice. It was a Nazi submarine base on the western coast of France. Funny—a year ago Danny had hardly been out of Philadelphia. Now he'd been to England and France and Germany. He liked Philadelphia better.

Danny looked across the field. A wounded man was being removed from a plane. The man's arm was bloody, but someone was lighting a cigarette for him, so maybe he'd be all right.

"Fourteen!" Virge shouted, spotting another plane. "Fourteen or fifteen? I've lost count."

"Fourteen," Eugene said, "but there's fifteen right there." Another sea gull had appeared on the horizon.

Saint-Nazaire was not an easy target. The submarine pens were made of concrete ten feet thick. It was said that the bombs bounced off those submarine pens like rubber balls. There were German fighter squadrons and antiaircraft batteries all around Saint-Nazaire. It wasn't easy. It wasn't as easy as going to the soda fountain to get a malted, that's for sure.

But at least Saint-Nazaire was in France. Going to France was a picnic compared to going to Germany. Last week Danny and his crew had bombed Wilhelmshaven in northern Germany. The trip had taken seven hours. The sky was full of fighters and flak almost the whole time.

Now there was a rumor that Bomber Command was going to start sending the crews even deeper into Nazi Germany—maybe all the way to Berlin. Danny was glad he wouldn't be here for that.

Danny and his crew were almost finished. The Air Force had put a limit on the number of bombing missions the men could fly. The magic number was twenty-five. The crew of the *Memphis Belle* had completed twenty-four. One more and they would go home.

No crew had ever made it to twenty-five. Danny and his crew were kind of famous for having flown twenty-four missions without getting killed. It was said that the average flier was shot down on his sixteenth mission. Some made it to twenty, others went down on their first mission, but one thing was for sure: Everyone got killed sooner or later.

If the crew of the *Memphis Belle* survived their last mission, they would be the first crew in the Eighth Air Force to complete their tour of duty. Everybody said that the last one would be a "milk run"—a trip as safe and simple as a milkman's route through the neighborhood.

"Sixteen! Seventeen! Eighteen!" The planes kept coming in. The men kept calling out the numbers.

Colonel Craig Harriman was trying to keep his temper. He wanted to be out on the balcony of the control tower as he always was when the planes came back. Instead he was inside the tower listening to General Markham tell him that tomorrow's mission would be the toughest one yet. A lot of boys were going to get killed, and Harriman

7

better be prepared for it. Craig felt that ulcer eating away at his stomach.

"Sir, they're still coming in. How can I promise you twenty-four planes tomorrow when they're not even back from today's mission?"

"I need every plane you've got, Craig. If you have to stick them together with chewing gum, I want them in the air tomorrow. We're attacking Bremen and . . ."

"Where?" Craig asked. He was sure he had heard wrong. The security scrambler on the telephone made the bad connection even worse.

"Bremen!" Markam repeated. "This is the big push."

"But we hit Bremen a month ago," Craig started to say, but Markham interrupted. Craig pictured his superior officer: a big, bullish man with a bullying personality.

"We've got to hit it again. Intelligence says the Focke-Wulf plant is up and running again. Tomorrow we're going to make mincemeat of it once and for all."

"General, I know we have to put the pressure on, but I lost almost a quarter of my men last time—" General Markham interrupted again. He didn't want to hear about casualty figures. He only wanted to know how many planes Colonel Harriman could put in the air tomorrow morning. He used his line about chewing gum again.

One month ago Craig Harriman had stood on the control-tower balcony and counted the planes as they returned from their first mission to Bremen. Twenty planes went up that day. Sixteen returned, but one was so badly battered that it was only good for parts. The thought of returning to Bremen made Craig Harriman's neck tighten like steel cable.

"Yes, sir," he repeated automatically to Markham's comment that the Air Force had sustained acceptable losses on the last Bremen sortie. Craig hated that phrase, "acceptable losses." He wondered if the loss of any young man's life was "acceptable," but he didn't contradict General Markham. Craig was used to following orders.

Craig Harriman was a career man. He had joined up in 1933, when his father's shoe manufacturing business collapsed in the third year of the Great Depression. Jobs were scarce and the Army promised a regular paycheck. Craig had a wife and two small children—two boys.

"Yes, sir, I'll have my ground crews working all night on the planes. I was hoping to give them a little break. We're having a dance tonight. It's the Group's first anniversary . . ." he started to say, but General Markham didn't care about the dance or the Group's first anniversary. He kept talking about the big show tomorrow. He wanted a sky filled with planes.

Comstock, the S-2 Intelligence officer, came into the control tower from the balcony. He had been identifying the planes as they returned, checking them off on his master list. Craig was anxious to know the count, so he hurriedly wrapped up the conversation with Markham.

"Yes, sir, I'll give you an update as soon as I know more. Good-bye, sir," he said, and hung up before Markham could use his line about chewing gum for the third time.

"Sir, eighteen planes have returned. Three are still out," Comstock reported. Craig hurried out the glass doors to the narrow balcony overlooking the field. Below was a green lawn crowded with fliers watching the planes return. To the left of the tower an American flag rippled in the light breeze.

"So that's them," said the man from Washington as he leaned on the railing, looking down at the men below. "The crew of the *Memphis Belle*."

Craig Harriman had completely forgotten about Bruce Derringer. Derringer had just flown in that morning from Washington. He was a big man, half a foot taller than Craig, impeccably dressed. After a twenty-hour flight from the States he looked spruce and refreshed. Harriman wondered how Derringer did it. Perhaps the fellow Derringer had brought along was his personal valet. No, Craig re-

9

membered, the young man was a photographer from *Life* magazine.

Derringer was looking down at the six boys who had been playing football when the planes started coming back. "Those are the enlisted men," Craig Harriman told Derringer. "You're meeting the officers this afternoon."

"They must be the ten luckiest sons of bitches in the world," Bruce Derringer said with a smile.

Bruce Derringer said everything with a smile. Derringer had been a Madison Avenue advertising man before the war. The Army enlisted him to help salvage their public relations efforts. In one year Bruce completely revamped the Army's war bond campaign, raising heroic sums of money. He was honored at the White House for his work and was promoted to colonel. Derringer never even went through boot camp, Craig thought bitterly. He was handed his commission on a silver platter because the Army needed him.

Now they had assigned Derringer to the Eighth Air Force, a division of the U.S. Army, and put him in charge of a new public relations campaign: to convince the American public that daylight bombing was essential to the war effort. The ten-man crew of the *Memphis Belle* was the key to the campaign.

"They're ordinary men, Colonel," Craig said.

"Are you kidding? First they volunteer for this, then they fly twenty-four missions without a scratch. They don't sound very ordinary to me—"

"Two more, sir," Comstock interrupted, nodding toward the horizon.

Harriman raised his binoculars and looked out over the gently rolling landscape. There they were, two Flying Fortresses flying side by side. Now only one was unaccounted for. Craig felt his neck relax a little. Perhaps today all of his men would return. But then he remembered that tomorrow he would be sending them to the most dangerous target of all—Bremen.

"You know, people at home are getting pretty discouraged by our losses," Bruce Derringer said, putting a relaxed foot up on the railing. "They're starting to think that daylight bombing is a mistake. It's too dangerous. They're saying we should bomb at night, like the RAF."

"Daylight bombing is the only way we're going to win this war, Colonel," Craig said automatically. It was an old argument, whether to bomb at day or at night. Daylight bombing was more accurate but far more dangerous. Night bombing was safer but often missed the target.

"You're right," Bruce said with typical enthusiasm, "and we've got to get that message across. That's where I come in. The nation's going to fall in love with those boys. The first crew in the Eighth Air Force to complete their tour of duty."

"They haven't done it yet," Craig Harriman warned. He was superstitious and didn't believe in counting on anything until it happened. Ten years of Army life had made Craig a realist. Bruce Derringer wasn't a realist, but he hadn't been in the Army very long. Give him time.

"They will," Bruce said. Then he added, with a significant glance at Craig Harriman, "You'll make sure of it."

Craig was reminded of his first conversation with Bruce Derringer. Derringer tried to make him promise that the *Memphis Belle*'s final mission would be a milk run to insure that the plane and its crew returned safely. Craig was as anxious as anyone to have the *Belle* survive its twenty-fifth mission, but he had made no promises to Bruce Derringer.

And now he knew that tomorrow's target was Bremen. HQ wanted him to put twenty-four planes in the sky. Craig had a total of twenty-five planes on the base. If even one ship failed to return from today's mission, tomorrow he would be forced to send the *Belle* to Bremen. Craig Harriman was not a religious man, but he prayed that the final plane would come home. If it didn't, he had the feeling that Bruce Derringer was going to cause a lot of trouble.

"One more. Just one more." On the lawn below the control tower balcony, Danny and his crew scanned the skies for the last plane. "Wouldn't it be great if everyone came back today? I mean, with the dance tonight and everything."

"I give them four to one," Clay said, lighting a cigarette. Clay took odds on everything—craps or men's lives, it was all the same to him. "Any takers?"

"Me," said Jack. Jack bet on everything. He didn't care if the odds were terrible, he just loved the whole notion of betting. Jack was always broke.

Jack wasn't much bigger than Rascal, but he had a big man's personality. He had a compact, punchy body, a gravelly voice and teeth so crooked and spaced out that nobody could figure out how he ate with them. Jack came from a tough neighborhood in Chicago, so fighting the Germans was just like being back home.

"Show me your money, Jack," said Clay.

"Gene, lend me some money," Jack said, turning to his partner without missing a beat.

"What do I look like, Wells Fargo?" Eugene acted annoyed, but he was already dipping into his pocket.

Eugene McVey was as quiet as Jack was loud. He was the kind of kid everyone picked on in school: skinny, funny-looking, and always sick. He was the last person you'd think would be a waist gunner. He looked like someone who would work in the mess hall or have a job swabbing out the latrine. But two of the seven little swastikas painted on the side of the *Belle*'s nose were Eugene's. They represented the two Nazi fighters he had knocked out of the sky. Eugene McVey was a hell of a shot.

Jack and Eugene were like an old married couple who fought about everything but couldn't live without each other. Danny once told Jack and Eugene that they re-

12

minded him of his parents, and they pounded him into the ground.

Danny saw something on the horizon. At first he thought it was a plane, but no, it was just a bird. It was looking like that last ship wouldn't be coming back. That was too bad. Those guys would miss the first dance they'd had in five months.

Danny wondered if they would play "In the Mood" tonight. "In the Mood" was Danny's favorite song. He didn't really care what they played, as long as they didn't play "Danny Boy". "Danny Boy" was the song he hated the most.

Then Danny realized that even with twenty-twenty vision, he couldn't see a bird so far away on the horizon. "There they are!" he shouted. Sure enough, it was an olive-drab Flying Fortress, all thirty tons of it. On the ground a B-17 looked too heavy to get up in the air, but once it was up, it was magnificent.

The boys were relieved to see the last plane appear, and they pushed each other around and tried to trip one another. Then they started walking across the base, back to the barracks. They had three and a half hours to kill before the dance.

"I heard they brought in a swell band for the dance tonight," said Virge.

"Clay, maybe they'll let you sing with them!" Danny said. Big bands had come to the base twice before, and both times Danny had tried to get Clay up on the bandstand to sing. Both times Clay refused. Nobody could understand why Clay wouldn't sing in public. He was a great singer.

"No siree. You got the wrong man."

"You sing to us in the plane all the time," said Eugene.

"Yeah, but you guys ain't got no taste."

"Clay, do 'Roll Me Over in the Clover!' " suggested Rascal. Rascal couldn't open his mouth without mentioning sex. He was always telling stories about his sexual adventures, and nobody knew whether to believe him or not. He told everyone that he had lost his virginity when he was sixteen to a snake charmer in the circus. Nobody really believed it. On the other hand, who would make that up?

Danny heard the sputtering and coughing of an engine behind him. He turned to look. The last plane was coming in to land, but only one of its two front landing wheels were down. Virge also turned around to look. Virge was a flight engineer, and the moment he saw the crippled plane, he knew it was in trouble.

The plane touched the runway with its left wheel, immediately tipped to the right, and began scraping its belly on the tarmac of the landing strip. The prop blades bent back and sent a shower of sparks into the air. The big plane spun around on its one wheel. It wasn't a graceful landing, but at least it was on the ground.

Then it exploded. The first blast blew the right wing off, sending it twisting through the air like it was made of balsa wood. The second blast disintegrated the plane. Danny was two hundred yards away, but he felt the scorching heat of the explosion on his face. It felt like someone had opened an oven door.

On the control tower balcony, Bruce Derringer was reeling from the explosion. Ten men were aboard that plane. Bruce had never seen a man die before. He had only one previous experience with death. When he was ten, his puppy had been put to sleep.

"Come on, Bruce," Craig Harriman said, stone-faced and seemingly not affected by the disaster. "You wanted to meet the officers of the *Memphis Belle*."

"Jesus, what happened?" Bruce asked in shock. "They were home."

"The pilot came in on one wheel. He should have belly-landed," Harriman explained.

"Are they all dead?" Bruce asked. Black smoke was streaming upward from the wreckage and gathering in a

14

big cloud above the airfield. Fire engines and ambulances were racing toward the crash site.

Craig Harriman didn't answer. No answer was needed. "Let's go, Colonel," he said, walking toward the glass doors of the control tower.

Bruce was as stunned by Harriman's attitude as he was by the horror out on the field. Ten men had died in front of Harriman's eyes, yet the commanding officer hadn't even blinked. *What kind of man am I dealing with*? Bruce Derringer asked himself as he followed Harriman into the control tower.

In fact, Craig Harriman was terribly shaken by the explosion, but he would not allow himself to show it—not to Bruce Derringer or to anyone. These days he couldn't afford the luxury of sorrow. He had a base to run and a war to win. Feelings only got in the way.

It was best to put the accident out of his mind, at least until he wrote the letters. He would have to write ten letters of condolence to the families of the men who died in the explosion. He always wrote to the families of the dead or missing. Craig Harriman wrote a lot of letters.

He forced himself to concentrate on tomorrow's mission. His orders were to put twenty-four planes in the air. If all of the ships had returned today, he would have been able to spare the *Memphis Belle* from the Bremen sortie and give them a milk run for their final mission. But Craig Harriman had just lost his twenty-fourth plane. Tomorrow the *Memphis Belle* would have to fly.

2

Captain Dennis Dearborn sat stiffly in the straight-backed chair in the officer's club. He wanted to cooperate with the man from Washington, but something about Bruce Derringer got under his skin.

"So you named your plane after your girl back home. That's a great angle," said Derringer, glancing at his notes. "But you don't sound like you're from the South, Captain Dearborn."

"I met her when I was in Memphis on business," Dennis replied. He didn't like to talk about Margaret. Other men discussed their wives and girlfriends as if they were public property, but Margaret was nobody's business but his own. They had met when she was a telephone receptionist at a Memphis furniture store and Dennis was working as a sales representative for his father's company.

Dennis had begun working for Dearborn Furniture immediately after he graduated from Michigan State with a business degree and a 4.0 average. He expected to be given an executive position in the firm, but his father made him

17

a junior sales rep instead and Dennis went on the road. He spent two years driving all over the country in his 1937 Packard which had a tendency to overheat. Five years after he started with Dearborn Furniture he was promoted to vice president of Marketing.

On December 1, 1941, Dennis and Margaret became engaged. On December 7, 1941, the Japanese bombed Pearl Harbor, and the following day Dennis enlisted in the Army.

Dennis Dearborn was twenty-six years old and stood exactly six foot tall, which was really too tall to fit comfortably in the cockpit of a B-17. He volunteered for the Air Force because, after all that driving around the country, he was sick of being on the ground. The sky would be a nice change. He passed pilot school with flying colors, but there was shortage of planes and he waited almost a year before he got his own ship. He named her *Memphis Belle.*

Dennis was self-conscious about his height, so he carried himself very straight and held himself very still. He kept his hands at his sides because he thought they were too big for his body. When he spoke, he looked you straight in the eye. He almost never smiled.

"I bet the real Memphis Belle's a living doll, huh, Dennis?" said Bruce Derringer with a sly grin. He was trying to get Dearborn to loosen up so the *Life* magazine photographer could get a decent picture of Dennis. Dennis was so expressionless, he could have been carved in stone.

"She's a very fine woman, sir," Dennis replied stiffly.

The photographer took the picture, and Dennis blinked from the flash. He hated having his picture taken. He hated the whole idea of making a fuss about the *Memphis Belle.* He and his crew were nothing special. They were just doing a job.

But if the photo turned out well, he would send one to Memphis. For some reason Margaret couldn't get enough of his pointy, boyish face.

• • •

From his years in advertising Bruce Derringer had learned to rely on first impressions. His first impression of Dennis Dearborn was that the young pilot took himself very seriously. He had a U.S. Army Air Force regulation poker up his ass.

Luke Sinclair was something else again. The copilot was as relaxed as Dennis was tense and as friendly as Dearborn was standoffish. Luke almost preened in front of the camera. He ought to be a movie actor, Bruce thought. He even has a little bit of a tan.

"So you were a lifeguard before the war," Bruce said, picturing Luke on the beach surrounded by adoring women and only occasionally glancing at the water to see if anyone was drowning. "That's a pretty responsible job, Luke."

"Yeah, it's rough basking in the sun all day, having girls swarming all over you," Luke said with a grin as the *Life* magazine photographer focused his camera on him. Luke turned a little to the left so the lens could catch the angle of his jaw. His jaw was one of his best features.

"Getting a golden tan. Being out in the fresh air every day," Luke continued the list. "Yeah, it's rough. That's why I decided to enlist in the Air Force. I had to get away from all that."

Luke smiled. His teeth were another of his good features. They were very white and perfectly even. He brushed his teeth for a half hour each night to get rid of the cigarette stains. He had blond wavy hair. His hair was another of his good features.

The photographer snapped the picture. Luke knew it was a good one. To tell the truth, he rarely took a bad picture. There was just something about his face that loved the camera. He imagined the photo on the cover of the popular weekly magazine. That wouldn't exactly hurt his acting career.

Yes, Bruce Derringer thought to himself, *you can al-*

19

ways trust your first impressions. My first impression of Lieutenant Luke Sinclair is that this guy is a winner.

I wish I could be more like Luke, Val Kozlowski thought as he waited for the *Life* photographer to take his picture. *Luke practically made love to the camera. I've never been more nervous in my life. I'm more nervous than I was on my first bomb run.*

"Val. That's an unusual name. What's that short for, Valentine?" Bruce Derringer asked. Val didn't answer. He pulled at his cuffs, then straightened his tie. How come his collar suddenly seemed so tight? He had worn this shirt a million times.

"I bet the women love that name," Bruce added, trying to elicit a response from the twitchy bombardier.

Val hated his name. What kind of a name was Valentine for a fellow? The only thing it was good for was toughening him up in the playground after school. He'd learned how to fight real fast.

"You're the bombardier," said Bruce, referring to his notes. He had to find something in Kozlowski's file to engage the bombardier's interest and take his mind off the picture-taking session. Kozlowski was a good-looking guy. He had an almost matinee-idol handsomeness, with dark, wavy hair slightly receding at the temples and a pencil-thin mustache.

"It says here you've got four years of medical school under your belt," Bruce said, hoping this would get a response and make the bombardier stop fidgeting.

Val shifted uneasily, reached down, and pulled up his left sock. Christ, he thought, how did Colonel Derringer find out about that? It was true that he had gone to medical school, but not for four years. He had attended classes for exactly two and a half weeks.

The rumor that Val was a doctor had started nine months ago when the crew first arrived in England. Eugene, the right waist gunner, had fallen off his bicycle and twisted his ankle. He was convinced it was broken. Val examined him and saw that it was only a slight sprain. He told Eugene to keep the leg elevated and to soak it in cold water every two hours.

When the ankle healed, Eugene acted as though Val had cured him of leprosy. He started calling him Doc and told the crew that Val could cure anything. Now, whenever anyone got as much as a hangnail, he came running to Val. Val didn't exactly lie that he had attended medical school for four years, but when the rumor spread, he didn't deny it.

Two and a half weeks after Val started medical school his father died of a heart attack while working a double shift at the shipyard. His father was working extra hard in order to earn the money for Val's schooling. Val had wanted to be a doctor ever since he was a kid, but money was tight.

When his dad died, Val couldn't afford to continue his studies, so he quit school and enlisted in the Army. After the war the Army would help Val pay for medical school, but that seemed very far away.

"Believe me," Bruce Derringer said cheerfully, "when your picture comes out in *Life* magazine, every man, woman, and child in America is going to want you to be their doctor."

Val hadn't thought about this. He considered this whole business of being the first crew to finish twenty-five missions a damn nuisance. But if Derringer was right, it might work in his favor. Perhaps the Army would even let him return to medical school before the war was over. Just the thought of being out of the Army and back in school made him smile.

"That's the way," said Bruce and the *Life* photographer snapped the picture. It was a beauty.

Try to think of all the good things about dying, Phil told himself. *Make a list. First, you won't have to shave every morning. Shaving is a real bore; it will bring relief never to have to do that again. Second, you won't have to worry*

about dying, because you'll already be dead. Third . . .
But Phil Lowenthal couldn't think of a third good thing about dying.

"Phil, look right at the camera," Bruce Derringer coached, but Phil barely heard him.

Phil had never thought about death until after their twentieth mission. On their twentieth mission they bombed Lorient. Plane after plane went down that day, but the *Belle* returned to base without even a flak hole. That's when everyone started talking about the *Memphis Belle* being charmed, and that's when Phil started to believe he was going to die.

He just wasn't lucky. He had never won a single thing in his life. As a kid in Rochester, New York, he'd entered every contest that came along. He cut out entry blanks from newspapers and magazines, filled them out, and sent them in. He never won. At Cornell he was the star of the track team. The coach had great hopes for him and even talked about the Olympics, but Phil never won a single medal. Someone else was always just a little better.

So when he started hearing that the crew of the *Belle* might be the first to crack twenty-five missions, Phil began to sweat. He knew that he would never make it. He just wasn't the hero type. He was the type that the folks back home remembered as "a nice kid." He was the type of guy about whom people said, "Oh, what a shame."

Phil did not take heart from the fact that he and the crew had survived twenty-four missions and had just one more to go. It only meant that he would fuck the whole thing up by getting killed on the last one. That was his luck.

"Sit up straight, Phil. Smile," Bruce said, trying to get the glum navigator to look at the camera.

"What's there to smile about, sir?" Phil asked.

"Well, you guys have finished twenty-four missions," Bruce said in his relentlessly cheerful voice. "One more and you get to go home. That would sure make me smile."

"Well, you're not me," Phil said. He looked down at his fingers. Lately he had been biting his fingernails. They were bitten down to the quick, and he had also been chewing on the skin around his nails. His fingers disgusted him.

"Please, just take the picture," Phil said, as if he were sitting in the electric chair and had grown tired of waiting for the executioner to throw the switch. Bruce realized that he would never get a smiling, Luke Sinclair kind of picture from Phil, so he nodded to the photographer. The bright flash went off.

Phil imagined the photo in a silver frame on his mother's dressing table, a little piece of black crepe draped over the top.

"You'll go back home in your own plane and fly all over the States making speeches, getting people to buy more war bonds, work longer hours, and turn out more planes. And believe me, you'll be wined, womened, and songed from one end of the U.S. to the other. It'll be tough, but we all have to make sacrifices."

Bruce laughed at his own joke and looked at the four officers of the *Memphis Belle*. They were a hodgepodge, all right. The pilot, Dennis Dearborn, was twenty-six going on sixty. Phil, the navigator, was so gloomy he made Frankenstein's monster look like Bob Hope.

Val Kozlowski, the bombardier, had possibilities, but Luke Sinclair was the real prize. The copilot had all-American good looks and boundless enthusiasm. It was no surprise that Luke responded first to Bruce Derringer's pitch.

"Sir, you mean we're going to be famous?" he asked.

"Afraid so, Luke," Bruce replied, and Luke let out a whoop of joy. He pounded on Val, but Val shoved him away. Luke ruffled Phil's hair but Phil ignored him.

Dennis Dearborn shifted slightly in his seat and cleared his throat before he spoke. "Colonel Derringer . . ." he began. Dennis had a surprisingly high voice for someone so tall.

"Call me Bruce," Derringer said with an easy smile, but Dennis didn't call him anything.

"We'll follow your orders to the best of our abilities—" he said, and Bruce quickly interrupted him.

"It's not an order, Dennis. We're working together."

"Yes, sir," Dennis said with a slight hint of disapproval in his voice. "But I would prefer if the enlisted men don't find out about this yet."

"Their pictures in *Life*?" Luke asked incredulously. "Wine, women, and song? You've got to tell them! They'll go nuts!"

"I don't want them going nuts," Dennis said evenly. "Right now I want them thinking about their jobs and that's all."

"Come on, we could do our jobs in our sleep! Why can't they know?"

"Because I said so."

"My father used to say that," Luke said contemptuously. The tension between pilot and copilot didn't escape Bruce Derringer's attention. There's no love lost between these two, he thought.

"Okay, Dennis, you're the boss," Bruce said before a fight could break out between the two young men. "Tell your crew when you think it's right. Gentlemen, thank you for your time."

Dennis, Luke, and Val got to their feet, but Phil remained sitting in the dark green easy chair, his shoulders slumped and his head down. He looked like he just lost his last friend in the world. Val clapped him on the shoulder.

"Come on, Phil, I think you need a drink," he said.

"No I don't," Phil replied, finally struggling to his feet. "I need about ten."

• • •

24

The barracks resembled a huge tin can cut lengthwise and set down in a sea of mud. In the center stood a hissing, potbellied stove that either gave off too much heat or none at all. The concrete floor was littered with cigarette butts and pinups papered the walls. The hut smelled of dirty socks, sweat, cigarette smoke, farts, and an occasional whiff of after-shave.

The radio was tuned to a London station but these days there was more news than music. Nobody was interested in the news. It was never good news, anyway.

"London was bombed last night in what is believed to be a reprisal for the RAF attack on Berlin Saturday night," the newscaster said in his proper British accent. "Air raid sirens sounded in the capital shortly after midnight, and the final all-clear was not heard until several hours later. German bombs exploded in several parts of the city, but casualty figures are not known at this time."

Originally the *Memphis Belle* crew had bunked in with the men from a plane called *Ready, Willing, and Able*, but that plane went down over Hamm a month ago. Now there was a mixed bag of men in the hut—one from this plane, two from that plane. When a man didn't come back from a mission, his bunk was stripped, his possessions removed, and a fresh-faced rookie took his place.

"Clay, shouldn't you let the sergeant go through Becker's stuff?" Danny said as Clay Busby wrenched the lock off the dead man's locker. Becker had been on the plane that came in on one wheel and exploded.

"The sergeant'll just send it all to Becker's widow," Eugene told Danny. "We don't want her getting anything embarrassing. We better do it."

The men were getting ready for the dance: shaving, polishing their shoes, and gluing down their hair with Brylcreem.

Clay sorted through the contents of Becker's locker. Danny didn't know Becker very well. They talked a couple of times, that's all. Becker had only been in their hut for two weeks. He was the same age as Danny, twenty-one,

25

and wore thick, silver-rimmed glasses. He had gotten into the Air Force by memorizing the eye chart.

"Hershey bar," Clay said. Becker's widow wouldn't get much comfort from a candy bar, so it was fair game.

"Me, me!" Virge shouted eagerly, and Clay tossed it to him. Then Clay set some things aside for the widow: a Bible, an extra pair of eyeglasses, a couple of initialed handkerchiefs.

"Danny, which one's better?" Virge asked, munching on the chocolate bar and showing Danny some sketches of the restaurant he planned to open just as soon as the war was over. "This one's all shiny aluminum, very modern. And this one is more homey, with the brick and little bushes. . . ."

Virge was obsessed by his plans for his restaurant. He was always drawing floor plans, making up budgets, and creating menus. The guys made fun of him, but it didn't seem to bother Virge. He had a dream.

"They both look good to me," Danny said, and they did.

"After the first restaurant's open, I'm going to open a whole bunch of them, exactly like the first one. So you can go to Detroit and get the exact same hamburger you got in Baltimore."

"Virge, nobody wants the same old food everywhere they go," Danny said.

"Sure they do," Virge replied, looking lovingly at his drawings. "It's comforting."

Danny wished he knew what he was going to do after the war. Before he'd enlisted in the Army he had worked in a library, but he didn't see much future in that. He liked to write, but he didn't know if he could make a living at it. He wrote poetry sometimes, but mostly he crossed it all out. Danny had high standards.

"Love letters," Clay said, pulling a thick batch of letters from the dead man's locker.

"Wife or girlfriend?" Eugene asked, and Clay opened

one of the letters to find out. They were on blue paper. Danny thought he could smell one of the love letters from across the hut, but it turned out to be Rascal patting on some cologne.

"Read 'em out loud!" Rascal shouted. "Get me in the mood for tonight!"

"Girlfriend," Clay determined after quickly scanning one of the letters. He tossed the pack to Eugene who lifted the lid of the potbellied stove and dropped the letters inside. They flared up with a blue flame.

"Does Becker have any clean socks in there?" Eugene asked, putting the lid back on the stove and walking over to the locker. His own socks stank to high heaven.

"Air medal, photos, pocketknife." Clay continued to itemize the contents of Becker's locker. He put these in the pile for the widow, then he pulled a paperback book from the locker. "Dirty book!"

"I'll take it," Danny said. He needed something to read. He was reading *Great Expectations* for the third time. He liked it, but not enough that he wanted to read it three times. Clay tossed him the book. It was titled *Hothouse Flower*. The cover showed a picture of a woman with her clothes half torn off and a man standing over her with a whip. It looked promising.

Danny paged through the book. A four-leaf clover was stuck in the middle at page 63. It was a real one, wrapped in cellophane.

"Look, Becker forgot his good-luck charm," Danny said, showing it to Virge.

"Poor slob."

"He should've worn it around his neck. Then you never lose it," Eugene said, holding up his St. Anthony medal. Eugene didn't go anywhere without his St. Anthony medal, not even to the latrine. Nobody made fun of him. Almost everyone had some kind of good-luck charm.

Danny glanced down at his left wrist. There it was, his lucky rubber band. The day after he got to the base, somebody asked if he had any cards. He pulled out his deck; they were his mother's and had pictures of two poodles on their backs. They were kind of embarrassing, but they were cards. He took the thick red rubber band off the deck and slipped it around his wrist so he wouldn't lose it. For some reason Danny didn't understand, he had worn the rubber band ever since.

"Rubbers!" Clay called out as he held up a little foil packet.

"Dibs!" Rascal shouted, and Clay tossed him the contraceptives. Rascal examined them with an expert's eye.

"We know Virge the Virgin won't need them," he said. Virge was munching contentedly on his Hershey bar. "Virge, you gotta promise if you ever lose your cherry, you'll tell me about it."

"I'll send it to you. COD," Virge replied.

Danny laughed. Rascal was always tormenting Virge about never getting laid, and it was nice to see Virge have a sense of humor about it. Virge said that he wanted his first time to be with a woman he loved, not a prostitute or tart. Danny thought Virge was probably just scared. Danny had been scared his first time, but it had worked out all right.

Down at the other end of the hut a poker game was going on. It seemed like there was always a poker game going on, and Jack Bocci was always in the center of it. Now he came strolling up and took a ten-dollar bill from the pile of Becker's possessions.

"Becker owed me ten."

"Jack, don't take his money!" Danny complained.

"He owed it to me!" Jack growled. Jack reminded Danny of Popeye the Sailor Man in the funny papers. He was always mad. Even when Jack was happy, he seemed mad.

"Hey, what do you guys know about Germany?" Jack asked.

"Pretty women," Eugene said.

"Good beer," Danny said.

"The hamburger's named after a town here," Virge said. Only he would know a thing like that.

"Well, a little birdie told me that's where they're sending us tomorrow."

There was a moment of shocked silence. The crew assumed that their last mission would be a joyride, a milk run to a French target right across the Channel. This would be their reward for having survived so many missions. It never occurred to them that the last one would be rough.

"You sure?" Eugene asked.

"We ain't going to Krautville," Rascal said confidently. "Our plane's broke."

"No, it's fixed," Virge said.

"Christ, let's go break it!" Rascal exclaimed, and he wasn't joking.

"They wouldn't send us to Germany our last time, would they?" Eugene said, fingering his lucky St. Anthony medal.

"They'll give us a milk run to France, don't you think?" added Danny.

No one had an answer. Last week they had gone to Wilhelmshaven. A month ago they had gone to Bremen, which was even farther into Germany and twice as dangerous. Once they had gone to Hamm, and when they came back, half the bunks in their Nissen hut were empty. The crew of *Ready, Willing, and Able* had gone down before they'd even reached the target. Only one man got out of the plane, and when he opened his parachute, it was on fire.

"Anybody want the rest of this stuff?" Clay asked. He was down to the bottom of the locker. Without a word the boys drifted over to Becker's stripped bunk.

"Deck of cards." Rascal took that.

"Razor blades." Jack needed razor blades.

"Lucky Strikes." Danny could always use another pack.

"Shoelaces." Eugene's were about to break.

"Pack of Doublemint." Virge wanted the gum.

That was it. Becker was gone. All that remained of him was a small pile of possessions on his stained mattress that would be sent home to the widow. Danny wondered if he should put the four-leaf clover in the pile, but he was afraid that Becker's wife would be angry at her husband for forgetting his good-luck charm. Maybe she gave it to him to keep him safe.

No, it was better to let her think that Becker had died for no good reason. It was a bad break. It had nothing to do with good luck or bad luck or four-leaf clovers or lucky rubber bands. It was the way things went. Danny slipped the four-leaf clover into his pocket. It might bring him good luck tonight. Maybe he'd get a girl at the dance.

3

The sharp sound of the trumpets bounced off the corrugated tin roof as the band played "Underneath the Spreading Chestnut Tree." The airplane hangar was swinging. The girls were wearing their prettiest dresses and their best nylons. The airmen looked sharp: uniforms pressed, shoes shined, hair slicked down.

A new B-17 named *Buckaroo* was parked behind the bandstand. Above it hung the bomb group symbol—a red shark in the shape of a bomb, its sharp teeth bared—and a sign reading, HAPPY 1ST ANNIVERSARY. A giant net of sixteen thousand red, white, and blue balloons hung from the ceiling. The bar stretched the entire length of the hangar, and almost everyone had a glass of beer or whiskey in hand.

The dance floor was packed. Servicemen were throwing their girls in the air and catching them as they came down. The girls kicked their legs and showed their garters. The hangar smelled of perfume, cigarette smoke, liquor, and

31

sweat. Tonight they were the four sweetest smells in the world.

Jack Bocci was a surprisingly graceful dancer. His partner, a petite girl with raven-black hair, had no will of her own. She was a puppet in Jack's arms as he swung her out and under his arm and flung her around his back. He could do nothing wrong.

Nearby, Eugene was dancing with Louise. Louise was a short, fleshy girl with a wide, bright smile. Her breasts bounced up and down, left and right as she danced. Eugene could hardly keep his eyes off them. They seemed to have a life of their own.

Eugene swung Louise under his arm, and there it was, Jack's big fat butt. It practically had a sign on it saying "Kick me." Eugene couldn't resist. He planted the shiny toe of his shoe in Jack's right cheek, then whirled back into big Louise's protective embrace. Jack angrily looked around to find the source of the kick, but Eugene had already spun off into the crowd.

Across the room, Rascal was chatting to a doll in a pink-and-green flowered dress. She had milk-white skin, silky blond hair, and a spattering of freckles across her nose and cheeks. She was the sexiest thing Rascal had seen in months, and he was determined to land her. Her name was Faith.

"I heard them saying maybe we're going to Germany tomorrow. . . ." Rascal paused, letting the significance of this sink in. "My short, young life could be snuffed out in an instant. I volunteered for the Air Force because I thought it would be fun. I never dreamed I could get—"

He choked up, and a tear sprang to his eye at the thought of his own death. He was quite proud of himself. *If I don't have this girl in the sack by midnight*, Rascal thought, *they should take away my dick.*

Blimey, this boy is a bore, Faith was thinking. *I wonder how many times he has used this line and if any girl was silly enough to fall for it.*

32

Faith looked away from Rascal. She had to—she was going to laugh right in his face. Across the room by the refreshment table, a young man was standing all alone. *Now he's adorable,* Faith thought. *How come he's by himself and I'm stuck with this silly twit?*

"Oh, Faith, when I think I might never see the stars again or hear good music or talk to a beautiful girl like you . . ." Rascal continued. The tear was trickling down the side of his cheek. He wiped it away but not too quickly. He wanted to make sure Faith got a good look at it.

"You need a drink," Rascal said, taking Faith's empty glass and getting up from the table. "I'll be right back."

He hurried toward the bar, reminding himself to give the bartender a tip so he would pour a little extra gin into Faith's drink. Yes, it looked like Rascal was going to get lucky tonight. Becker's rubbers would come in very handy.

Virge knew he should be asking a girl to dance, but he thought he'd have one more beer first. Maybe that would give him courage. He wasn't much of a dancer. Something always happened when he tried to jitterbug. Someone always got injured.

That's why he froze when the pretty girl in the flowered dress came up to him. He was sure she was going to ask him to dance, and how was he going to turn her down without hurting her feelings? Virge didn't know why girls made him so nervous, but they did. He felt his legs start to tremble, and his face flushed bright pink before Faith even said a single word.

She didn't ask him to dance. She asked him to get her a drink, and then she asked him where he came from, and when he told her, she asked where Minnesota was. She asked him about his family, and that relaxed him a little because he liked talking about his family. Before he knew it, he was telling her about his plans for the restaurant.

"You've never had a hamburger?" Virge's eyes almost popped out when Faith expressed ignorance of his specialty. "That's unbelievable. You don't know what you're missing."

"They sound wonderful. It's been so long since I've had any meat." Rationing had been in effect for so long, Faith could barely remember what it was like to have food that wasn't canned. Just hearing Virge talk about hamburgers made her mouth water.

"See, what I do is . . . May I?" Virge reached for her hand. His hands were broad and smooth. Little blond hairs were sprinkled across the back of them, and one big blue vein ran down the center of each hand.

"I work the meat very slowly. Very tenderly. That's the secret." He closed Faith's hand into a fist and demonstrated his technique, gently massaging her fist.

"Rub in a little Worcestershire, a little garlic, a little thyme." His fingers rubbed in the imaginary ingredients. "Then I ease it into a patty." He loosened her fingers so that her hand opened slowly. He pressed it flat. "Gently, gently," he said, "so I don't bruise the meat."

"Virge, you're making me so hungry," Faith said a little breathlessly. *He doesn't know what he's doing to me,* she thought. *I've got to get him alone.* Faith wanted Virge's hands all over her. She wanted him to treat her whole body like a hamburger.

Five minutes later, when Rascal emerged from the crowded bar with Faith's drink, she was nowhere to be found.

"Phil, come on, you've had enough," Val said as his partner stepped up to the bar for his fifth whiskey of the evening. Val had bought Phil two shots in the officers' club after the meeting with Bruce Derringer. They discussed everything but the bond tour and the spread in *Life* magazine. The whole thing stunk of bad luck, and neither man wanted to think about it. Then they came to the dance and Phil immediately knocked back two more whiskeys.

Phil had the look of a man determined to get blind

drunk. "How come they brought *Life* magazine over and everything?" he asked, slurring his words a little. "Are they trying to jinx us?"

"Just forget it," Val said, looking out at the dance floor. "Let's find us a couple of girls."

The bartender set a brimming glass of whiskey on the bar. Phil drank half of it in one swallow, then, weaving a little, spoke thickly in Val's ear. "Val, tell me the truth. The truth. Are you scared?"

"I'm Val. Come on." Val took the glass from Phil, set it on the bar, and pushed his partner out on the dance floor. Maybe some jitterbugging would sober him up.

"Luke, ever done any public speaking?" Bruce Derringer shouted above the noise of the band. Bruce and Luke were sitting at a table with two very pretty girls. Bruce's girl was named Helen. Or was it Ellen? The music was so loud, he didn't hear her clearly. It didn't matter because Helen or Ellen was far more interested in Luke than she was in Bruce. She could barely take her eyes off the handsome copilot. The girl had good taste.

"A little acting," Luke replied. "Amateur stuff," he added modestly.

"I bet you were good," Bruce said. "We're going to have to excite people on this bond tour. Inspire them. Dennis is a fine man, but he doesn't have your enthusiasm."

"I'm a qualified pilot, too, same as him," Luke said, trying not to whine. "They just didn't have a plane for me. So he's the big-shot pilot and I'm sitting in the dummy seat."

Luke drained his drink. *I probably shouldn't be telling Colonel Derringer all of this*, he thought. *The last thing I need is for this to get back to Dennis*. But Luke felt he could trust Bruce Derringer. The guy seemed pretty smart.

"You're no dummy, Luke," Bruce said, putting a hand on Luke's solid shoulder. "We both know that." Yeah, Luke thought, this guy is pretty damn smart.

• • •

Across the room, Dennis Dearborn was speaking to Pete Bogard, the rookie pilot of a brand-new B-17 called *Mother and Country*. On the nose, instead of a painting of a sexy girl, the plane sported a picture of an eagle perched on an American flag. That afternoon Dennis had seen the ground crew polishing that eagle until it shined.

"Being pilot is . . ." Dennis hesitated, trying to come up with the right words to convey to Bogard the incredible responsibility that would be his when Bogard took his plane up for the first time. "Well, you'll see. You've got nine men depending on you for their lives. You've got five thousand pounds of explosives in the bomb bay. You're flying thirty tons of machinery into enemy territory to defend your country. It's—"

Dennis broke off in mid-sentence. He simply couldn't put it into words. Bogard was staring blankly, as if Dennis were speaking in Hindi. *He must be only two or three years younger than I am,* Dennis thought, *but he makes me feel like I'm his father.*

"What did you do before the war?" Dennis asked, but kept right on talking without giving the rookie lieutenant a chance to answer. "I was in the furniture business. Family business. Dearborn Furniture. Maybe you've heard of it." Bogard didn't reply; obviously he hadn't. "Well, this isn't like making furniture, that's for sure."

Dennis laughed a little. Bogard still didn't say a word. *He thinks I'm crazy,* Dennis suddenly realized. *Either that or I'm boring him to death.*

"Am I making any sense? I bet I'm not," Dennis said. A nervous chuckle came out of his mouth. It surprised him.

"Sure, Captain," Bogard said after a pause. He looked down at his empty glass. "Say, I'm going to get myself a refill. Thanks for the talk." Bogard gave a quick, unnecessary salute and hurried away to the bar.

Dennis was disappointed in himself. He wanted to explain to the young man that flying the plane was only one of a pilot's responsibilities. He also had to be father, confessor, referee, and banker to his men. Dennis knew he could pass on some useful information to the rookie pilot, but when he tried to speak, he found himself hopelessly tongue-tied.

Dennis wished he had taken that public speaking class at Michigan State. He had elected for volleyball instead. Now he was a lousy public speaker, and a lousy volleyball player as well.

He was worried about the upcoming bond tour. Colonel Derringer would probably expect him to make a lot of speeches, and the idea made him nervous. *I should learn to be more spontaneous,* Dennis thought, *be a little more like Luke.*

He spotted Luke sitting with Bruce Derringer across the hangar. Bruce and Luke were acting as if they had known each other their entire lives. Dennis couldn't remember the last time he felt as relaxed as Luke looked right now. Well, we're not here to have fun, Dennis reminded himself. We're here to win a war.

Suddenly the hangar seemed unbearably noisy and smoky, so Dennis walked to the door.

Outside, it was cool and damp. A thick layer of fog had settled over the base like a white blanket. Usually Dennis hated the fog—it was a pilot's worst enemy—but tonight it was comforting. It was like walking in a cloud. He took a sip of his beer and headed for Hangar B.

Three planes were parked inside the huge hangar. Ground-crew members were swarming over them, patching flak holes, working in engines, changing tires. Even after all this time Dennis was still amazed by the manpower required to keep a B-17 in the air. Each plane had mechanics, instrument specialists, radiomen, armament crews, and electricians assigned to it, all under the supervision of the ground-crew chief. The ground crews were the unsung heroes of the war.

Les Enright was a pear-shaped man with a pockmarked face, but he was the best ground-crew chief on the base. He knew the *Memphis Belle* backward and forward. The fact that Dennis and his crew had survived twenty-four missions was in large part due to Les Enright. Perhaps that's why Dennis felt a surge of jealousy when he walked into Hangar B and saw Les working on someone else's plane.

Is You Is Or Is You Ain't My Baby? had really taken a beating. The pilot's window was shattered, the left front tire was flat, and a big chunk was missing from the tail. The ball turret was broken in half and covered with dried blood. A mechanic was hosing it out. A red stream ran across the floor to the drain.

"Les, what are you doing here?" Dennis asked. "You're *my* ground-crew chief. You're supposed to be working on *my* plane." It came out harsher than he intended.

"Sir, I'm just helping out a little with . . ." Les started to say as he helped roll a dolly supporting a new ball turret over to the damaged aircraft.

"You should be giving the supercharger on Number One your full attention." Dennis knew he sounded testy, but he couldn't help it. Engine One worried him.

"The supercharger's fixed."

"Okay, but how about the cowl flaps on Number Three?" Dennis started to ask, but Les answered before he got the words out.

"Number Three's fixed. It's all fixed. You don't have to tell me my job, Captain," Les said. He said it respectfully, but he couldn't hide the edge in his voice. "Watch your feet," Les added, pointing to Dennis's polished shoes.

Dennis looked down. The drain in the floor was plugged, and a dark red pool of blood was gathering right at his feet. He stepped back, slightly nauseated.

"The *Belle*'s in mint condition," Les said. "If you don't believe me, go out and look at her. She's right outside."

Dennis realized that he had jumped on Les. He should have known that Les wouldn't work on any other plane until the *Belle* was shipshape, every nut and bolt of her. Les probably hadn't gotten any sleep for the past twenty-four hours.

Dennis opened his mouth to apologize but stopped himself. *I have nothing to apologize for,* he thought. *My job is to make sure the plane is in perfect working order, even if I have to ruffle a few feathers to get the job done.*

"Okay. Thanks, Les" was all he said, then Dennis left the hangar.

The plane looked beautiful, wrapped in fog. A scaffold was set up under the left wing, and Dennis climbed up to look at the painting on the side of the nose: a shapely girl in a bathing suit with a telephone receiver to her ear. It didn't much look like Margaret, but it was a pretty painting all the same.

"Well, I'm going to miss you, girl." Dennis was surprised to hear himself talking out loud. He glanced around nervously to see if anyone heard him, but the airfield was deserted.

"We've been together a long time and you've never let me down. You know how to take care of your man, and that's just about the best thing a fellow can say about a gal, I guess." It felt good to talk to the plane after being so inarticulate with the rookie pilot and so testy with Les.

A little music was drifting across the field from the hangar. "I remember the first time I saw you," Dennis continued, "not even a year ago. It's hard to believe it's over so soon. It seems like we just got here and now we're going home."

He tried to imagine what home would be like. He would work in the family business and eventually take it over from his dad. He'd marry Margaret and have a family of his own. The base, the crew, and the plane would be just memories.

His life had changed; whether for better or worse, Dennis didn't know. Forty or fifty years down the road, when he looked back at his life, this would be one of the highlights. He loved his command. Much as Luke got under his skin, Dennis couldn't imagine being without him. He wished there was a way the crew could stick together after the war.

"Well, you're just as beautiful to me tonight as the first time I saw you," Dennis said, and raised his beer to take a drink. *Look at me,* he thought, *talking to my plane. The next thing you know, I'll be climbing on top of her to make love to her.*

Dennis had had enough to drink and poured the rest of his beer on the ground. He climbed down the scaffold and started to stroll across the field toward the barracks. It was time to hit the sack.

"I wish you'd talk to me like that, Virge," said Faith the moment Dennis was out of earshot, then kissed Virge in the hollow between his neck and shoulder.

Faith was lying under Virge on a hastily assembled bed of parachutes. Virge's shirt was open and his belt buckle half undone. He still couldn't figure out how this had happened.

They had been talking about hamburgers. Then Faith wanted a breath of fresh air, so he took her outside. Then she wanted to see the plane, so he took her out to the hardstand. Then she wanted to see inside the plane, so he helped her up through the hatch. Her waist was so delicate. As she pulled herself up into the plane he caught sight of her panties.

He scrambled up into the plane after her and closed the hatch. He really wasn't trying to kiss her when he bent his head down toward her; it was simply that he was so tall and he was going to bump his head on the roof. Somehow their lips met, and Virge had never felt anything so soft and tender and exciting before. It was better than food.

But the moment he heard Dennis's footsteps, all thought of losing his virginity vanished. He whispered to Faith to be still, but Faith didn't. She pulled up Virge's undershirt and put her hand on his stomach. She started playing with his belt buckle.

"You know what the captain would do if he caught us in here?" Virge said after he was sure Dennis was gone. "He'd murder me! Come on, Faith, let's just get this over with and get back to the dance."

Virge started to take off his pants. "Wait, there's something . . ." Faith said, wiggling under him. "Hold on. There! Sorry!" She pulled something out from under her. It was silver and shone a little in the moonlight.

"My wrench! I've been looking for that all over! Where'd you find it?" Virge said excitedly, grabbing the wrench.

"Under my bum."

"Boy, I thought someone stole it." Virge checked the wrench to see if it was okay.

"Virge, forget the bloody wrench." Faith pulled Virge's head down to hers and kissed him hard. A moment later the wrench fell out of his hands and hit the deck with a clank.

This wasn't the way Virge had planned it. He always thought his first time would be with his new bride in a four-poster bed in the honeymoon suite of a nice hotel. Here he was, on the floor of a B-17 with a girl he had known for twenty minutes. Right now it seemed like the most romantic thing that had ever happened to any young man.

"You've never done this before, have you?" Faith asked, touching the smooth side of Virge's carefully shaven face.

"Why, am I doing something wrong?" Virge asked worriedly. He pulled back in case he was hurting her or something.

"No," she said, putting her arms around Virge and pressing him close. "You're doing everything just right."

Later Virge and Faith walked back across the field to the hangar in silence. Virge felt that if he didn't hold on to Faith's hand, he would lift off the ground and float up into the sky, never to return. He wanted to shout and sing and tear off his clothes and show the whole world his new, nonvirginal body. But Faith was quiet, so Virge was quiet too.

Virge hoped that Faith didn't regret what they had just done. She seemed a little sad, but maybe that came with the territory.

They stopped outside the door to the hangar. Inside, the band was playing "Green Eyes."

"That was . . ." Faith started to say, but then didn't say what it was.

"Yeah, it really was," Virge replied. He didn't know what it was, either, except that it was swell.

"I wouldn't want this to get around."

"Around?" Virge didn't know if he had heard her right. Sometimes he had trouble understanding English accents.

"I know what you Yanks are like, always bragging about your women."

"Oh, no! Gosh, I wouldn't . . ." He pressed her hand to reassure her. "Not if you don't want me to," he added, hoping Faith would allow him to tell the crew, especially that smug bastard, Rascal.

But all Faith said was "Thanks," and she seemed grateful that he wouldn't brag about what they had done. So that was it. He couldn't tell anyone. He would have to go through life with everyone thinking he was still Virge the Virgin.

"Maybe I'll pop 'round for a hamburger someday," Faith said with the sweetest smile on earth, then she turned to go back into the hangar. Virge started to follow, but she put a hand on his arm.

"I'll go in first, if you don't mind."

"Oh, sure!" Virge said, even though he wanted to be with her the rest of the night, dancing and holding her in his arms. "Go right ahead."

She quickly kissed him, then disappeared inside. All of a sudden Virge knew he'd never see her again. She would slip away from the dance without even a good-bye. Even so, Virge swore that he would keep his promise. Faith had been gentle and patient with him. He would never tell a living soul that they had made love. It was nobody's business but his own.

But he had to do something to celebrate. He was alone. There was nothing to keep him from shouting or singing or tearing his clothes off now, but none of those things seemed right.

He looked up at the moon. It was diffused through a layer of fog, romantic and mysterious. It was the kind of moon you just had to howl at. So he howled.

There had never been a party like this before at Bassingbourn. The band was fine, the beer was flowing, and even the reserved English girls were letting down their guard. If this was war, war wasn't so bad, after all.

Craig Harriman sipped his coffee and looked at his watch. It was already ten minutes to ten, and the party showed no sign of slowing down. If he didn't signal the bandleader to start the last number, he was going to have a lot of hung-over fliers tomorrow on the mission to Bremen. But as long as the band played and the pretty girl sang, Bremen seemed far away, and tonight Craig Harriman wanted it to be as far away as possible.

At this time tomorrow night some of these young men would be dead. Some would be blown to bits in an instant, like the boys who died in the explosion that afternoon. Others would have to suffer before they died. Still others would have to bail out over Germany and spend the rest of the war in prisoner of war camps and perhaps die there.

Craig caught the bandleader's eye. They had arranged a signal. When Harriman rose from his chair and left the hangar, the band would begin the last number, "Auld Lang Syne." Craig stubbed out his cigarette. It was almost time.

Lieutenant Gregor asked Colonel Harriman if he wanted another cup of coffee. Craig didn't answer right away. The four cups he had already drunk were eating away at his stomach. His mouth was stale from the pack and a half of cigarettes he had smoked today. The muscles in his neck were so tight that it hurt to move his head. He needed rest.

But Craig Harriman knew he wouldn't rest tonight. He never slept the night before a mission. He stayed up as late as he could, busying himself with paperwork. When he finally went to bed at one-thirty or two o'clock in the morning, he lay wide awake until the adjutant knocked on his door at four. It was those sleepless nights in bed that Craig dreaded the most. He would do anything to shorten them.

So Craig Harriman didn't give the signal at 2200 hours as he had planned. Instead he accepted Gregor's offer of a refill and took another cigarette from the silver case that Comstock offered. At 2230 exactly, thirty minutes from now, he would signal the bandleader. He let Comstock light his cigarette, inhaled deeply, looked out at the dancers, and tried to forget about tomorrow.

"Is that yours, that brand-new plane out there?" Rascal asked the young man. There weren't many boys on base who looked younger than Rascal, but this rookie made Rascal looked like a grandpa.

"Yeah," the rookie answered. *"Mother and Country."*

The rookie had neatly combed blond hair and an angular face that he hadn't grown into yet. He was sitting at a table with his crew, none of whom looked much older. They looked more like a boys' choir than an aircrew.

"Mother and Country!" Rascal repeated. He glanced

at Danny, Eugene, and Jack. They sighed at the beloved words.

"Ain't that sweet?" Jack said.

"Brings a tear to the eye," added Eugene. They had been drinking.

"We had our first practice today," the rookie said enthusiastically.

"How'd it go?" Danny asked.

"We need a couple more," he replied, blushing a little. "If you guys have any advice for us or anything . . ."

"Get a gun, shoot your big toe off, and go home," Jack answered without missing a beat.

"That's good advice," Eugene said.

"Hallelujah, brother," Rascal added, then he put an arm around the rookie's bony shoulders and looked down at the boy's shoes.

"Are those size eights? How about leaving a little will saying that when you get your ass shot off on your first mission, those nice, shiny new pumps come to me?"

Color drained from the young man's face. He looked at Rascal with a hurt, betrayed expression. Then he put his hand to his mouth, jumped to his feet, and pushed through the crowd, trying to hold in the vomit until he was out the door.

"Touchy," Rascal said. Then he chuckled.

The boy was leaning over the toilet bowl when Danny came into the latrine. The latrine smelled of piss and ammonia. Danny assumed that somebody swabbed it out once in a while, but he had never actually seen anybody doing it. Pinups were pasted above the urinals and "Kilroy was here" was written at least twelve times on the wall.

"You okay?"

"Yeah. Nerves, I guess." The rookie was embarrassed. He came out of the stall. Danny went to the cracked, stained sink and filled a tin cup with water. He handed it to the shaky young man.

"They were just fooling around. I remember when I

45

first got here. Same thing.'' The rookie drank the water. His sharp little Adam's apple bobbed up and down.

"I'd give anything to be in your place," he said. "One more and you get to go home."

"Sometimes I wish I could stay," Danny replied. "Sounds crazy, but I'm used to it here. The guys are like brothers to me. I never had brothers. Four sisters." He laughed a little. "When we go back home, I don't know when we're going to get together again. We come from all over. I guess that's why I keep taking their pictures." Danny glanced down at his camera. He had three pictures left before he had to change the roll.

"That's the way you'll be with your crew," Danny said.

Some color had returned to the rookie's cheeks. He looked about twelve. *Did I ever look that young,* Danny asked himself. *Probably.*

Then he remembered that he still had Becker's four-leaf clover in his pocket. He bet the kid didn't have a good-luck charm, and you just had to have a good-luck charm over here. Everybody had one. The red rubber band never left Danny's wrist.

"Close your eyes," Danny said. At first the rookie was reluctant to do it. Maybe he thought Danny was going to play a trick on him. But he closed his eyes, anyway.

The charm was neatly wrapped in cellophane. Danny took it out of his pocket and tapped it on the young man's chin. The rookie opened his eyes and saw the four-leaf clover. It was a real one. He took it.

"Come on, let's get back to the dance," Danny said.

When they entered the hangar, the band was just winding up a number, so Danny hurried over to Clay.

"Clay, now's your chance! Get up there and sing!"

"Uh-uh, I'm not gonna make a fool of myself in front of all these folks." Clay was funny—he didn't bat an eye when ten Nazi fighters were coming at him from all angles, but he was too scared to get up on the stage and sing a song.

"Ladies and gentlemen, can I have your attention, please?" a voice said over the loudspeaker. Bruce Derringer had stepped up to the stage during the break between numbers and was speaking into the microphone. The hangar quieted down.

"There's ten very special men here tonight. I'm sure you know who I mean. They're just about to become the first crew in the Eighth Air Force to fly their twenty-fifth and final mission. Let's hear it for the crew of the *Memphis Belle*!" he said, then began a cheer. "Hip hip hooray!"

"Hooray!" the rookie started to shout, but Danny grabbed his arm to stop him. The young man looked at Danny in surprise, and Danny whispered in his ear.

"It's bad luck."

"Hip hip hooray!" Bruce shouted again. Some of the crowd had responded on the first cheer, but word spread quickly that to congratulate a crew on completing their tour before they had done it was as good as condemning them to death.

When Bruce Derringer went into a third cheer, an ominous hush fell over the hangar. In an instant the party turned from a celebration into a funeral. Everyone was looking at the crew of the *Belle*, wondering what they were going to do. Eugene was clutching that religious medal of his. Even Rascal was speechless.

Danny looked at Clay. He didn't need to say a word. Clay could read Danny's mind. He pushed through the crowd, hurried up the stairs to the stage, and took the microphone.

"This friend of mine keeps begging me to sing, and I guess I ain't gonna get out of it this time." Clay dragged the mike back to the piano, sat down, and did what he said he would never do—he sang.

"Oh, Danny Boy,
The pipes, the pipes are calling . . ."

Danny flushed bright red. If there was one song he wished had never been written, it was "Danny Boy." People had been teasing him about it ever since he was little. It wasn't his fault that he was Irish, had red hair, and his name was Danny. He tried to disappear into the crowd, but Eugene and Jack grabbed him and forced him to stay and listen.

> "From glen to glen
> And down the mountainside . . ."

The rookie watched Danny with his crew. They were teasing him, jabbing him in the ribs, and ruffling his hair while Danny squirmed. The rookie remembered what Danny had said, "The guys are like brothers to me. That's the way you'll be with your crew." Now he knew what Danny meant. It was all for one and one for all. The war seemed a little less frightening tonight.

> "The summer's gone
> And all the roses falling,
> It's you, it's you must go
> And I must bide . . ."

Then, as if it were planned, the band swung into an uptempo version of "Danny Boy," and Clay followed right along. The ominous mood vanished, and everyone started dancing again and having a good time. Eugene, Jack, and Rascal grabbed the nearest girls they could find, and suddenly a pretty brunette was in Danny's arms. He never considered himself much of a dancer, but tonight he was Fred Astaire.

Then the big net of red, white, and blue balloons came down. For an instant the crowd was buried in balloons, then the balloons started popping and it made everyone laugh and whoop with delight. Everyone was laughing and whooping, and it seemed like the dance would go on and on forever.

Outside, the fog was thick. The music sounded very far away, as if it were playing on the moon. The moon itself was a blurry disk in the sky. The popping of balloons sounded like distant artillery fire.

Phil was out in the middle of the airfield, alone with his bottle. He had stolen it from the bar when the bartender wasn't looking. He planned to drink the whole thing. Maybe then he could forget that tomorrow he was going to die.

He stumbled across the field, tripped, and fell on his knees in the grass. Just like a wino, he thought. He started to laugh, but instead of a laugh a shout came out of his mouth.

"I don't want to die!" The cry echoed across the empty field.

Never had Phil loved life so much as now, with the music in the distance, the big planes around him, and the moon shining through the fog. He took a deep breath of the thick night air. He shouted again.

"I don't want to die!" He didn't know who he was talking to, but he hoped somebody heard.

"I don't want to die!" he shouted again.

Phil wanted an answer—someone to say that he wasn't going to die, that he should throw away the bottle and hit the sack. If there was a God, now was the time for Him to speak.

Phil listened. Nothing. Only the band, far away, playing "Auld Lang Syne."

Phil stumbled to his feet, uncorked the bottle, and took a long drink. The whiskey burned his throat and made his eyes water, but it tasted good. He put the cork back so that if he fell, he wouldn't lose a precious drop. Then he stumbled off alone into the cool, opaque night.

4

Although Danny hadn't fallen asleep until well after midnight, he was already awake when Sergeant Pacovsky came into the barracks and shined the flashlight in his face. Danny always woke up early the morning of a mission and just stayed in his sack where it was warm.

"Daly, rise 'n' shine. Mission at 0800," said Pacovsky in his raspy voice. Danny smelled cigar smoke on the sergeant's breath. He imagined Pacovsky smoking cigar after cigar to make his voice more raspy.

"Okay," Danny said, squinting and holding up a hand to block the glare of the flashlight until Pacovsky moved the beam across the aisle and shined it in Rascal's face.

"Moore. Up and at 'em."

"I just went to sleep!" Rascal complained, and burrowed under the covers.

"Busby, Hoogesteger, Bocci, McVey!" the sergeant shouted. "Alla youse guys, get crackin'!" The blacked-out barracks was soon filled with the sounds of men groaning, hacking, and cussing. Clay sat bolt upright in bed and started to sing.

> "Grab your coat and get your hat,
> Leave your worries on the doorstep . . ."

A match flared as someone lit a cigarette. Danny swung his freckled legs over the edge of the bunk, and his toes touched the icy floor. This was the last time he'd have to do this. Everything he did today would be the last time he ever did it.

> "Just direct your feet
> To the sunny side of the street."

Somebody threw a boot at Clay and someone else uttered a string of obscenities, but Clay kept right on singing.

"Captain Dearborn, mission today," Pacovsky said, shining the flashlight in Dennis's face. "Breakfast 0600, briefing, 0645."

Dennis woke immediately. He was glad he'd called it quits early last night and gotten a good sleep. "Thanks, Sergeant," he said, then reached for his watch and started to wind it. He wound his watch every morning as soon as he woke, regular as clockwork. His watch had never stopped.

"Lieutenant Sinclair," Sergeant Pacovsky said, moving the flashlight to Luke's bed. The officers' quarters was less crowded than the enlisted men's barracks, with only six bunks instead of twelve. The four officers from the *Belle* bunked at one end; the other end was occupied by the pilot and copilot of *Windy City*.

"I'm up," Luke said. He had a big crease mark across his cheek where he had slept on his pillow wrong. He looked over at Dennis. Yep, Dennis was winding his watch. If Dennis woke up next to the most beautiful girl in the world and she laid back and begged him to make love to her, Dennis would wind his watch first.

"Where's Lieutenant Lowenthal?" Pacovsky asked, shining his flashlight on the empty bunk across from Luke's.

"I don't know," Dennis said. "Val, where's Phil?"

The moment Val saw the neatly tucked-in corners of Phil's regulation bunk, he knew Phil had been out all night. Val desperately tried to think when he had seen his partner last. It was too early to think clearly, but he remembered Phil knocking back whiskey after whiskey at the dance and talking about being jinxed.

"He's in the can," Val lied to Dennis. "Couldn't sleep. Nerves."

Sergeant Pacovsky grinned. He had a tooth missing. "I don't blame him. Give 'em hell today."

"Will do," Dennis said, then continued winding his watch. Val looked at Luke. Luke grinned back at him. Val knew Luke was thinking that Phil had gotten lucky last night. But Val wasn't so sure. He had just remembered the last time he saw Phil. Phil was staggering out of the hangar with a full bottle of Scotch under his arm.

Ten minutes later Val was dressed and jogging across the base in search of his buddy. The sky was blue-black and the stars were just clearing away. It had rained during the night and the ground was thick with mud. Men were hurrying to the latrine and the mess hall. Some were in uniform, some in battle gear, some still in their underwear. A jeep sped by, splashing mud.

It wasn't like Phil to disappear like this. Phil was a steady guy. One of the only good things about this damn war was working in the nose next to Phil. He wasn't a braggart like Rascal or a nervous Nellie like Eugene. A fellow could count on Phil.

Val ran around the perimeter track. Bomb carts and gas

trucks raced back and forth. Ground crews worked on their planes. Armament crews installed the guns and loaded boxes of ammunition. Everyone worked quickly and quietly. If they spoke, they spoke in whispers. Flashlights flickered all over the field.

Now that Val thought about it, Phil hadn't been himself for a couple of weeks. He was always downcast. He never laughed anymore; that pouty mouth was always set in a frown. He looked like a little boy who had just been spanked.

Val remembered what Phil had said last night at the dance: "Tell me the truth. Are you scared?" It was the kind of question you never asked.

Val headed for the airplane hangar where the dance had been held in the hopes of finding Phil passed out in a corner. Maybe the guy just fell over behind the refreshment table when nobody was looking.

All that remained of the dance was the sign HAPPY 1ST ANNIVERSARY and the beer bottles, cigarette butts, and broken balloons that littered the floor. The wreckage of the plane that had exploded the day before was parked inside the hangar and was being cannibalized for its parts. There wasn't much left of it, but what remained could be repaired, cleaned up, and used on another plane.

Phil was nowhere in sight. Val stood in front of the hangar doors, took out a pack of cigarettes, and lit up. He only had one more Lucky Strike left. He reminded himself to save it until after the mission. That would be something to look forward to.

Suddenly a voice shouted, "Bogey, six o'clock low!" and before Val could turn around or even snap his lighter closed, Phil tackled him. Val fell to the ground with a thud. Phil was on top of him, heavy as lead and laughing like crazy. He reeked of liquor. His breath could have knocked down a Nazi fighter.

Val scrambled to his feet and looked at his partner. One look was all he needed.

"You're drunk!"

"I rethent that inthinuation!" Phil said, deliberately slurring his words. He giggled at his own joke, then took a long swig of Johnnie Walker. There was about an inch of whiskey left in the bottom of the bottle.

"Are you crazy? We've got a mission!" Val snatched the bottle away from Phil.

"I know. Why'd you think I got drunk?" Phil said. Now he was slurring his words without even trying. "I'm gonna get it today, Val. My luck's up, my number's run out. I mean . . ." He was momentarily confused by his mixed metaphors.

"I'm gonna die and I want to give you something to remember me by." Phil heaved himself to his feet. Weaving dangerously, he took off his watch and held it out to Val with the most pathetic puppy-dog look. Val wanted to smack him.

"I don't want that piece of crap. You've got to get hold of yourself. Everybody's counting on you." Val tried to walk Phil toward the barracks, but Phil couldn't walk very well. His feet kept going in opposite directions.

"You want my cuff links? They've got my initials on them." Phil tried to take one off, but he couldn't get the clasp to work. His fingers felt thick, as if they belonged to a bigger guy.

"You know what's going to happen if Dennis sees you like this? What's got into you?" Val asked, but Phil wasn't even listening.

"How about my whole set of New York Yankee baseball cards?" he said eagerly, then just as quickly changed his mind. "Nah, then you'll just remember the Yankees and forget about me."

Val's head was spinning. What was he going to do? Phil had an hour-long briefing to attend, plus a specialized navigator's briefing after that. He had essential duties on board the aircraft. At the moment Phil couldn't even walk straight. He looked like a puppet whose strings were tan-

55

gled. He wouldn't shut up about giving something to Val to remember him by.

"I know, my fountain pen!" Phil said. "You could use it to fill out prescriptions and stuff."

"Shut up," Val said irritably. "Just shut up."

"Or you name it, Val. Anything you want. My dog tags? You want my dog tags or my Boy Scout knife? Or how about . . . ? How about . . ." Phil wrinkled his brow. He had forgotten what he wanted to give Val so Val would never forget him. Everything was a little fuzzy right now.

Five minutes later Luke and Val were in the latrine, watching Phil lurch toward a toilet stall. He misjudged the distance and banged into the partition.

"That's our navigator," Luke said cheerfully.

Men were hurrying in and out of the latrine, hastily shaving and relieving themselves. Nobody talked much. They wanted to do their business as fast as possible and get to chow.

"We better tell Dennis he's sick and get someone else," Val said as Phil disappeared inside the toilet stall.

"We can't! A new man is bad luck!"

"What's a drunk navigator, good luck?" Val glanced quickly toward the door to make sure Dennis wasn't coming.

"So you're the doctor. Sober him up."

There it was again, that awful phrase: *You're the doctor*. Whenever anything went wrong, the crew depended on Doc to fix it. For the hundredth time Val wished he had never let them believe he had finished medical school.

"What's happened to him?" Val said, ignoring Luke's suggestion. "He used to have the steadiest nerves in the crew."

"Come on, he's not so bad. He's just a little high." Right then there was the sound of a trickle from Phil's toilet stall. Val glanced at his watch.

"I timed that. Forty-five seconds to find his own dick."

56

If Val reported Phil's condition to Dennis, the poor slob could be court-martialed. It would be one thing if Phil was always like this, but he'd never gone on a bender before. It could have happened to anybody. What's a friend for if he doesn't help his pal when he needs it the most? In the end, Val had no choice. He had to sober Phil up.

"Okay, stick your finger down your throat," Val said to Phil after barging into Phil's toilet stall. Phil looked appalled, as if the mere suggestion made him sick. "Do it or I'll do it for you," Val threatened.

Phil tried to get away, but his reflexes weren't working as swiftly as usual, and Val was stronger, anyway. Val pushed Phil up against the partition between the stalls, pried Phil's mouth open, and stuck his index finger down Phil's throat.

It worked. Vomit spurted out of Phil's mouth and made a direct hit on Val's neatly pressed shirt and tie.

The next thing was to get him shaved. Phil, like everyone on board, would be wearing a rubber oxygen mask clamped tight against his face during the mission. If a man didn't shave closely, the mask would rub and rub at even the slightest bit of stubble until he was ready to jump out of his skin. You could always tell the new crews by the rashes on their faces.

Val didn't trust Phil to shave himself. The guy would probably slice an ear off. Phil had a dazed, almost comatose look. His face was puffy and pale. You could almost see the headache forming behind his eyes.

Val had the left half of Phil's face finished when Luke strolled back into the latrine after a reconnaissance trip around base.

"Coast's clear," he announced. "Dennis went for chow."

"Luke, I want you to have this," Phil said, digging in his pocket. "It's my penknife. It's real nice." He tried to press the well-worn Boy Scout knife into Luke's hand.

"Keep it. If Dennis sees you like this, you'll need it to

cut your throat with," Luke said, grinning. Val was annoyed at Luke. The copilot wasn't taking Phil's condition seriously enough. He treated it as lightly as he did everything else.

Luke opened a little packet, pushed Phil's head back, and emptied the contents into Phil's mouth. Tiny tablets of licorice fell onto Phil's white-coated tongue.

"Sen-Sen," Luke said, as if it were the solution to all their troubles.

Meanwhile the enlisted men had no idea that the man who was about to navigate them into enemy territory was so shaky, he couldn't even hold his own razor. They were dressing as quickly as possible so they could get to chow before the real eggs ran out. When the real eggs ran out, the cooks served powdered eggs. Powdered eggs slid down your throat like snot.

Danny took a picture. He wasn't sure there was enough light, but he risked it, anyway. This was his last chance to get a shot of the barracks on the morning before a mission.

"I can see it," Jack said. "I get back home, I'm making love to the wife, the door breaks open, and it's Danny, taking a fucking picture!"

Danny laughed. The crew made fun of him for taking so many pictures, but he didn't think they really minded. If they minded, you'd *know* they minded. Twenty years from now they would all want copies to show to their kids.

Across the aisle from Danny, Eugene was frantically searching his bunk area. He had torn his sack apart, and now he was tossing everything out of his locker. Eugene was always a little nervous, but right now he was in a complete state of panic.

"Anybody seen my St. Anthony medal?"

"Isn't he the patron saint of missing things?" Danny asked, remembering this from a distant Sunday school lesson.

"Yeah, I can't find him!"

Danny instinctively looked down at his left wrist. There

it was, his lucky rubber band. It used to be bright red, but it had faded to pink. He didn't know what he'd do if he ever lost it.

Then he remembered the bottle of champagne. A couple of weeks ago he had gone to Cambridge, the nearest big town, in search of a bottle of champagne to take along on their last mission. Champagne was rare—nobody much felt like celebrating these days—and Danny had to go to six pubs before he found a bottle.

It was against orders to take liquor on board the plane, but Danny didn't think the captain would object if they all had a drink of champagne on the way home, when it was all over.

"You're not thinking of sneaking this on the plane, are you?" said Rascal in mock horror, snatching the bottle of champagne away. "Danny, I am shocked! And Virge goes out for the pass!" Before Danny could protest, Rascal threw the bottle across the room like a football.

"Don't!" Danny shouted. That bottle represented two months' savings from his flight pay. But Virge caught the bottle easily, tucked it under his arm, dodged some imaginary offensive players, then sailed it back to Rascal.

"Hey, wise guys, cut the crap!" Jack snarled.

"I found it!" Eugene announced, discovering his St. Anthony medal, caught in the sagging springs beneath his mattress. He kissed the medal, put it around his neck, and said a little prayer of thanks.

At that same moment Val was also praying: praying that Phil's hiccups would go away. The hiccups had started three minutes ago. First Val tried making Phil drink water upside down. Then he made Phil hold his breath as long as he could. Then he had him breathe into a paper bag, but nothing worked.

"Hic!"

"Cut it out!"

Suddenly the door to the officers' barracks opened, and Dennis strolled in, puffing on his pipe. "There you are,

Phil,'' he said as he went over to his bunk, took a letter from his pocket, and placed it under his pillow. This was Dennis's ritual. It was a letter to his girl back home. It would be sent to her in case he didn't come back.

"I just want to remind you both to keep it quiet about you know what,'' Dennis said.

"What?'' Val asked, his mind on the hiccup that he knew would be popping out of Phil at any moment. Then Val remembered the press guy from Washington and the *Life* photographer. Dennis didn't want the six enlisted men to know that the entire crew was going back to the States together to raise money for war bonds. Dennis would tell them when today's mission was over.

"Oh, sure,'' Val said.

Dennis took an extra pack of pipe tobacco from his locker, then looked around his bunk to see if he had forgotten anything. He smoothed down an almost invisible wrinkle in his meticulously made bunk. He opened his locker once more and took out an extra pencil. Val was in agony, waiting for that telltale hiccup.

"Well, see you at briefing,'' Dennis said, then he finally went out the door. Val looked at Phil in amazement.

"You did good!'' Val said. In response Phil let out the biggest hiccup Val had ever heard.

The mess hall was enveloped in a cloud of smoke. It stank of burned toast and grease. The mess was divided into two sections, the smaller for the officers and the larger, more crowded area for enlisted men. Men were talking more than eating. Nobody had much of an appetite before a mission. Usually hunger struck you halfway to the target when it was too late to do anything about it.

Val led Phil down the service line. Phil was no longer hiccuping or talking about dying. He was in a daze. He shuffled behind Val like a chastised puppy.

"Give him extra," Val said to the hairy cook behind the counter. "He's real hungry."

The cook dumped a heaping spoonful of runny eggs on Phil's plate, then dropped some strips of fatty bacon on top. Phil felt his stomach turn over. He had nothing left to throw up, but he felt like throwing up, anyway. *At least a guy on death row gets to choose what he eats for his last meal,* Phil thought. *I don't even get that privilege.* He grabbed the plate before the cook could insist that he take two gray, obscene sausages linked by a string of tough gristle.

Down two steps in the enlisted men's section, Clay, Virge, Eugene, Jack, Rascal, and Danny were crowded together at a table. They were smoking and drinking the thick, stomach-corroding coffee, letting their greasy food congeal on the tin trays. Only Jack was eating. He was a bottomless pit.

"These eggs would gag a buzzard," he said, and grabbed some neglected bacon off Eugene's plate.

"It's gonna be a milk run today, boys," Clay said lazily. Clay's drawl sounded good in the morning; he had a morning-type voice. "I feel it in my bones."

"That's what you said when they sent us to Wilhelmshaven," Danny reminded him.

"God, I hope we don't have to go back there," Eugene said, fingering his St. Anthony medal.

"They wouldn't do that. Not to my mama's baby boy," Rascal said. Then he saw Captain Dearborn coming, immediately straightened up, and wondered if he had done anything in the past twenty-four hours he could be in trouble for. The captain always made you feel like you had done something wrong.

"How are we doing this morning, men?" Dennis asked as he came up to the table. Luke was following right behind. He sneaked up behind Rascal and put a hammerlock on his neck.

"Stop it!" Rascal complained, struggling to get out of the hold. Sometimes Luke treated him like that stupid dog of

61

his. "You won't have a chance to do that after today, Luke, sir."

"Oh, I wouldn't be so sure of that. Right, Dennis?" Luke smiled at Dennis, daring him to tell the enlisted men about the bond tour, but before Dennis could react, there was a huge crash and clatter. All eyes turned toward the service line.

Val was scurrying to recover a tub of silverware that Phil had accidentally knocked to the floor.

Luke held his breath. He watched Dennis watching Phil. All you had to do was look at Phil to see that something was wrong with him. His face was swollen and fish-belly white. If Dennis realized that Phil was hung over so badly that he couldn't even tie his shoes, they were in big trouble. The Army didn't have a sling big enough to hold Phil's, Val's, and Luke's asses.

Dennis didn't say anything right away. He watched Val scrambling to collect the silverware. Phil just stood there, acting as if he had never seen knives, forks, and spoons before.

When Dennis finally did speak, all he said was "I guess we've all got the jitters this morning. See you after briefing." Then he walked out the door. Luke let out his breath. They had gotten away with it so far, but they still had a long way to go.

The briefing room was even more smoke-filled than the mess hall. It was a long, round-topped Nissen hut with a small stage at the far end. On the stage, a black curtain covered a large map of England and northern Europe. At the edge of the curtain was a spool of red yarn. The spool was the first thing the men looked at when they poured into the briefing room.

The yarn stretched behind the curtain and traced the path to the target. The men could gauge how difficult the mission would be from the amount of yarn left on the spool. If a lot of yarn was left, the line didn't stretch very far across the map, and the mission would be to a city nearby, just across the Channel in France. In other words, a milk run. But when very little yarn remained on the spool, the crews knew that the target was far, probably in Germany.

Today the yarn was almost entirely used up. Just one red thread remained on the spool. It wouldn't be a milk run, after all.

"How the hell's Phil going to get through the navigator's briefing afterward?" Luke asked as Val pushed Phil into a seat. The six cups of thick black coffee that Val had poured down Phil's throat made little difference. His eyelids were drooping and his head nodding on his chest.

"On a wing and a fucking prayer," Val answered.

In the back of the room the radio operators were gathering. It turned out that the young rookie from *Mother and Country* whom Danny had befriended at the dance last night was also a radio operator. He was a little nervous.

"I thought we'd have a little more practice before we went up," the rookie said to Danny. The crew of *Mother and Country* had only done two practice flights since they arrived in England three days ago. They didn't expect to be sent on a mission for another week.

"You'll do fine," Danny reassured him. The rookie took the four-leaf clover out of his pocket and showed it to Danny. Danny smiled. He never told the rookie where it came from, and the rookie didn't ask.

A voice cried out, "Ten-hut!" and one hundred and twenty men shuffled to their feet. Colonel Craig Harriman entered the briefing room and stepped up on the stage.

"At ease, gentlemen."

Harriman looked out at the sea of faces before him. Every time he stood on this stage to announce the day's target he had the same thought: They're so young. Some of them still had acne. Others had hair that stuck straight up in back no matter how much hair cream they put on. Some looked a little hung over.

"I hope you all had a good time last night," Craig Harriman said. A murmur of assent ran through the room. Craig allowed the laughter and nudging to continue for a moment before he spoke again. "But now it's back to business." The room quieted. The men knew that this was the moment when the commanding officer would announce the target. Eyes flickered over to the spool of yarn. That single red thread was not a good sign.

"The target for today is . . . Bremen."

The S-2 pulled the black curtain. The red yarn stretched from their base in eastern England across the wide North Sea, turned sharply south, and penetrated sixty miles straight into Germany.

The room erupted into gasps and groans. Some fliers cracked jokes. Some swore. Some just stared at the map in horror. They had gone to Bremen a month ago. When they returned, a quarter of the bunks on base were empty.

Phil was probably the only man in the room who wasn't surprised. He had expected this all along. He never fooled himself for a moment that they would be given a milk run for their last mission. He knew it would be the toughest one yet, and he knew, wherever they went, that he would die there.

He closed his eyes. He wanted to stay awake for the briefing, but he was so damn tired. *I'll just close my eyes for a moment,* he thought. It was the last thought he had for a while.

Colonel Harriman waited until the men had gotten over their shock before he spoke again. When he did speak, it was in a curt, businesslike voice. *Don't show your feelings,* he reminded himself. *If they know you're as scared as they are, they'll be twice as scared.*

"This is the most important target we have ever been given. Bremen is home to the Focke-Wulf Flugzeugbau

64

factory, where they assemble FW-190 fighter planes. The FW-190 is one of the deadliest weapons the Germans have, so we want to hit this target hard and accurately. The S-2 will give you all the details, and I'll be back to say a few words at the end."

Colonel Craig Harriman stepped off the stage and walked quickly to the door. He knew the men were watching him, so he allowed not the slightest trace of emotion to cross his face. But his mind was racing, circling around one question: What do you say to your men when you're sending them out to die?

5

Bruce Derringer was steamed. First Craig Harriman wouldn't tell him the name of the target, then he was refused entry to the briefing room. Harriman told him that this was for security reasons. What did they think he was, a Nazi spy? Bruce wasn't going to let himself be treated like this. His job was to protect the crew of the *Memphis Belle*, and he was going to do it.

"Are you crazy? Bremen's one of the most heavily defended cities in Germany!" Bruce shouted at Craig Harriman as they strode briskly along the wooden slats set down in the thick mud outside the briefing room. Bruce had cajoled a young lieutenant from Intelligence into telling him the target, and after Bruce recovered from his shock he set out to find Craig Harriman.

"They'll get blown out of the sky. You've got to pull the *Memphis Belle* from this mission."

"No," Harriman said without even a moment's consideration.

67

"I need those men," Bruce pleaded. "This whole public-relations junket depends on them."

"I have orders to put every plane up there I can."

"Craig, we had an agreement," Bruce said, trying to remind Harriman of yesterday's discussion. "The *Belle* was going on the next milk run."

"I agreed to nothing," Harriman replied in his usual tight-lipped manner.

"The whole base is counting on those boys to make it. Washington's counting on it." If Bruce had to drop FDR's name, he would.

"Colonel, all available crews are going on this mission. There is nothing more to discuss." Harriman stepped up his pace to get away from Derringer. He wanted to be alone to compose something to say to the men after the briefing. The briefing was half over; in another thirty minutes he would be standing in front of them again.

Bruce jogged up in front of Harriman. "Craig," Bruce said conspiratorially, "if we present a united front, the two of us, we can get the *Belle* pulled. You talk to HQ. I'll talk to Washington."

"I promised General Eaker twenty-four planes today. I lost one yesterday. The *Memphis Belle* has to go." Harriman didn't even stop to deliver this verdict. He kept striding along the temporary wooden walkways, which were already sinking into the gummy mud.

Harriman was everything Bruce hated about the Army. He was power mad, callous, and unreasonable. As far as Bruce could tell, Harriman had no friends on the base. At the dance last night the CO sat at a table with his men, as grim as if he were attending a funeral.

Perhaps if Harriman got to know some of the men on a personal basis, he wouldn't be so quick to send them to Bremen. Bruce thought of Luke Sinclair, Val Kozlowski, and the red-haired, freckle-faced radio operator named Danny dying over Germany in a few hours, and he felt like slugging Harriman in the middle of his tight, chiseled face.

"You don't really care if those men live or die, do you?" Bruce said. "They're just another plane to you. Just so you can reach your quota."

Craig Harriman stopped. He turned and looked at Bruce, his dark eyes burning. "Colonel, I'm in command here, and I've made my decision."

"Your decision is inhuman and irresponsible, and I'm going to make sure everybody knows about it, starting with General Eaker!" Bruce shot back at him, then set off across the field in search of a phone.

Talking to Harriman was pointless, but Bruce had a lot of friends in Washington. He would get the *Belle* pulled from this mission if it was the last thing he did. *The Army is a load of horseshit,* he thought as he dodged a jeep streaking by. *I'm sure glad I'm in advertising.*

"This is our target right here," said the S-2 in a dry, matter-of-fact tone. The briefing room was quiet and dark. The light from the overhead projector was the only one, and it caught swirls of smoke drifting up from a roomful of cigarettes.

An overhead view of the outskirts of Bremen was projected on a screen. "It's a square building, the only square one in the area, so you can't miss it." Comstock tapped the square, gray building with his pointer, then pointed to the surrounding area.

"Note these railroad tracks on the east and this long rectangular building on the north. That's a hospital. These are houses here. This is a school and a playground."

Great, thought Val, if the bombs don't fall on the Focke-Wulf factory, they'll fall on sick people or kids. Val was relieved not to be the lead bombardier. *Windy City* would be leading the group. When the bombardier on *Windy City* pressed his bomb release button, all of the bombardiers in the group would press theirs.

Even so, Val stared at the target photo, trying to burn it into his eyes. There was no telling what might happen over Bremen. You had to be prepared for anything.

"The strike force will be composed of two combat wing formations, each consisting of three groups. Our group will be leading the first wing in the middle, forward position. Each plane will carry the maximum load: eight five-hundred-pound, general-purpose bombs or four one-thousand-pounders."

Beside Val, Phil was fast asleep. His head rested on his chest and his breathing was labored. At one point he started to snore, but Val jabbed him in the side and he quit. Val was taking notes for Phil, as well as for himself.

"A fighter escort of P-47 Thunderbolts will meet up with you as you cross the English coast, and take you as far as their tanks will allow. They'll be turning back here." The S-2 tapped the easternmost island of the long, thin string of Frisian Islands that skirted the northern coast of Holland and Germany. "They'll meet you again over the North Sea on your return."

The small fuel tanks of the P-47 prevented it from going all the way to the target. The friendly fighters hightailed it back to England, refueled, and then met the B-17s on the return trip. Everyone loved the friendly fighters and dreaded the moment when they had to turn back.

"There's an estimated force of two hundred seventy FW-190s and ME-210s in the Bremen area, so you'll probably be seeing plenty of action. Also, there are about two hundred flak batteries around Wilhelmshaven and Bremen, and these antiaircraft gunners are pretty accurate. So wear your flak helmets and jackets at all times."

Everyone agreed that the flak was worse than the fighters. The little Focke-Wulfs and Messerschmitts could fly rings around the heavy B-17s, but at least you could fire back at them. You couldn't do anything about the flak gunners. You just had to hope they missed.

While the briefing continued with weather and formation information, the gunners were suiting up for the mission.

"It was such a beautiful dream, Virgey," Rascal told Virge as they entered the locker room. "I walk in the barracks, I look, and guess who's lying in my bunk? Betty Grable!"

"Rascal, your sheets are so dirty, the Bride of Frankenstein wouldn't get in your bunk."

"Well, she was there and she was naked and she was gorgeous. So I slip in beside her and take her in my arms and she kisses me and wraps those long legs around me. And then guess what happened?"

"You woke up," Virge guessed.

"Yeah, I woke up," said Rascal sadly. The two young men started stripping down and putting on their many layers of flight gear. They would need every layer. It would be thirty degrees below zero over the target.

First they put on long underwear. Over that they wore bright blue heated suits, nicknamed "bunny suits." The suits had long cords that plugged into an electric outlet in the wall of the plane. The bunny suits worked pretty well, except that when a man sweated too much, the circuits shorted out. It was also not a good idea to wet your pants.

Next came the heavy, fleece-lined leather pants. Then the leather flying jackets with their wide sheepskin collars. Some guys, like Rascal, had the name of their plane painted on the back. On their feet they wore thick, fleece-lined boots. These were also heated and attached with plugs to the bunny suits.

On their hands they wore thick, clumsy gloves. They were very awkward, but if a man touched his gun without gloves, his skin would stick to it the way fingers stick to a metal ice-cube tray when it comes out of the freezer. More than one man had lost his fingers that way.

They wore wool scarves around their necks, where they also wrapped their microphones. Finally, every man wore a leather helmet on his head, a bulky parachute on his back and a bright yellow life jacket on his front. The life jacket was called a Mae West. When inflated, it resembled the famous sex symbol's monstrous bust.

Clay was singing as he pulled on his gray long johns. They were white once upon a time, but that was a long time ago. For good luck, he never washed them.

> "I'm putting on my top hat,
> Tying up my white tie,
> Brushing off my tails . . ."

> "I'm duding up my shirt front,
> Putting in the shirt studs,
> Polishing my nails . . ."

"There he goes," Rascal said, "the human jukebox."

The briefing room smelled of leather jackets and was warm now with the bodies of one hundred and twenty worried young men. They were quiet now, waiting for the commanding officer to speak.

Craig Harriman didn't know what to say. He gladly would have traded places with any man in the room. Craig had flown one mission back in December. He liked it much better than waiting on the ground, but General Eaker had begged him not to fly anymore. The Air Force couldn't afford to lose Craig Harriman.

"Today they've given us a chance to really make a difference in this war," Colonel Harriman began. He spoke quietly and forced himself to look at their faces. Was it his imagination or were the pilots getting younger every day? He remembered that at least one new crew was flying its first mission today. They called their plane *Mother and Country*.

"Let's do this job the best we can and leave the rest in the hands of God. With luck it'll all be over soon and we can go back home to our families."

They were listening, drinking in every word. Craig Harriman wanted to tell them, "I don't know any more than you do. I don't have any answers. I'm flying by the seat of my pants too."

"My thoughts will be with you, and I won't rest until you're back." He remembered Bruce Derringer's accusation that he cared only about statistics. "Each and every one of you," he said, and he meant it.

"Dismissed."

At the same moment, in Harriman's office, Bruce Derringer was shouting into the phone. "I've talked to six different people and been cut off twice! I want General Eaker on this phone *now*, or I want your name, Corporal!"

The distant voice on the other end said something about holding on. The connection to Pinetree was so static-filled that Bruce could only understand every third word.

"I'll hold," Bruce said suspiciously, "but you better not cut me—" Before he could even finish the sentence, there was loud interference on the line. When that abruptly stopped, there was silence. He jiggled the phone cradle.

"Hello? Hello?" he shouted, but the silence continued. He had been cut off again.

"You'll have nil to three-tenths low clouds at takeoff with visibility one to two miles," the pudgy, balding group navigator read from the latest weather report.

The navigators were gathered together in the front of the briefing room for their specialized session. In the back of the room copilots and bombardiers were lined up to receive their flimsies, which contained more detailed information about the day's mission. The flimsies were printed on heavy rice paper. If you bailed out over enemy territory, you were supposed to eat them.

"So far, so good," Val said to Luke as he watched Phil across the room. Phil had slept soundly through the regular briefing but was alert now. Val could see him scrutinizing the diagrams projected on the screen and studiously taking notes.

What he couldn't see was how Phil was keeping himself awake. He had never felt so tired, but he couldn't nod off no matter how much he wanted to. So he took the sharp end of his compass and jabbed it into his forearm. The sting jolted him awake every time he started to doze. It hurt like hell and he was probably giving himself blood poisoning, but he was staying awake.

"We're dead men! We're dead!" was Rascal's reaction when Danny said they were going to Bremen.

"Shut up, Rascal!" Virge said irritably.

"You shut up, Virgin!" The word *virgin* was like a slap across Virge's face. He started to spit back that he wasn't a virgin anymore, but the words froze in his mouth. He had promised Faith that he wouldn't brag about last night, and he was determined to keep his word, even if it meant a lifetime of insults from Rascal.

"Cut it out, guys," said Eugene. Eugene, Danny, Jack, Clay, Rascal, and Virge were piled into a jeep, waiting for the four officers to join them. "Clay, what're our odds today?" Eugene asked, fingering his lucky St. Anthony medal.

"Well, they'll overload us with bombs, so it's about thirty to one that we'll crash and blow up on takeoff," Clay said in his thick Southern drawl. "Then the Gerries will throw every fighter they've got at us, so, five to one against us even gettin' to Bremen. Then you've got your flak batteries . . ."

"Skip the gory details," Jack growled. "What's our chances?"

"Basically we're fucked." Clay shrugged as if it didn't matter one way or the other.

Luke's dog, Bucky, came bounding up to the jeep, announcing the arrival of the four officers. The enlisted men

74

straightened up, stopped grousing, and pretended to be happy to be going to Bremen.

Virge studied the officers' faces, but he couldn't tell what they were thinking. Luke was smiling and petting his smelly dog as usual. Dennis was stone-faced, but this, too, was usual. Val seemed a little worried, but then Val always seemed a little worried. Phil's eyes were bloodshot, his face was pale, and his hand shook as he pulled himself into the jeep. None of them said a word.

Then they were speeding down the perimeter track to the plane. Clay started singing "Amazing Grace," and they all chimed in. Nobody but Clay was much of a singer, but they stayed almost on pitch, anyway.

> "Amazing grace
> How sweet the sound
> That saved a wretch like me . . ."

All around the track you could see armament crews bombing up the planes, fuel crews filling gas tanks, and ground crews doing their final checks. Jeeps and bomb carts and tractors raced up and down the perimeter track. No matter how scared you were about the mission, you couldn't help but be just a little excited too.

> "I once was lost,
> But now I'm found.
> Was blind, but now I see . . ."

My God, our plane is beautiful, Danny thought as the jeep skidded to a halt in front of the *Memphis Belle*. It never ceased to amaze him that the plane was so big on the outside and so cramped on the inside.

It weighed thirty tons and had a wing span of one hundred and three feet. There were four huge engines, two on each wing. The plane was painted olive green on top

75

and gray underneath, but the tips of the propellers were a festive bright yellow.

The nose was Plexiglas. Beside the nose was the painting of the leggy girl in a bathing suit with a telephone receiver to her ear, and next to her a row of twenty-four bomb symbols for the twenty-four missions the *Belle* had flown. Below the bombs was a line of seven little swastikas representing the number of enemy fighter planes the crew had shot down. Two were Eugene's, two were Clay's, and one each for Rascal, Virge, and Jack.

The four officers entered the plane through the nose hatch while the gunners headed for the waist hatch at the rear of the plane. Luke was the first into the cockpit. He vaulted his body into the right seat and plugged himself into the interphone system.

There were dozens of dials and switches on the instrument panel, and more on the left and right walls below the pilot's and copilot's windows. Between the seats was the control box, which contained the ignition switches, engine controls, and throttles. Below that were the trim tab, elevator, and rudder controls. The windshield looked out over the nose, and an overhead window gave a good view of the sky.

"Soon as you're ready, call in," Luke said, pressing his throat microphone button and speaking over the intercom.

Down in the nose, Val and Phil were setting up their stations and also plugging themselves in. The nose was the most spacious part of the aircraft. A man could almost stand up straight without bumping his head.

The Norden bombsight, the secret weapon of the Eighth Air Force, was perched in the very tip of the nose. The bombsight automatically computed the speed of the plane, the weight of the bombs, barometric pressure, wind speed, and drift in order to determine the exact dropping point for the bombs. At the start of the bomb run, four minutes from target, the pilot relinquished control of the plane to

76

the bombardier. For those four minutes the bombardier flew the plane through the bombsight.

Val Kozlowski sat on a small, cracked seat behind the bombsight. On the right front wall of the nose was a panel of bombing instruments. Directly above his instruments was a .30-caliber machine gun. When Val wasn't working the bombsight, he was manning his gun.

There were more instruments on the left, including the bomb-bay door control and the bomb release button. The release had a protective cap, like the safety on a pistol, to keep the bombs from being released accidentally.

"Bombardier checking in," Val said as he affectionately patted the bombsight.

Phil Lowenthal sat farther back at a little desk that jutted out of the left wall of the nose. Above and behind the desk was his navigational equipment: radio compass receiver, drift meter, tuning controls. In the ceiling was a small glass dome in case the navigator needed to steer by the stars.

Phil carefully arranged his materials on the desk: pencils, ruler, maps, flimsies, and logbook. He plugged in his throat mike and tested it.

"Navigator checking in."

Up the stairs from the nose and directly behind the cockpit was the top turret. This was Virge's territory. Two powerful .50-caliber machine guns jutted out of the Plexiglas dome above. Hand controls rotated the turret; other hand controls aimed and fired the guns.

"Top turret checking in," Virge said. The crew was all business now. There was no horsing around. Even though the crew chief and armament crew had checked the equipment, the crew checked it again. Nothing was left to chance.

Directly behind the top turret was the bomb bay. Eight fat olive-drab bombs with yellow markings hung above the doors, four on each side. A narrow catwalk, little more than a metal tightrope, stretched from one end of the bomb bay to the other, connecting the top turret with the radio room.

Danny felt safe in the radio room. It was not large but it was all his. Danny's desk was bolted to the left forward bulkhead wall and held his receivers, transmitters, and Morse code key. More equipment was attached to the right bulkheads, fore and aft. There were two small windows, one on the port side of the fuselage and one on the starboard. A .50-caliber machine gun stuck out of an opening in the ceiling. This was Danny's gun.

"Radio operator checking in," Danny said, then opened his logbook and wrote at the top of a fresh page: "Date: May 17, 1943—Target: Bremen, Germany."

Behind the radio room was a small area that contained the ball turret mechanism. The turret itself, a small round ball of aluminum and Plexiglas, clung to the belly of the plane. Rascal knelt in the ball turret compartment, checking his ammunition boxes. He wanted to make sure the ropes of ammo led easily into the turret. If they jammed, he was a sitting duck.

"Ball turret checking in."

The plane narrowed toward the back. Jack and Eugene, the waist gunners, didn't even have enough room to stand back-to-back at their stations. The stood hip-to-hip. When the action was fast and furious, they couldn't help bumping into each other.

"Right waist gunner checking in," Eugene said, looking over the big rope of copper bullets that rose from the ammo boxes on the floor, looped through a sling in the ceiling and fed into his heavy .50-caliber machine gun.

Jack was lovingly stroking his gun. He had named it Mona. No one knew why. Jack's wife was a real dish and looked like her name should be Mona, but it wasn't. Her name was Patsy. Jack kept a picture of his wife and two kids on the fuselage wall. Nobody could figure out how a grouch like Jack had gotten such a swell looking dame. Everyone was a little jealous.

It was hard to say which was the worst position on the plane, the ball turret or the tail. The ball was uncomfortable and claustrophobic, even for a little guy like Rascal. But the ball was flexible, and because the German pilots usually didn't attack from below, it was one of the safest stations. So it was probably the tail gunner who got the rawest deal.

Clay knelt in front of his guns. There was a little seat to sit on when he wasn't in action, but the tail gunner had to be on his knees to fire his twin .50s. Clay's shoulders just fit in the narrow space between the fuselage walls. His head stuck up into a glass-enclosed box that gave him a spectacular view of the formation behind the plane but also a spectacular view of the Nazi fighters trying to kill him. The tail was cramped, dangerous, and lonely.

The tail gunner was separated from the other men on the plane, but Clay Busby didn't mind too much. He kind of liked it back there. He could sing to his heart's content. "Tail gunner checking in," he reported over the intercom, then hummed a snatch of "Let's Call the Whole Thing Off".

"Inverters," Dennis said, looking at his preflight checklist despite the fact that he had it memorized backward and forward.

"On."

"Generators."

"Off." *This is the last time I have to answer Dennis like a schoolboy reciting his multiplication tables,* Luke thought as he checked the instruments one by one. *Hooray.*

"Fuel booster pumps."

"On."

Virge stepped down from the top turret and crouched behind the control box. This was his takeoff position. Virge was flight engineer as well as top turret gunner, and it was his responsibility to fix anything that went wrong with the plane during flight. Fortunately not much went wrong on the *Belle*.

The engine they had lost over Saint-Nazaire on their last mission was practically the only serious trouble they'd ever had. That wasn't too serious, because a Flying Fortress could stay in the air on three engines, even on two. It was said that a Fortress could fly on one engine, but nobody wanted to try it.

"Good," Dennis said, completing the last item on the checklist. He put down his clipboard and spoke to the crew over the interphone. "Assume positions for take-off."

Virge was the first to see the jeep speeding down the perimeter track. He tapped Dennis on the shoulder and pointed. Dennis slid his side window open as the jeep skidded to a halt in front of the plane. Lieutenant Gregor—stocky, neatly dressed, and perpetually cheerful—shouted up at Dennis.

"Captain, there's a delay. We've got nine-tenths cloud cover over the target. But it might blow over. Stand by your plane until further notice."

"How long?" Dennis asked.

"They don't tell me doodly, sir," Gregory replied, then sped away to the next plane.

Dennis pressed the button on this throat mike and addressed the crew. "Men, we're delayed. There's cloud over the target. They're asking us to stand by until further notice. Danny, tell the others."

Clay, Rascal, Eugene, and Jack weren't on their headsets; they were getting their takeoff positions in the radio room, the safest section of the plane. Danny relayed Dennis's message to the four gunners.

"The target's clouded up. We're delayed."

Nobody said anything for a moment. Frankly they didn't know whether to be overjoyed or disappointed. Nobody much wanted to go to Bremen and be pummeled by two hundred and seventy fighters and two hundred batteries.

But nobody much relished the idea of sitting around the base all day with nothing to do. There had been a lot of days like that.

"SNAFU," said Rascal after a pause.

"Situation normal," Jack added, then Clay, Eugene, and Danny chimed in on the familiar, oft-repeated refrain:

"All fucked up!"

The moment Phil heard about the delay, he knew what he was going to do: sleep. If he just got an hour or even a half hour of sleep, he would be fine.

He pulled off his headphones and throat mike and set them on his desk. A few steps and he was at the nose hatch. He opened it and dropped down onto the pavement. The fresh air smelled good. Behind the base, a farmer was mowing a field of hay. That smelled good too. It was warm and sunny.

Phil ducked under the belly of the plane and climbed up to the left wing. He took off his parachute and set it down. He was so tired that his body was trembling. He laid down and was asleep before his head even hit the parachute.

6

May 17, 1943, 0825 Hours

"Dammit!" Luke said, pounding the steering column in frustration. "Why do they always do this?"

"Okay, Luke, let's do the preflight check again." Dennis ignored his copilot's fury and picked up his clipboard. "We can use this extra time to double-double-check everything. Brakes," he said, reading the first item on the list. Dennis's calm, his lack of any reaction to the standdown, was just the kind of thing that drove Luke to distraction.

"Didn't you hear?" Luke said. "There's a complete cloud cover over Bremen. We're not going anywhere!"

"Brakes," Dennis repeated, as if he hadn't heard.

"Set! They were set before! They're still set!" If Dennis had his way, Luke thought, he'd do the preflight check all day long. That's his idea of fun.

"Hydraulic pressure."

"Check!"

"Fuel transfer valves."

"Off!"

• • •

Clay came out of the plane for a smoke. He certainly wasn't going to sit in that tin can of a tail section a moment longer than he had to, so he jumped out the waist hatch, stretched his cramped leg muscles, and lit up. As he drew deeply on his cigarette he looked over at the farm on the other side of the fence. The hay was pure gold in the morning sun. In the distance, a church spire stuck up like a needle.

Clay didn't have any burning desire to go to war. He never thought the war would be glamorous and exciting. He figured it would be a lot of hard work, and if he was going to work hard, he'd rather do it on the farm where you feel like you're getting something done.

When his second daddy had told Clay that if he didn't join up to defend his country he'd be horsewhipped, Clay didn't put up a fight. He enlisted straightaway. A man had to die sometime; it didn't really matter if it was in the sky above Germany or down home in Louisiana. There was no use worrying about it.

But Clay missed the farm. Shooting a gun was all right, but it couldn't compare with driving a tractor or plowing a field. So when Clay saw the old farmer in worn tweeds bent over an ancient horse-pulled combine baler, Clay found himself walking toward the rickety wooden fence that separated the base from the farm.

"Busted?" Clay called to the old farmer. The baler was parked at the edge of the field. The four workhorses were chewing lazily at the hay while flies buzzed around them.

"I don't know what's wrong with it, Yank," the farmer replied, scratching his head like a character in the funny papers. He had the look of a man who had to get his field mowed today, and of course today was the day the baler chose to break down.

"I've got one just like it at home," Clay said, tossing away his cigarette. "Let me take a look." The fence was strung with a roll of barbed wire. Clay walked along the fence until he found a break in the wire.

The old farmer watched the young man scrambling over the fence. Clay was a sight in his heavy leather pants, suspenders, and blue bunny suit, but if he could fix the baler, the old man would take back everything he'd ever said about the American fliers.

The quiet little town of Bassingbourn had been invaded by Yanks at about this time last year, but the farmer had little contact with them. Once in a while he'd be in the local pub having a drink with the locals when a squadron of unruly fliers would come tumbling in. They would get very drunk very fast and start buying drinks for the house. They usually got in a fight before time was called.

There was a saying about the Yanks: "The only thing wrong with them is that they're overpaid, oversexed and over here."

"I sure miss it," Clay said to the farmer, crouching down to look at the baler. "Sometimes I stand over there and just smell your farm. Takes me right back home. I hope you don't mind my smelling your farm for free."

Clay's Southern accent was so thick, the farmer understood only part of what he was saying. He couldn't be more than twenty-one or twenty-two, the farmer guessed, but he seemed to know what he was doing. He handled the gears of the baler with ease and confidence. Maybe the boy could fix it, after all.

The stand-down was the answer to Bruce Derringer's prayers. He had been unsuccessful in his attempts to reach General Eaker, but now he was talking to Washington. The fact that it was three o'clock in the morning there didn't bother Bruce.

"Well, wake him up at home!" he shouted to the flunky in the State Department who had answered his call. Bruce had a personal relationship with Henry L. Stimson, the Secretary of War, and he was positive that Hank would bar the *Memphis Belle* from going to Bremen. But Bruce had to work fast. There was no telling how long the hiatus would last.

Craig Harriman stopped dead in his tracks when he came into his office and saw Bruce behind his desk, talking on his phone, drinking his coffee, and probably smoking his cigarettes.

"Washington," Bruce said to Craig, as if this explained everything.

"Colonel, I won't tolerate this." Craig Harriman felt his temper flaring. There was something about Bruce Derringer that simply rubbed him the wrong way. "If I have to, I'll have you arrested and locked up until takeoff."

"There won't be any more takeoffs if we can't convince people back home that daylight bombing makes sense," Bruce said, ignoring the threat of arrest. "The *Belle* is the way to do it. I can take it around the States and say look, they made it, they survived twenty-five missions, so can others. . . ."

"Bruce, they're going. That's final," Craig said, cutting Bruce off in mid-sentence. Before Bruce could respond, the door opened and the S-2 came into the office.

"Sir, the cloud cover over Bremen is breaking up. HQ will make a decision in the next ten, fifteen minutes," Comstock reported.

"Thank you, Corporal," Craig Harriman said. Comstock saluted and went out.

"A lot can happen in fifteen minutes," Bruce said to Harriman, and a moment later the fuzzy voice of the State Department flunky came over the phone.

"Yes, I'm still here!" Bruce shouted into the receiver. "Great! You bet I'll hold!" Bruce shot a triumphant look at Craig Harriman while he waited to be put through to the Secretary of War.

Boy, oh boy, this feels good, Clay Busby thought as he rode the antique baler through the hay field. Clay had fixed the contraption in no time, and the old farmer was so grateful that he let Clay drive it for a few minutes. The baler cut the hay, bound it into sheafs, and deposited them on the field fifteen feet apart.

When Clay saw Luke Sinclair jogging toward him, he thought he was in big trouble. He wasn't supposed to leave the base without permission, even if the base was just across the fence. But Clay should have known that Luke didn't care about rules. He had something more important on his mind. He wanted to shoot Clay's gun.

"All you do is call up on the interphone and say you're having trouble in the tail. I'll come back and you let me have the guns for five minutes," Luke said, his shaggy, musty dog trotting happily behind him.

This wasn't the first time Luke had tried to persuade Clay to let him shoot the tail guns. Luke had suggested it on the mission to Hamm one month ago. Clay wouldn't have minded, but he knew that if the captain ever found out, his ass would be placed permanently in an Army-issue sling. So Clay turned Luke down. Now Luke was after him again with the same request.

"It's against regulations, sir," Clay said.

"Screw regulations."

"If they found out, they'd put my hot dog in a bun and chow down," Clay said, watching the neatly tied packages of hay fall out of the baler at regular intervals.

"Nobody's going to find out," Luke said. Luke threw a stick, and Bucky tore ahead of the baler to retrieve it.

"It's just between us," Luke said conspiratorially. "This is my last chance to get my hands on a gun. How am I going to get girls back home if I haven't killed a single Nazi? Clay, you don't know what it's like being a copilot. I don't do anything. I don't shoot a gun. I don't fly the plane. I sit there and take orders from Mr. Perfectionist."

Bucky came racing back and jumped into Luke's arms. Bucky was hot, sweaty, and stinky, but all he had to do was lick Luke's face and he was the most perfect dog God had put on this earth.

"I'll do anything you say, Clay. I mean it. Name your price," Luke said.

Clay stopped the baler. He watched while that dumb, smelly mutt slurped away at Luke's face. Luke was so happy, you'd think he was being kissed by Rita Hayworth.

"Okay. You got a deal," Clay said. "Give me your dog."

Luke's mouth dropped open in shock. He'd never heard of anything so barbaric. He couldn't give Bucky away, not even for the chance to shoot down a Nazi fighter. Maybe Clay was joking, Luke thought. He had to be joking. But Clay kept puffing on his cigarette and eyeballing the dog. Luke began to have this terrible feeling that Clay was serious.

"You're flight engineer—" Rascal started to say, but Virge interrupted.

"I'm flight engineer *when we're in flight*. Les is ground-crew chief. He checked the ball turret and it's okay."

"I know, but just look at it," Rascal asked, stroking the dull silver exterior of the ball turret.

"I just did," Virge said, exasperated. Virge had gone over the turret inch by inch, but Rascal still wasn't satisfied. He kept insisting that something was wrong with it. "Rascal, you're just nervous," Virge said, trying to calm Rascal down. It didn't work.

"I'm not just nervous!" Rascal exploded. "It jammed last mission! I'm the one who has to sit in this rat trap!"

The turret was literally a ball hanging from the belly of the plane. Rascal had heard all the jokes about being the scrotum of the airplane, but it was no laughing matter when you were sitting inside and the turret wasn't responding to the controls. Your mama had better start getting out her black dress.

On their twenty-fourth mission the ball turret simply

froze. Rascal twisted the hand controls again and again, but the turret simply wouldn't move. A fighter came barreling in at five o'clock, firing right at the turret. There was nothing Rascal could do except pray the Nazi bastard was a bad shot.

He was. The fighter zoomed harmlessly by, and a moment later the turret started working again. It was frozen for only fifteen seconds, but they were fifteen of the most terrifying seconds of Rascal's life. He didn't want the same thing to happen again.

"Rascal, I checked it, top to bottom. It's okay," Virge said, trying to reassure the little ball-turret gunner. "Take it easy," he added, then started to pack up his toolbox.

"Gee, thanks, *Virgin*," Rascal said sarcastically.

"The name is Virgil."

"Not to me." Rascal smirked.

Virge flushed with anger. No matter how much you tried to help Rascal, no matter how friendly you were with him, he wouldn't let up. For nine months Virge had endured his sarcasm and taunts, and he was sick of it.

"You know, Rascal, I could tell you something," he said, slamming the lid down on his tool box.

"What? Tell me, *Virgin*," Rascal sneered.

Virge wanted to tell Rascal about Faith so bad, he could taste it. Rascal had wanted Faith for himself, and it would kill him to find out that she had gone with Virge instead.

But Virge had promised Faith that he wouldn't brag about last night. He'd probably never see her again, but that didn't make it any less of a promise. She made him feel like the greatest lover in the world, and all she asked in return was that he didn't announce it to the world. It was a small price to pay. Much as Virge would have enjoyed rubbing it in Rascal's face until the dwarf screamed for mercy, Virge couldn't do it.

"Nothing," he said to Rascal, then picked up his toolbox and walked away.

• • •

Forty-five minutes went by and HQ still hadn't decided whether they were going to Bremen or not. The crew of the *Memphis Belle* was gathered on the flat, grassy area next to the hardstand.

Val was compulsively doing sit-ups, one after the other, trying to put his nervous energy to good use. Rascal shuffled and reshuffled a pack of cards. They were Becker's cards, the dead man's cards. Luke played with his dog. Jack practiced magic tricks. Virge cleaned his tools.

There was almost no breeze and just a few clouds. A cow mooed, although there were no cows in sight. Someone slapped at an insect and the slap sounded like a gunshot.

Then Virge's monkey wrench slipped out of his hands, dropped in his toolbox with a loud clang, and all hell broke loose.

"Jesus!" Rascal said, startled by the bang.

"Virge, do you have to?" Eugene complained.

"Sorry, I just . . ." Virge started to apologize, but then Eugene shouted at Jack and pushed him away.

"Stop it! Leave me alone!" he said. Jack had just pulled a half crown out of Eugene's nose. He was an amateur magician.

"Seven to one we're not going," Clay said calmly, as if it didn't matter one way or the other. He was whittling. Clay was always either whittling or singing or both.

"Let's just go. Let's just get it over with," Val said in the midst of another sit-up. His shirt was off. His stomach had more ripples in it than the English Channel.

"I'd rather get it over with by going to a nice little French target," Jack said, producing a coin out of nowhere, then making it disappear again.

"Yeah, so if we have to bail out, we can hide in some little French girl's hayloft!" Rascal said excitedly.

"Is that all you think about, Rascal?" Virge said. Virge realized he sounded like his father, and he hated himself for it.

"I have to make up for you, *Virgin*," Rascal said, taunting him again. "Take up the slack."

"Why don't you shut up, Rascal?" Virge asked, not politely.

"Why don't you shut up?" Rascal replied, and then the two of them went for each other. They wrestled around in the grass.

"Why don't the both of you shut up?" Jack shouted.

"Okay, men, calm down," said Dennis easily. Virge and Rascal separated. "Getting excited isn't going to do any good," Dennis added. "Relax. Be more like Phil."

He pointed a thumb toward the wing of the plane, where Phil was still fast asleep. Luke and Val looked at each other. The same thought crossed their minds at the same time: If Dennis only knew . . .

"What are you writing, Danny Boy?" Jack said, snatching Danny's notebook from him. "Poetry!" he exclaimed, opening the book and seeing some verses written inside. "We have a poet on the plane!"

"Give it back, King Kong!" Eugene said, grabbed the book from Jack, and handed it back to Danny.

"Thanks, Gene."

"Read us something you wrote, Danny," Val said, sitting up and staying up this time.

"No . . ." Danny started to say, but then the entire crew started begging him to read something. He couldn't tell if they were kidding or not.

"Come on. Come on, Danny."

"It's poetry time!"

"I wanna hear some poetry!"

"Nothing's finished," Danny explained, but now even Dennis was encouraging him to read aloud.

"Don't be shy, Danny," he said. Danny knew he was blushing. Then Jack took out his harmonica, started playing a little of "Danny Boy," and Danny blushed more.

Danny wouldn't have minded reading some of his poetry if it was any good. The problem was, it stank. If he

91

read one of his poems, the crew would laugh, and he wouldn't blame them. Danny opened his notebook to see if there was anything he was proud of, but page after page of his writing was crossed out.

He wanted to be a writer, but he never seemed to finish anything. He got discouraged easily and gave up too quickly. His notebook was filled with half-completed poems. Danny would have given anything to write like Robert Frost or Hart Crane or William Butler Yeats.

That's when the idea came to him. He knew a Yeats poem by heart, a beautiful poem about flying. What would be the harm in pretending that he had written it? He didn't want to lie to his buddies, but he didn't want to disappoint them, either.

He looked down at his notebook. For a panicky second he couldn't even remember how the poem began. Then the first line came back to him: "I know that I shall meet my fate . . ." He was nervous that Dennis or another crew member would have read the poem before. Danny's voice shook a little as he started to recite.

> "I know that I shall meet my fate
> Somewhere among the clouds above;
> Those that I fight I do not hate,
> Those that I guard I do not love . . ."

During the first couple of lines the guys joked around and made fun of the poem, but by the end of the first stanza they had quieted down. Danny was surprised. They were listening and really believed he had written it. He continued.

> "Nor law, nor duty bade me fight,
> Nor public men, nor cheering crowds,
> A lonely impulse of delight
> Drove to this tumult in the clouds;

"I balanced all, brought all to mind,
The years to come seemed waste of breath,
A waste of breath the years behind,
In balance with this life, this death."

That's exactly what I was trying to tell the rookie pilot from *Mother and Country* last night, Dennis thought after Danny had finished. *Everything I've ever done before in my life is insignificant compared to being in command of the* Memphis Belle. *Nothing I will ever do in the future will ever be so important. The war is important. I hate the killing and the suffering, but as long as there is a war and I'm part of it, I want to have an impact. I want to count.*

It was very quiet after Danny finished reading. Even the cow stopped mooing. A little breeze came up and pushed some puffy clouds through the sky. The smell of the hay farm was very strong and sweet. The rest of the world, and the war, seemed far away.

Then all of a sudden a jeep skidded to a halt in front of the plane and the lieutenant who had told them they were delayed shouted, "Captain, you're going up! Takeoff's in five minutes!"

In no time the crew threw their flight clothes back on and were running toward the plane. Val woke Phil. Rascal gave the ball turret one last check and then jumped into the plane. Luke said good-bye to Bucky.

"Okay, Lieutenant, it's a deal," Clay said to Luke as he pulled on his sheepskin jacket and put his cap with the two funny earflaps on his head. "You can shoot my gun for two minutes. Just two."

"I'm not giving you my dog," Luke replied, nuzzling Bucky's mud-encrusted fur.

Clay wrinkled his nose. "I don't want that flea-bitten, mangy pooch, anyway," he said, then jogged off toward the tail. Luke set Bucky down and the dog went tearing off across the field. Luke ran to the nose hatch and hoisted himself into the plane.

He climbed into the cockpit, dropped into his seat, and plugged in his interphone cords. "Let's do the preflight check again for good luck," he said to Dennis. Dennis picked up his clipboard but didn't read the first item on the checklist as Luke expected. Instead he spoke in a quiet, reflective voice.

"Luke, if we could decide right now—do we go to Bremen or stay down—what would you choose?"

"Go! Are you kidding?" Luke said excitedly. "I can't wait!" He was already picturing a Nazi fighter falling out of the sky, riddled with his bullets.

The control tower balcony was crowded with men. So was the lawn below. Colonel Craig Harriman looked at his watch, then nodded to the S-2. Comstock fired a green flare. It arced over the field.

Captain Dennis Dearborn flipped a switch on the control panel. Engine One coughed, belched a blue-white cloud of smoke, and the propeller blades started to turn. They turned slowly and jerkily at first but soon gained momentum and whirled into invisibility.

Clay, Eugene, Jack, and Rascal gathered in the radio room. No one was allowed in the narrow tail of the plane during takeoff; the extra weight caused it to drag. The radio room, positioned between the two wings, was the most solid part of the aircraft.

Rascal nervously shuffled his deck of cards. Clay whittled and hummed. Eugene clasped his hands and moved his lips in silent prayer. Jack practiced his magic tricks.

Engine Two roared into action. The fuselage started to vibrate from the whirling of the propellers. In the nose, Phil was having difficulty keeping his desk in order. His pencils rolled off the desk; as soon as he picked them up, his maps fell to the floor. So he bit off a piece of chewing gum, attached it to a pencil, and stuck it to the desk. In no time he had every pencil, map, and flimsy gummed down. You learned these little tricks after twenty-four missions.

Dennis flipped another switch and Engine Three began to turn. Then Engine Four started up. Engines were pounding all over the field. Clouds of dust whooshed into the air, and the grass whipped frantically back and forth. The air was wrinkled with gasoline fumes.

Bruce Derringer hurried onto the control tower balcony, followed by the *Life* photographer. Bruce had spoken to the Secretary of War, but Stimson had refused to interfere with Colonel Harriman's decision to send the *Belle* to Bremen. Bruce made the case that the future of daylight bombing depended on the *Belle*'s survival, but Hank would not change his mind. If Harriman said the *Belle* had to go, it had to go.

In a moment the S-2 would fire the second flare, which signaled the planes to start lining up on the runway. This was Harriman's last chance to change his mind. He could radio orders to Captain Dearborn to shut down his engines. In a few minutes it would be too late.

Bruce looked at Harriman. His face was tense, his mouth drawn in a tight line. A muscle twitched in his left cheek. Bruce realized that Harriman would never back down, no matter how much Bruce pleaded. It was now a matter of pride. Harriman wanted to put twenty-four planes in the air, and now twenty-four planes were revving their engines, waiting for the signal to move onto the runway.

It came. The second flare streaked over the field. Les Enright, the crew chief of the *Belle*, shouted to his ground crew to pull the chocks. Two men ducked behind the whirling propellers and dragged the triangular wooden blocks out from under the huge front tires.

"Let's move it!" Les motioned to Dennis to pull forward.

"Unlock tail wheel!" Dennis said over the thundering of the engines. Luke reached down to the lower control pedestal and released the tail wheel brake.

"Tail wheel unlocked!"

Dennis gently released the front wheel brakes, keeping his right hand on the throttles. Without the slightest bump or jerk the plane rolled off the hardstand and onto the perimeter track. They were on their way.

7

Windy City, Mama's Boys, C Cup, Mother and Country,
and *Memphis Belle*—the planes lined up one after another
on the runway. The Flying Fortresses looked ungainly on
the ground, leaden and cumbersome. It was hard to believe they could fly.

Craig Harriman glanced at his watch, then nodded to
the S-2. Comstock fired another flare. As it rocketed over
the field the green flare split into two prongs. It was the
signal for the lead plane, *Windy City,* to take off.

Windy City hurtled down the runway. The sheer weight
of the plane seemed to hold it down. Thirty tons of machinery was never meant to fly. But at eighty miles per
hour its front wheels rose up a little. For an instant the
plane hovered a few feet above the runway, as if unable
to make up its mind whether or not to take to the sky.
Then it simply lifted into the air.

Thirty seconds later *Mama's Boys* sailed away, looking
no heavier than a balsa-wood airplane. Then came *C Cup.*

Then the new plane, *Mother and Country*. Its takeoff was so smooth, the rookie crew seemed like old pros.

"Ten, nine, eight." Luke counted off the seconds. Dennis's right hand was tight on the throttles, his eye fixed on the runway ahead.

"Seven, six . . ."

In the radio room, Jack, Eugene, Clay, and Rascal were sitting on the floor in their takeoff positions. Danny sat at his desk. He pressed his headphones hard against his ears, listening for transmissions from the control tower.

"Five, four . . ."

Val was also in his takeoff position, his back against the aft bulkhead wall of the nose. Phil sat in his chair, his hand gripping the cold metal edge of the desk. Takeoff could be the most dangerous part of the mission, especially when the plane was carrying the maximum load of explosives. Three weeks ago a plane lost an outboard engine on takeoff, plunged to the ground, and blew up. They were still filling in the huge hole it left in the earth.

"Three, two, one! Go!" Luke shouted.

Dennis eased the throttles forward. The *Belle* started to move down the runway. Dennis cocked his ears for any unusual noise or vibration, but the plane sounded good as new. Dennis remembered having unfairly reprimanded the ground-crew chief last night for neglecting the plane. He meant to apologize to Les, but it had slipped his mind. It was too late now.

The *Belle* picked up speed: forty, fifty, sixty miles per hour. Dennis kept his eye on the instruments. Luke watched the runway. Virge was crouched behind them, his eye darting across the instrument panel, searching for anything amiss. Everything looked good. Seventy miles per hour. Seventy-five. Eighty. Eighty-five.

The plane took a breath. That's how Dennis always thought of it. She always took a little breath right before she lifted up. It was like the breath a man takes before he dives into a pool of water. Dennis eased the throttles forward a fraction of an inch to encourage her.

That was all she needed. The two front wheels left the ground, the huge wings felt the air underneath them, and the plane rose into the sky, headed for a bank of perfect clouds.

Luke grabbed Virge by the collar of his Mae West, yanked him down, and shouted happily in his ear, "This is what sex is like!"

Virge, who now knew what sex was like, didn't contradict him.

"Wheels!" Dennis ordered.

"I know," said Luke, flipping a switch on the throttle box. There was a high-pitched electric whine as the landing gear retracted up into the bottom of the plane.

"Watch the cowl flaps," Dennis said.

"I know!" Luke said irritably. Luke wondered, *Does he think I'm a moron? We've only done this a hundred times.*

Those perfect, fluffy clouds were right ahead. They were bigger than they appeared from down below. Clouds are pretty to look at, but they're not pretty to fly through, especially in a sky full of planes. All it took was one pilot not sticking to his predetermined altitude and climbing speed and there could be a deadly midair collision.

They entered a cloud. Dense white fog enveloped the plane. Visibility was zero. Dennis kept his eyes on the instrument panel to make sure that he was at the correct speed and altitude. Luke monitored the sky ahead. He shifted nervously in his seat. He couldn't see a thing. *I might as well have my eyes shut,* he thought. *I hope to God everybody knows what they're doing up here.*

And then they were flying right into the belly of another B-17. It was so close, Luke could see the faces of the crew members through the windows.

"Look out!" he screamed.

Dennis pushed on the control wheel and the nose of the

Belle dropped down. Virge was thrown off his feet and hit his head hard on the back of Dennis's seat. The renegade B-17 roared overhead, missing the *Belle* by a few feet. Luke looked through the overhead window and saw a painting on the nose of the plane: an eagle perched on an American flag and the name, *Mother and Country*. It was the rookies.

"Jesus, that was close," Luke said as Dennis pulled the plane up. It had all happened so fast, it was hard to believe it had happened at all. Two minutes into the mission and they had almost been killed. Luke wondered what else was in store.

As much as Dennis got under Luke's skin with his superior attitude, Luke had to admit that he was capable of making very quick decisions. If Dennis had waited a half second longer to drop the plane, they would have crashed into the rookies. Even Luke was impressed.

Virge sat back on his heels, touched his forehead and got blood on his fingers. He knew the cut wasn't serious— it was just a bump—but this was the first time anybody had ever been wounded on the *Memphis Belle*. He hoped it was also the last.

Then they were out of the clouds and flying through dazzling blue, blue sky. The sun was so bright that the three men in the cockpit had to squint. Below, the English countryside was a green and brown and yellow patchwork quilt.

A B-17 eased up on the left side. *Baby Ruth* had been around almost as long as the *Belle*. This was *Baby Ruth*'s twenty-second mission. It was a good sign to have such an experienced crew as their left wingman.

"Who's our right wingman?" Luke asked.

"Mother and Country," said Dennis.

"Swell. The rookie crew," Luke said with a groan.

"Luke, take over for a second," Dennis said. He released the control wheel and Luke grabbed hold of it. Steering the plane was nothing like steering an automobile; it took brute strength to hold the plane steady. The Fortress moved up and down in the air; it needed constant adjustment but Luke loved it. Dennis didn't let him take control often enough.

Dennis opened a thermos and poured steaming tomato soup into the cup. He offered some to Virge, but Virge shook his head. The soup reminded him of his wound. He touched the cut on his forehead and felt a dried crust. It had already stopped bleeding.

In the waist, Jack was lovingly stroking the long black barrel of his gun.

"Okay, Mona, let's get us a nice little 109 today," he cooed romantically to the .50-caliber. "We got us one a couple of months ago. Let's do it again."

Eugene watched. *My partner is crazy,* he thought. *He talks to his gun like it was a beautiful woman. If he kisses it, I'm bailing out.*

"Sweet-talking your gun won't help, Jack," Eugene yelled above the roar of wind coming in the open windows of the waist. "Just straight shooting."

"Butt out, Gene," Jack snarled.

"You know, when I got my *two* Nazi fighters . . ." Eugene said proudly, holding up two fingers just to drive the point home.

"You're asking for it!" Jack threatened. Eugene laughed. He loved to rub in the fact that he had two confirmed kills while Jack had only one.

It wasn't enough for a gunner to shoot down a fighter. The kill also had to be confirmed. Two men, members of your own crew or crew members on another plane, had to witness the kill.

The problem was that everything happened so fast in the sky that it was hard to tell who had shot what. A gunner might destroy ten fighters, but if nobody saw him do it, he wouldn't get credit. Eugene had been lucky: both times he scored a direct hit on enemy aircraft they were confirmed, once by Virge, once by Rascal. That really got Jack's goat.

Still chuckling, Eugene turned back to the right waist window. The minute his back was turned, Jack clipped him behind the knees. Eugene crumpled and almost fell to the floor. Jack laughed loudly at his practical joke.

I've got to think of a good trick to play on Jack, Eugene thought. *This is our last mission together. I want to come up with something that he will never forget, the practical joke to end all practical jokes.* Eugene started sifting through the possibilities.

"Captain, okay if I arm my bombs?" Val asked over the interphone.

"Go ahead."

Val pulled his interphone cord from the jack box and walked toward the hatch leading up to the cockpit. Phil caught hold of him.

"Here, take this," he said, pulling a gold class ring off his finger and pressing it into Val's hand.

"Phil, look, you're not going to die," Val said.

"Just in case. I want you to have it to remember me by," Phil said, pressing the ugly ring into Val's hand.

Val was sick and tired of babying Phil. First he had to find Phil, then he had to sober him up, then he had to cover for him. He felt like hitting the navigator on the side of the head. Maybe it would knock some sense into him.

"You're flak-happy," he said. "We took a big chance on you. Now do your job and shut up!" Val disappeared up the hatch before Phil tried to give him something else to remember him by, like his dirty underwear. Val wondered if his friend had lost his mind. He wouldn't be the first flier who went flak-happy, the Air Force equivalent of battle fatigue.

Val kind of wished that he had gone flak-happy just once during his tour of duty. He would have been sent to the flak shack, a beautiful English estate where you did nothing but lounge around and be waited on hand and foot by pretty nurses.

But Val was not a candidate for the flak shack. His nerves were much too steady. Steady hands and steady nerves—those were good qualities for a bombardier to have. They were even better qualities for a doctor.

In the bomb bay, Val gently eased the cotter pin from the nose of one of the big olive-drab bombs. This was the first of three stages in the arming of a bomb. The second stage occurred when the bomb was released. An arming wire leading to the bomb rack was disconnected as the bomb fell from the bomb bay. The third stage happened as the bomb dropped toward the target. A silver pinwheel on the bomb's tail started to twirl. As it twirled, the pinwheel unscrewed. Only when the pinwheel fell off the end of the bomb was the bomb fully armed.

That was not to say that the bombs were perfectly harmless before they were armed. More than one plane had blown up when a German antiaircraft gunner scored a direct hit on the bomb bay. Maybe that's why Val always patted the bombs a little after he removed the cotter pins. He liked to think of them as his friends.

While Val was arming the bombs Virge was helping Rascal drop down into the ball turret. The ball-turret gunner never got into position until the plane was safely off the ground. It was much too dangerous to ride in the turret during takeoffs and landings. Anyway, the ball was so cramped and uncomfortable, even for a small guy like Rascal, that the gunner always waited until the last possible second to get into the turret.

"Rascal, there's nothing wrong with it," Virge said, supporting Rascal under the armpits as Rascal inserted his legs through the small entry slot.

"Don't worry your pretty head about it, Virge," Rascal replied sarcastically.

"I'm just doing my job."

"Now you do it. Thanks a lot," Rascal said, then

slipped down into the turret. Virge closed the hatch over him, and a moment later the turret started turning smoothly with a high-pitched whine. *It looks fine to me,* Virge thought, giving the gears one last check. Although Virge knew the mechanics of the ball turret like the back of his hand, he had never actually sat inside. It scared the pants off him.

In the ball turret, Rascal was like a baby in a womb—an aluminum and Plexiglas womb. There were small windows all around the turret and one large circular pane of armored glass in the front, which gave a good view of the sky and the ground below. Two .50-caliber machine guns jutted out of the turret, one on either side of the main window.

The Sperry ball turret was tight and claustrophobic. The gunner laid back in the curve of the ball with his legs cocked and spread in front of him. His head was almost completely hidden by a complex panel of hand controls and firing switches. At the same time the turret was insubstantial, nothing more than a little pouch clinging to the belly of the plane.

Rascal worked the turret back and forth, up and down, testing it, almost trying to find something wrong with it. The turret had jammed once before. The fact that neither the ground-crew chief nor Virge could find anything wrong didn't satisfy Rascal. Your tooth always stops aching the moment you step into the dentist's office; you still have a cavity.

"Boys, we're at ten thousand feet," Rascal heard Luke say over the interphone. "Let's hear your oxygen checks."

Rascal clamped his oxygen mask to his face. This was the part he hated most. It was worse than the fighters and the flak. It was even worse than hanging outside the plane in a plastic scrotum.

The mask fitted so tightly over your face that when you finally took it off, your skin was rubbed raw. Your sinuses ached after breathing pure oxygen for hours on end; a long mission like today's could give you a headache that would last a week.

"Clay, how are you doing back there?" Luke asked, and right away Clay's smooth singing voice came over the interphone:

> "Don't worry 'bout me,
> I'll get along . . ."

Clay had a million songs, and somehow he always found one that fit the occasion.

"Captain, we're exactly five miles south-southwest of Great Yarmouth," Phil reported from the nose. "This is the rally point. We're in formation."

From his vantage point under the plane Rascal could see B-17s spread out all over the sky in perfect little *V*s. The planes flew as tight to each other as possible. The closer you flew, the more your gun power counted. The Gerries were less inclined to come in close when the planes were clustered together. Flying tight formation was exhausting and dangerous, but it helped keep the Germans at bay.

"Okay, boys," said Dennis, "we're on our way."

The formation was composed of three groups, eighteen planes to each group. The *Memphis Belle* was in the first group.

The first group was divided into three squadrons. The high squadron flew above and a little to the left, the lead squadron flew underneath and slightly forward, and the low squadron flew below and slightly to the right.

The *Belle* was lead plane of the second element of the lead squadron. The first element flew above and just ahead of the second.

Windy City was the lead plane of the first element. It led the entire group. Its wingmen were *Mama's Boys* and *C Cup*.

Memphis Belle was lead plane of the second element,

105

with *Baby Ruth* as its left wingman and the rookie plane, *Mother and Country*, on its right.

Nearly three hundred planes were in the air, flying thirty thousand feet above the cold North Sea. Contrails—wide, beautiful white strips of vapor—streamed from each engine on each plane. The contrails striped the sky.

"Listen, men," Dennis said over the interphone, "I'm showing almost thirty below zero up here, so keep your gloves on. Don't touch your gun with your bare hands or your fingers will stick right to it. I don't want anyone losing any fingers."

Dennis always gave the same speech every time. It didn't matter if it was their first mission, their tenth, or their twenty-fifth. It was always the same. He started out with the rule about keeping their gloves on and then told them always to check their masks.

"Keep checking your masks for frozen saliva. That stuff gets down there and freezes up and blocks up your oxygen flow. The last thing I need is someone passing out on me."

"In short," Rascal said, "don't drool."

"In short," Dennis said, "check your masks."

In the radio room, Danny was wrapping the bottle of champagne in an extra pair of long johns he had brought along to keep it warm. He hoped the champagne wouldn't freeze and explode. He really wanted to surprise everyone by popping it open on the trip home.

"Keep the interphone free and call out those fighters," Dennis said, continuing his instructions. "Make it short and sweet and let the next guy say his piece. And don't shout on the interphone. We can hear you loud and clear."

Down in the nose, Phil was trying to decide how to distribute his possessions to the crew. He wanted everyone to have a little something to remember him by after he got killed. He was a little hurt that Val didn't want his watch, his cuff links, or his ring, but he felt sure that the other men would appreciate a little memento.

"This is for Virge," he said, setting his lucky rabbit's foot to one side. Then he decided that Clay might appreciate the rabbit's foot more, because of his farm background. He set the rabbit's foot aside for Clay. He would give the class ring to Virge.

"Let's make this our best run yet," Dennis said, as if he had never said this before. "One we can really be proud of."

"Right in the pickle barrel, huh, Dennis?" Val said, anticipating Dennis's next line.

"*Only* in the pickle barrel. Let's keep our minds on our jobs, work together, and stay alert." Dennis always finished his little pep talk with this advice.

"Captain, I'm getting Gracie Allen here," Danny said. He started hearing Gracie's funny, high-pitched voice over the radio while Dennis was giving his speech. "Can I put her on?" he asked.

"Yeah, yeah!" Rascal said excitedly.

"Please, sir!" This was Virge. Gracie Allen was just about the only thing Virge and Rascal agreed on—they both thought she was swell.

"All right, Danny," Dennis said reluctantly, like a parent whose kids were begging to stay up late. "But when I say that's enough . . ."

Danny was so afraid he would lose the radio signal that he flicked the switch before Dennis even finished speaking. The voices of George Burns and Gracie Allen came in loud and clear on the interphone. Gracie's wacky voice made everyone smile before she even told a joke.

". . . my family is putting on a backyard circus, just like we did when I was a kid," she said.

"Every spring you kids used to put on your own circus?" George asked. George always asked the questions and Gracie always gave the answers. She always was mixing things up and getting things wrong. That was the fun of Burns and Allen.

"Yes. Of course, admission was free, but that was only

for people who could afford it." It was the kind of joke that was so dumb, you had to laugh. Danny laughed.

While Burns and Allen continued their routine Eugene was making a little joke of his own. This was the last chance to play a trick on Jack that he would never forget. It would pay Jack back for all the time Jack had made a fool of him or called him Geenie the Weenie.

On the back of an old flimsy Eugene wrote in big block letters, COULDN'T GET LAID LAST NIGHT! He attached two pieces of electrician's tape to the flimsy, and when Gracie told a particularly funny joke, Eugene slapped the sign on the back of Jack's flight jacket.

Jack turned and smiled, thinking that Eugene was just enjoying Gracie's joke with him. Jack had no idea that the joke was on him. COULDN'T GET LAID LAST NIGHT was attached to his back for all the world to see. Eugene giggled. He couldn't wait until Jack found out about the sign.

There was a loud burst of static over the radio and George and Gracie's voices started to fade. Danny fiddled with the frequency dial, trying to get the signal back, but the two comics kept disappearing. They were right in the middle of another joke when they disappeared altogether.

Everyone was disappointed. Now they would never know the punch line. But that wasn't the only reason the crew was silent when the signal faded away. Now they were too far from England even to pick up a friendly radio signal. It meant they were getting closer to Germany with every minute.

"Okay," Dennis said, "enough fooling around. Test-fire your guns."

8

A moment later the plane thundered with the sound of machine guns.

Rascal spun the ball turret around, firing in a complete circle. The vibration of the guns went right through him and rattled the turret so hard, it felt like it would drop right out of the plane.

In the waist, Jack and Eugene both opened fire. They stood hip-to-hip in the narrow compartment. Shells spit out of their guns and fell to the floor. By the end of a mission the deck would be covered with spent cartridges. Stepping on them was like stepping on loose roller skates.

Down in the nose, Phil and Val also tested their guns. When the navigator and bombardier weren't busy with their individual tasks, they were expected to man their guns. On the bomb run, when the bombardier was too busy to worry about fighters, the navigator was expected to cover both guns.

Clay Busby woke up. He had dozed off during Dennis's little speech, and when Clay heard the firing of the guns, he thought they were already in action. He looked around for bandits, but the sky was clear. He realized that the firing was a test. He knocked off a round with his twin .50s just for good luck.

"Little friends, three o'clock high!" Virge announced, and everyone looked up to see a squadron of P-47 Thunderbolts streak across the sky above the formation.

The Thunderbolts were one-seat fighters powered by a single propeller mounted in a round, blunt nose with a white ring painted around the cowling. Four machine guns were mounted in each wing. The Thunderbolts could do anything. They twisted and turned and dived and banked with ease. They made the huge B-17s look like dinosaurs.

"I'd give anything to fly a Thunderbolt," Luke said enviously as he watched the little fighters. "You're all by yourself, you can do anything you want. That's flying."

The little friends would escort the formation as far as their small gas tanks would allow, then they would return to their bases, refuel, and meet the formation on the way back from the target. It was a great feeling knowing that the little friends were nearby, ready to leap to your defense. It was a terrible moment when they wiggled their wings, disappeared, and left you to fight the enemy alone.

"It's the best pen money can buy," Phil said as he presented the shiny black fountain pen to Eugene. Phil's father had given it to him for graduation, and it was one of his most treasured possessions. He couldn't understand why Eugene was looking at it like it was a chewed-up pencil Phil had found on the floor.

"Why can't I have the baseball cards?" Eugene asked, looking at the complete set of New York Yankee cards Phil held in his other hand. They were especially precious now because of the paper shortage. Baseball cards hadn't been made since 1941, and wouldn't be made again until after the war, whenever that was.

"They're for Jack," Phil said, presenting the cards to the left waist gunner. Jack scratched his neck.

"I'm really more of a football fan myself," he said, eyeing the fountain pen.

Goddammit, Phil thought, *I'm going to die and they're already bickering over who gets what!* He grabbed the baseball cards from Jack, thrust them into Eugene's hand, snatched the fountain pen from Eugene, and gave it to Jack.

"Happy?" he screamed, then turned on his heel and walked toward the front of the plane.

Danny watched Phil as he angrily stomped through the radio room on his way back to the nose. Danny sensed that something was wrong and was just about to ask Phil if he could help when he heard a crackle over the radio and a high, nervous voice speaking to him.

"*Mother and Country* calling *Memphis Belle.* Come in."

Danny quickly flipped a switch and glanced out the window at *Mother and Country* to see what was wrong. Radio operators were only supposed to communicate with each other in very serious emergencies. The Germans might be listening. But the rookies' plane was flying nice and tight to the right side of the *Belle,* like it was supposed to. It looked fine.

"Read you, *Mother,*" Danny replied. "What's wrong?"

"Nothing, Danny," said the rookie radio operator with whom Danny had made friends at the dance last night. "I just had a question—"

Danny interrupted. "We're not supposed to use the radio unless it's an emergency."

"Oh, s-sorry," the rookie said, stammering. "It was just about my logbook, whether I should write down every radio communication I hear or just ones about us."

Danny didn't want to come down hard on the rookie. Danny remembered his own first mission. He felt he was doing everything wrong and would get in trouble when he got back down to the ground. It took a while to figure it all out. *Tonight I'll take the rookie aside and give him some pointers,* Danny thought.

"Write down everything at first," Danny said quickly, "then later you can decide what's important. Look, we better sign off."

"Okay. Thanks, Danny," said the rookie. "I won't bother you again."

Danny's camera was in the corner of his desk. He brought it along so that he could take pictures on the way home. He wanted to get a shot of the crew popping open the champagne and maybe an overhead photo of the base, although that was against regulations.

He thought that perhaps the rookie would like a picture of himself on his first mission when he was green and didn't know what he was doing. Danny stood up and aimed his camera out the right window. He could see the rookie bent over his desk, making an entry in his log-book.

"I'm taking your picture. Smile," Danny said, and clicked the shutter.

They were out over the cold, gray North Sea. It was a long flight to Germany. There wasn't much to do except wait and worry about what was to come. Every so often Dennis would speak over the interphone, just to keep the crew alert.

"We're getting close to enemy territory," he said. "Be on guard. Call out those fighters as soon as you see them."

Mostly it was quiet, except for the constant pounding

of the engines. The gunners watched the sky, knowing that at any moment it could begin.

"I wish they'd come," Jack said.

"The man wants to be shot at," Rascal commented.

"It's better than waiting."

Each gunner had his own area of the sky to patrol. The sky was a big clock with the nose of the plane pointing to twelve. The right side was one o'clock to five o'clock, the tail was six, and the left side of the plane was seven to eleven o'clock.

If a fighter was headed straight at the nose, it was coming in at twelve o'clock. If it was flying down at the nose, the gunner would call out "Twelve o'clock high." If it was at the same altitude as the plane, the gunner would call "Twelve o'clock level," and if it was coming from below, the call would be "Twelve o'clock low." The calls were the same all around the clock.

When Val wasn't stationed at the bombsight, he manned his gun on the right side of the nose. He covered the sky from twelve o'clock to three o'clock—high, level, and low. On the left side of the nose Phil checked the sky from nine o'clock to twelve o'clock—also high, level, and low.

Virge, his head stuck up into the dome of the top turret, had a bird's-eye view of the entire sky above. The turret revolved three hundred and sixty degrees, so his territory was all positions of the clock high. He kept particular guard over the cockpit; neither pilot nor copilot had weapons.

The opening in the roof of the radio room afforded only a limited view of the sky, so Danny could only watch the clock from four to eight high. Danny knew he was a good radio operator but a lousy gunner. As far as he knew, he had never hit an enemy aircraft.

The ball-turret gunner had a spectacular piece of the sky below. Revolving his turret in a circle, Rascal watched for enemy aircraft at all low and level positions. Rascal kept the ball moving; it was never still.

The big open windows in the waist allowed Jack and Eugene to patrol large portions of the sky on both the port and starboard sides of the aircraft. Jack, on the left, checked for Gerries from eight to ten o'clock. Eugene, on the right, watched from two to four.

From his narrow perch in the tail, Clay Busby kept watch over the entire area behind the plane. He was isolated from the other gunners, but he didn't mind that too much. Clay was a little bit of a loner, anyway. He found himself humming, ''I'll go my way by myself . . .''

It was hard to say which was the hardest part of a mission. Some said it was having that oxygen mask clamped to your face for so many hours. Others said it was the fighters; still others said it was the flak. But most said it was the waiting.

There was a lot of waiting, and waiting got a man into trouble. It gave him time to think, and when a man began to think, he began to worry. He worried about the plane getting hit and going down. He worried whether he could get out of the plane and whether his parachute would open. He worried about being caught by the Gestapo. He worried about spending the rest of the war as a POW.

The crew thought about home. It seemed impossible that life was going on without them back in Duluth and Seattle and Philadelphia. They wondered what their mothers, girlfriends, and ex-girlfriends were doing right at this moment. They wondered what on earth they would do with their lives once the war was over.

''Clay, you really sang great last night,'' Eugene said as he watched the bright sky for fighters. ''You should do like we keep saying. After the war go to Hollywood and get a record contract like Frank Sinatra.''

''Yeah, so we can say we knew you when,'' Jack added. Clay was whittling while he waited for the action to begin. "Nah. I'm gonna get me a nice little farm and a nice little wife and settle down," he said. "Luke's the one who should go to Hollywood. He could star in the pictures."

"Maybe, maybe," said Luke, contemplating the possibility of being another Cary Grant. "I don't know what I'm going to do after the war. Except not work."

"Yeah, Luke, why go back to the daily grind of being a lifeguard?" Rascal said sarcastically. "Take it easy!"

"I'm not going to do that anymore."

"Yeah, I'm not going back to the pharmacy, either," said Eugene.

"I know exactly what I'm going to do after the war," Virge piped up.

"Virge, if I hear one more word about that stupid restaurant of yours," Rascal said impatiently, knowing that Virge was about to tell them for the millionth time in boring detail about his plans to open a hamburger restaurant back home in Minnesota.

"It's not stupid!" Virge said angrily. "At least I've got a plan. What are you going to do after the war, Rascal?"

"Come to your restaurant and rob it!" Rascal replied. Everyone laughed, and Virge felt his face flush. *Well,* he thought, *they can laugh all they want, but I'll have the last laugh.* Virge pictured a string of identical restaurants all over the country, each one bearing his name in neon lights.

"Val's the smart one," said Jack. "He's got it all mapped out. All he needs is another year or so and he'll be a doctor. We'll all still be picking our noses, wondering what to do with ourselves."

Val didn't answer. He was thinking: *I wish I'd never let them think I finished medical school when I only went for about two and a half weeks. I'll be so glad when I don't have to lie about it anymore.*

"What kind of doctor are you going to be, Val?"

"A rich one," Val said, and got a laugh. Actually he

115

wanted to be a general practitioner and treat all kinds of patients, but it made a better joke if he pretended he was in it for the money.

"What about Phil?" he asked, changing the subject as quickly as possible and looking over at his partner. "What should he be after the war?"

Phil's skin was so pale, it was almost transparent. A bead of sweat was sliding down the side of his face. He might as well have a tattoo across on his forehead reading, "Scared shitless!"

"A mortician?" Val suggested, looking at Phil to see his reaction. Phil said nothing; he just turned away.

He'll be sorry he said that when I get hit in the chest with a .50-caliber bullet, Phil thought morbidly. *Or maybe a piece of flak will slice off my head and it'll go rolling across the floor and stop at Val's feet.* It comforted Phil to think of the worst possible scenario.

"Fellas, think about this," Dennis said to the entire crew. "My family has a furniture business. We make furniture and sell it. It's a big venture. We need a lot of help. You can all come work for me."

There was complete silence. Not a word was said. Not a single member of the crew volunteered to work for Dennis. Feeling ridiculous, Dennis spoke again.

"Like I said, don't give it a thought."

Dennis was hurt. He hadn't made the offer on a whim. He had been thinking about it for a long time and was waiting for the right moment to pop the question. He got along well with the crew. They were a team. Why not continue the good work after the war? They could transform Dearborn Furniture into a major national corporation.

"That's just what we need, you ordering us around the rest of our lives," Luke said. He imitated Dennis's voice: "Let's do the preflight check again for the twentieth time."

Then all of a sudden the whole crew was imitating Den-

116

nis, poking fun at the instructions he gave them every mission without fail.

"Don't hog the interphone!" Rascal said.

"Keep your gloves on!" Virge said.

"Check your masks!" Danny said.

"Call out those fighters!" Jack said.

"Let's make this our best one yet!" Clay said.

"Right in the pickle barrel!" Val said.

Everybody laughed.

Dennis said, "I'm not that bad." He tried to be good-natured about the teasing, but in truth Dennis was a little stung. He repeated the warnings time after time, not because he thought his men were stupid but because he didn't want a single one of them getting hurt.

They can rib me all they want, Dennis thought, *but I'm responsible for my men and my ship and I don't want anything going wrong. Maybe I'm a little bit of a stuffed shirt at times, but that's a small price to pay for getting everyone back home safe and sound every time.*

Dennis's thoughts were interrupted by Clay's voice on the interphone. He addressed Danny. "Danny Boy, you didn't say what you're going to do when it's all over."

Danny honestly didn't know what he was going to do after the war. Before he had enlisted, he'd worked in the public library, but that was just a summer job. He had studied English literature in college, so he could always teach. Being a teacher didn't sound so bad, although it didn't sound as good as being a famous writer.

"I don't really like even thinking about it," Danny said. "I mean, what if something happens to us?" This just slipped out; he didn't mean to say it. It was bad luck to think that they might not make it. Sometimes it seemed like everything was bad luck.

"What I mean is, it just seems so far away, that's all," Danny added.

A silence fell over the plane, as silent as it could be with the constant pounding of the engines and the wind

117

rushing through the open waist windows and the open hatch in the radio-room roof.

Danny was right, there was no telling when the war would be over. Daylight bombing was supposed to stop the Nazis, but the Luftwaffe was as strong as ever. Hitler still occupied Poland and France and was bombing London almost every night.

When the crew of the *Memphis Belle* returned from Bremen, the war would be over for them. They would go back to the States and train other young men to be gunners and bombardiers and pilots. But the war would keep going on and on until somebody won. In the spring of 1943 it was a close call. Even Clay Busby didn't take odds on who would win. America had never lost a war before, but there was always a first time.

For the first time in his life Danny was glad that he had sisters instead of brothers. If he had brothers, they, too, would have to risk their lives over Germany or in Italy or in the South Pacific. It was better never to have brothers than to have brothers and lose them in the war.

The silence continued. It was strange to hear the interphone so quiet. Somebody was always making a joke or calling out a fighter or singing a song. Danny kicked himself for spoiling the mood. Before, they were fooling around and having a good time making fun of the captain. Then he'd brought everyone down by suggesting that the war would never end.

"Sorry," Danny apologized, but no one said, "That's okay," or "Don't worry about it." No one said anything. *I hope they're not mad at me,* Danny thought, worrying. *I couldn't stand it if the fellows were mad at me.*

Suddenly Eugene shouted, "Bandits, five o'clock high!" Danny looked up through the opening in the radio-room roof. There they were, six little black specks in the sky. Danny swung around his machine gun and sighted them in. They were too far away to fire at right now, but give them time.

Virge turned his handgrip, and the top turret spun to face the fighters. He aimed his guns. He wished he had a candy bar to fill the hole in his stomach. He hadn't eaten anything at breakfast.

In the waist, Eugene made a quick check of his gun and ammunition rope, then he sighted in the fighters too. His finger tightened on the trigger. He glanced down to see if his lucky St. Anthony medal was still around his neck. It was. As long as he had his medal, he'd be all right.

"Go get 'em, little friends!" Luke shouted, and the friendly fighters peeled away from the formation and eagerly climbed up the sky to attack the Germans. The party was about to begin.

9

"Hold your fire until Gerry's in range," Dennis warned the gunners over the interphone. "Don't waste ammunition."

As soon as he said it, though, there was the rattling of a machine gun from the rear of the plane. It made everyone jump.

"I said, hold your fire!" Dennis shouted, and a moment later the firing stopped.

"That was Geenie the Weenie," said Jack, looking over his shoulder at Eugene. "Hosing the air, like always."

Eugene felt his face turn bright red, even though his skin was practically frozen stiff. He knew he was trigger-happy. He couldn't help it. He wanted to fire at them before they fired at him.

Jack was laughing at him, so Eugene faked a kick to Jack's groin. Jack didn't even flinch. I guess I've used that trick too many times, Eugene thought, but wait until Jack sees the sign, COULDN'T GET LAID LAST NIGHT!, taped to his back. That will make him madder than hell. Just thinking about his partner's fury made Eugene smile.

The little friends and the Nazi fighters rushed at each other at a combined speed of over six hundred miles per hour. Twinkling lights appeared on the wings of the planes—machine-gun fire.

"They're ME-109s," Virge said. Enemy aircraft identification classes were the most important part of a gunner's training. He learned the characteristics of each German airplane—Focke-Wulfs, Messerschmitts, Junkers—and how to distinguish them quickly from the friendly fighters.

The classes were easy. It was simple to sit in a comfortable classroom and spot an ME-109 or a FW-190 from a picture projected on a screen. Real combat was different. The gunners were cold and cramped and nervous. The sun was bright, and the Gerries flew in front of it to blind the gunners. A man had only seconds to determine if a fighter was ours or theirs, friendly or unfriendly, a Spitfire or a Focke-Wulf. More than one gunner had made a fatal mistake.

The Thunderbolts and Messerschmitts were on a collision course, their machine guns blazing. The 109s were smaller and more sleek than the Thunderbolts, with long, thin bodies and cone-shaped noses, like cigars with wings. Messerschmitts could do anything, and do it faster than any plane in the sky. The Gerry fighter pilots were fearless. You had to admire them, even when they were trying to kill you.

Just when it looked like the two fighter squadrons would collide in midair, the Thunderbolts veered off, swooping straight up into the sky. The Messerschmitts kept coming. The enemy squadron split apart in order to penetrate the formation, and suddenly there were Messers everywhere you looked.

"They're a-comin'," Clay said over the interphone.

Even Clay, who never got excited about anything, sounded a little excited. It was the first attack of the day.

"Call them out," Dennis said, and immediately voices tumbled over each other on the interphone.

"Six o'clock high!"

"Nine o'clock high!"

"Ten o'clock high!"

"Three o'clock high!"

"They're all over the place!"

Jack opened fire. A half second later Eugene opened up. The narrow waist compartment throbbed from the reverberation of the guns. Long tongues of flame shot out of the barrels. Shell casings spit out of the chambers and clattered to the floor.

In the top turret, Virge followed a fighter down from five o'clock high to two low. He warned Val that it was coming.

"Val, watch this guy on the right."

"I see him."

"Breaking low to four o'clock!" Eugene shouted. "Ball turret, look out, look out!"

"Don't shout on the interphone!" Dennis reminded the crew.

Rascal spun his turret and pounded his guns at the Messer as it appeared on the starboard side of the plane. The fighter was in range and the turret was responding beautifully, so Rascal had a good chance of a kill. Bagging his second confirmed fighter would be a great way to finish his tour. The bandit was so close that Rascal could see the features on the pilot's face.

"That guy had blue eyes," Rascal said. The ME zoomed by without being touched.

In the cockpit, Luke was turning and twisting in his seat, trying to see the action. He hoped that soon Clay would call him back to the tail and let him shoot the guns. Even though Luke had never fired a .50-caliber machine gun, he was certain that he could get one of the Nazi fighters. He once won four stuffed animals in a single night at a carnival shooting gallery.

"Luke, do your job. The gunners will do theirs," Dennis said to the copilot.

Enemy fighters were buzzing around the formation now, but the first element was bearing the brunt of the attack. The Nazis knew from the position of the first element, above and ahead of the *Belle*, that those three planes would be leading the bombing raid. It was Gerry's first order of business to knock *Windy City*, *Mama's Boys*, and *C Cup* out of the sky.

"They're leaving us alone," said Eugene, touching his St. Anthony medal just to make sure it was there. He did this whenever there was a little break in the action. It calmed him down.

"They're going after the first flight," said Val. From the nose he had a good view of the attack. The Gerries were really giving it to *Windy City*. The lead plane had a fine picture on the side of its nose: a girl caught in a strong wind with her dress blowing up over her bare bottom.

But the girl was taking a pounding. Machine-gun fire ripped through the side of the plane and smoke started twisting out of Engine Two. The little friends were working hard to drive the bandits away, but they kept coming back for more. When Gerry wanted to knock a plane down, he usually succeeded.

"*Windy City*'s on fire!" shouted Luke, seeing Engine Two of the lead plane burst into flame. An engine fire was the most serious of all emergencies on a B-17. The pilot and copilot had to work quickly to cut the fuel line, put out the fire, and feather the prop.

"Why aren't they doing anything?" asked Luke. The fire was burning hot and steady on *Windy City*'s left wing. "Are they asleep?"

"Bail out, you guys!" Val said. If a fire couldn't be extinguished, there was only one thing a crew could do: jump.

"Come on, get out of there!" Phil repeated, but still nothing happened.

"Jesus, there's a hole in the pilot's window!" Val said. The left cockpit window was blown away. He couldn't see the pilot. He wondered if anyone was flying the plane.

Then it exploded. One minute *Windy City* was thirty tons of machinery, the next moment it was a massive fireball. It exploded with a sound like the loudest clap of thunder ever heard. The *Belle* rocked from the blast, and Dennis struggled to hold the plane steady. A second later the ball of flame became a huge black cloud full of whirling pieces of plane. It was dead ahead.

"Watch out!" Luke said, and immediately put his feet on the instrument panel to brace himself.

"Hold on, everyone!" Dennis shouted, and tightened his grip on the control wheel.

There was no way to avoid it. The *Belle* flew straight into the giant black cloud that used to be *Windy City*.

Smoke streamed in the open waist windows. Eugene caught a blast of it right in the face. The soot blinded him and he screamed in pain.

The moment Dennis heard the scream he said, "Call in!" and the crew immediately began calling out their positions from the back of the plane to the front.

"Tail," Clay said.

"Right waist," Eugene said, although his eyes were stinging and watering from the soot.

"Left waist," Jack said.

"Ball turret! Get us out of here!" Rascal shouted. Bits of metal were clicking against his turret. Any second a sharp metal shard could break through the Plexiglas and hit him in the face.

"Radio operator," Danny said.

"Top turret," Virge said.

When Luke opened his mouth to say "Copilot," there was a loud thunk on the bottom of the plane and the *Belle* rocked violently back and forth.

125

"Jesus fuck!" Luke cried out. "What was that? Copilot!"

"Bombardier," Val said, and in that instant the plane emerged from the black cloud into white, chilly sunshine. The light was so bright, it hurt to see.

"Navigator, call in!" Dennis said when Phil didn't report from his position in the nose. No matter what you were doing, when the captain said to call in, you called in.

Phil still didn't answer. "Navigator!" Dennis repeated. *"Navigator!"*

Val spun around to look at Phil. As he did, he remembered how Phil kept saying that he was going to die today, that he was sure he was going to die. Val felt his stomach clench, fearful of what he was going to see when he looked at his partner.

Phil was absolutely still. His eyes were open and he was staring at the Plexiglas nose. Val quickly scanned Phil's body to see where he was wounded, but the navigator seemed to be in one piece.

"Phil!" Val shouted, but Phil didn't respond. Val couldn't figure out what was wrong. Phil wasn't dead. He didn't look wounded. He seemed paralyzed. His face was ghostly white and his eyes were fixed on a point behind Val's head. He didn't even blink.

"Phil!" Val shouted again, and punched him in the arm. Phil looked at Val as if he didn't recognize him. This is it, Val thought, Phil has finally lost his mind.

"Navigator. Sorry. I'm fine," Phil said to Dennis over the interphone, finally emerging from his trance.

"When I say call in, I mean right away."

"Sorry. I'm okay," Phil said again.

Val didn't understand his partner. Disgusted, Val shook his head and started to turn back to his gun. That's when he saw what Phil had been staring at all along.

Somebody's insides were all over the nose. It was covered in blood and there were pieces of human tissue stuck to the Plexiglas. Val saw a piece of intestine and a slice of gray, porous tissue. Val guessed that it was part of a lung.

"Fuck!" Val exclaimed.

"Bombardier?" Dennis asked.

"Somebody's guts are all over the nose!"

"Any damage?" Dennis asked. "Crew, check your stations."

The blood was blowing back toward the edges of the Plexiglas and freezing. It made a bright red collar around the nose cone. When the blood froze, it glinted in the sun. It was almost pretty. Val couldn't take his eyes off it.

"Radio room okay," Danny reported.

"Waist okay," Jack reported.

"Tail okay," Clay reported.

Val tore his eyes away from the blood long enough to check whether the Plexiglas nose cone had been cracked or broken.

"Nose okay," he said, then he glanced over at Phil. Phil had been nervous before the liquefied remains of one of *Windy City*'s crew hit the nose and stuck there, but now he was visibly shaking.

Val wanted to tell Phil that he wasn't going to die, that his guts weren't going to be splattered all over the sky, but it would be an empty promise. Anything could happen between here and the target. Whatever private terror Phil was going through, he was going to have to go through it alone. Val turned back to his gun and searched the starboard side for fighters.

"Call out those bandits," Dennis reminded his men.

"They're gone," Virge reported from the top turret. The turret whined and clanked as it turned. The sky above was empty. The sun was bright. Ahead, *C Cup* and *Mama's Boys* were peacefully flying along as if nothing had happened. It was hard to believe a plane had exploded only a moment before.

"Captain," Danny said over the interphone. "I just heard from *C Cup*. They're taking over the lead."

"Hear that, Val?" Dennis asked.

"Roger."

"*C Cup* is lead plane now. When they drop their bombs, so do we."

"Got it," Val replied. That was Dennis, always telling you what you already knew. It was annoying, but at the same time it was reassuring to know somebody was in charge. Dennis never overlooked anything. Maybe that's why they had made it this far.

On their first few missions the crew was sloppy and careless, but Dennis drilled his men over and over until the checks and rechecks were a way of life. Nothing was taken for granted. The men made fun of Dennis, but they didn't mind his attention to detail nearly as much as they pretended.

"Any chutes from *Windy City*?" Dennis asked. At debriefing after a mission the pilots and crews were expected to report any B-17s that went down and how many men had escaped.

"Those guys didn't have time to pee their pants."

"If you gotta go, that's the way."

"Here one minute, gone the next."

"Do we have to talk about it?" Phil asked. He was still quaking from the sight of the blood on the nose and didn't want to hear anybody's theory of a good way to die.

"Hey, I heard a good one from the waist gunner on *Windy City*," Rascal said excitedly. Rascal was a joke machine. He knew all the jokes that were floating around the base, and he told them over and over whether anyone wanted to hear them or not. Once in a while there was a funny one.

"What was his name?" Rascal asked. "The waist gunner on *Windy City*?"

"Cooley," Jack told him.

"I mean, the left one."

"Cooley!" Jack insisted.

"I mean, the right one," Rascal said, correcting himself. There was a little pause as the enlisted men tried to think of the gunner's name.

"I know the guy," Virge said. "The name's on the tip of my tongue. I can see him."

"Tall guy," Rascal said.

"Not so tall."

"Everyone's tall to me," Rascal replied, so no one disputed it.

"Lindquist!" Virge suddenly remembered.

"No, no, Virge," Rascal said. Rascal knew Lindquist. He was the right waist on a plane called *What-A-Dame!* Lindquist liked to get into fights. Rascal had been in a fight with him in a pub in London. It was about the best time Rascal had ever had.

"Something like that," Virge said uncertainly.

"Virge, you're not even close." There was another little pause as the gunners tried to think of the fellow's name. Nobody could come up with it, so Rascal just went ahead and told the joke, anyway.

"Okay, a plane gets shot down. This guy bails out. The Gestapo gets him. His leg's broken and they have to amputate. He says, 'Do me a favor. After you cut my leg off, give it to one of your pilots and have him drop it over my base in England.' So they do it."

"Rascal, don't tie up the interphone," Dennis interrupted.

"This is real quick," Rascal said, then spoke a little faster.

"A week later they have to take off the guy's other leg. Same thing. 'Could you have someone drop it over my base in England?' And they do it." So the next week they've got to cut off his arm. He asks them again, 'Could you please have someone drop it over my base in England?'

"This time they say . . ." Rascal imitated a German accent. " 'Nein. Zis ve can't do anymore.'

"The guy says, 'Why not?'

"And they say, 'Ve sink you're trying to escape!' " Everyone laughed and Rascal was pleased. He hated it when he told a really good joke and somebody, usually Eugene, said "I don't get it" or somebody, like Jack, already knew the punch line. This joke made everybody laugh, and Rascal immediately wanted to tell the joke all over again.

"Pretty good, Rascal," Luke said. "I think even Dennis liked that one."

"Stoller! That was the guy's name," Eugene said, but immediately Virge contradicted him.

"Stoller wasn't on *Windy City*."

"You sure?"

"I'm sure."

"Wait, it'll come to me," said Jack, scratching his head. Jack was the kind of guy who really did scratch his head when he was trying to think. That happened in the movies, especially in Three Stooges movies, but you never saw anybody do it in real life.

"I can see the guy's face," Clay said, picturing the right waist gunner on *Windy City*. He was kind of an ugly guy with a nose spread halfway across his face. It had been broken when he was a kid. He had a habit of pulling at his hair when he was nervous. Clay would see him across the mess hall before a mission, pulling on his hair. It was amazing he had any hair left. Clay had seen him that very morning.

"Well, whatever his name was, it's a good joke," Rascal said. It was too bad. Five minutes after the gunner had been blown to smithereens no one could remember his name. It gave everybody a sour feeling.

"Okay, men, let's stop horsing around," Dennis said. "The Gerries are out there somewhere. Be on guard, look sharp, and call out those fighters as soon as you see them.''

A moment later Luke saw the Thunderbolts peel off from the formation. He thought the attack was on again, and he eagerly looked around for Gerry fighters. There were no Gerries to be seen. Then he remembered that the little friends weren't flying all the way to Bremen. They were going back to England to refuel and would join the formation on the return trip.

''Damn, are the little friends leaving already?'' he asked. He glanced down and saw the long, skinny string of Frisian Islands skirting the coast of Holland. He recalled the S-2 pointing to them and saying that the escort would turn back here, just as the formation approached Germany.

''They sure know when to run out of fuel,'' Virge said.

''They ain't dumb,'' Clay remarked.

The pretty little Thunderbolts wiggled their wings to say good-bye, then zoomed away. The crew watched them until they became tiny specks in the sky.

When we see them again, Luke thought, *we will have bombed Bremen and I will have shot down a Nazi fighter with Clay's gun.* Luke couldn't wait. It almost made up for the fact that they were now defenseless against the entire German Luftwaffe.

''Navigator, give me a position,'' Dennis ordered.

Down in the nose, Phil was concentrating hard. As long as he kept busy, he didn't have time to think about dying. He extended the line he had already drawn from East Anglia across the length of the North Sea. It skirted the long string of Frisian Islands and crossed the border into Germany. His hand shook a little as he drew the line.

''Sir, that's the Third Reich down there,'' Phil announced. The formation would now make a forty-five-degree turn, straight into Deutschland.

Phil looked at the map. *Where will I get it?* he won-

131

dered. *What longitude and latitude? Before we reach the target or on our way home? Will it hurt? Will anyone remember my name when I'm gone?*

Phil wasn't the only man aboard asking himself these questions. Everybody was trying desperately not to think about the enemy, but all anybody could do was think about the enemy.

Bremen was a fortress defended by hundreds of fighters and some of the most accurate flak gunners in Germany. The Focke-Wulf plant was essential to the Nazi war effort, and one could be sure that the Germans weren't going to let the formation drop its bombs and go home without a fuss. The Nazis were going to put up a hell of a battle, and every plane in that cold, clear sky was going to have to fight for its life.

Jack summed it up: "Now the shit really hits the fan."

10

May 17, 1943, 1220 Hours

"Sweating it out" was what they called it. The men who
didn't fly that day had nothing to do but wait for the planes
to return. They played a little poker. They tried to read.
They wrote letters home. They worried. Everyone agreed
that sweating it out was harder than combat.

In the back of everyone's mind was the crew of the
Memphis Belle. Would they come back? If they did, there
was hope for everyone. If this crew could finish their
twenty-fifth mission, others could too. In the spring of
'43, the men of the Ninety-first Bomb Group needed all
the hope they could get.

They tried to keep busy. Someone started a softball
game. There was a bicycle race out on the runway. A few
men were playing horseshoes by the control tower. A
group was singing "Don't Sit Under the Apple Tree with
Anyone Else but Me" in four-part harmony. Others were
catching up on their sack time.

Craig Harriman was sharpening pencils. He lined them
up on his desk according to size, sharpened each one, and

then arranged them according to the sharpness of the point. There was paperwork to be done, but Craig couldn't concentrate on paperwork right now.

If Craig Harriman had been a man to break the rules, he would have gone to the radio shack and tried to contact the formation. Then he would know whether they had reached Bremen yet, if the bombing had been successful, and if the *Memphis Belle* was safe. But radio silence was strictly enforced and Craig Harriman was not the kind of man to break the rules.

He sharpened pencils instead. He tried to make them all the same size. It was difficult. If he sharpened one pencil a fraction of an inch too much, he had to start all over again. It kept him busy.

The rap on the door sounded like a gunshot. It startled Craig and he broke the lead on one of his pencils. "Yes?" he said.

Comstock, the S-2 officer, entered and saluted. Comstock had an annoying habit of clicking his heels when he saluted: salute, click—every time.

"Sir, you'd better come take a look at this."

"What is it?" Craig asked. He could tell from Comstock's tone that whatever it was, it wasn't good news.

"Sir, I think you'd just better come and look."

The minute Craig Harriman walked into the mess hall he knew that he was going to lose his temper. He heard it snap. It made a sound, a sharp little click like the heels of Comstock's shoes.

"We need more bunting along that wall," Bruce Derringer said, giving instructions to the *Life* magazine photographer who was organizing the decoration of the mess hall. American flags and colorful streamers hung from the ceiling. A platform had been set up in the corner of the hall for a small band. A banner stretched across the back of the hall: CONGRATULATIONS *MEMPHIS BELLE*—25 MISSIONS!

"Use everything we've got. Make sure the banner's cen-

134

tered. And move the piano up on the stage.'' The *Life* photographer nodded and began to carry out Bruce's instructions. About twenty enlisted men had been marshaled to help with the party preparations.

"What is the meaning of this?" Craig Harriman asked.

"Just a little party, Colonel," Bruce replied cheerfully as the banner was straightened and the piano moved to the stage.

"I didn't order this," Harriman said quietly, not wanting to make a scene in front of the enlisted men.

"Leave this stuff to me. The *Memphis Belle*'s my job," Bruce replied confidently. The welcome back party would provide a great opportunity for the *Life* photographer. Bruce could already see the magazine spread: the weary but happy faces of the young crew being toasted by the entire base. He reminded himself to put Luke Sinclair in front.

"And my job is to approve everything on this base," Craig Harriman said in a low, intense voice. "I did not authorize a homecoming."

"Craig, you work too hard at being a hardass," Bruce said with a smile. He didn't mean it as a criticism, but he could see the muscle twitching again in Craig's left cheek. "What's the harm in a little party in honor of these guys? They're special."

"I have twenty-four crews up there. They're all special to me," Craig Harriman replied.

"That's a great story, Craig, but baloney's my business and I know it when I see it," Bruce said. If Harriman was going to play hardball, so would Bruce. "All you care about is putting planes in the air. Getting results. Brown-nosing HQ. The only man on this base you care about is yourself—"

Harriman interrupted. "Come with me!" Nothing Bruce could have said would have tried Craig's patience more than the accusation that he didn't care. He cared too

135

much. That was his problem. Craig intended to show this pie-faced, blundering idiot once and for all what it meant to be a commanding officer.

Craig strode to the door. When he didn't hear Derringer's footsteps behind him, he repeated, "Come with me!" It wasn't an invitation. It was an order.

Bruce was taken aback by Harriman's reaction. The man hadn't blinked yesterday when a plane exploded with ten men aboard, but today he was a nervous wreck because of a little party. Bruce didn't understand the CO at all. It occurred to him that the man was mad.

When they entered Craig's office, Harriman said "Sit down!" with such force that Bruce found himself sitting automatically. Harriman yanked a drawer out of his desk and brought it over to Derringer. Bruce flinched, thinking that Harriman was going to smash the heavy drawer on his head.

He didn't. He turned it over and dumped the contents on the table in front of Bruce. Hundreds of letters spilled out. Some were in plain white envelopes, others in pastel envelopes. Some were written by hand, some were typed, but all were addressed to Colonel Craig Harriman, U.S. Army Air Force, Ninety-first Bomb Group, England.

"Start reading," Craig said. He picked a blue airmail envelope from the pile, opened it, and removed two sheets of paper covered with a neat, cursive handwriting.

"This one's from the father of a boy who got his head blown off over Lorient. Start with that." Craig held out the letter to Bruce.

"Craig, I think you're cracking up," Bruce said. Craig's normally unexpressive face was flushed, his eyes black, his whole body trembling.

"Read it!" Harriman said, and thrust the letter at Bruce. Bruce took it. Anything to calm Harriman down. The letter was dated April 15, 1943, almost exactly a month before. Bruce read.

Dear Colonel Harriman,

I want to thank you for your letter of sympathy about my son, Tommy. He was only at your base a month, but you described him right down to his boots. Tommy always made a big impression on everyone.

I know you can't tell me how my son died. We have to be careful about security these days. But I'm glad he was brave and did his job to the end. Maybe his mother and I raised him right, after all.

If I ever start to forget what Tommy was like, I can always read your letter and that will bring him right back.

Sincerely,
Thomas R. Maguire

"He was a top turret gunner," Harriman said. "Lorient was his third mission. It didn't even look like a body when they took it out of the plane. His head was gone. His right arm was gone from the elbow down. His chest was torn open and his intestines—"

"I'm sorry about the boy," Bruce interrupted, "but we have to expect losses. Acceptable losses, of course."

"Acceptable?" Craig asked incredulously. *"Acceptable losses?* Do you think any father or mother considers their son an acceptable loss?"

"I was speaking about statistics," Bruce said.

"These *are* statistics!" Harriman said, pulling a handful of letters from the pile. "Each one of these is a statistic."

Bruce was surprised at Harriman's attitude. It was Harriman who had shown no surprise or sympathy the previous day when the plane had exploded with ten men aboard. It was Harriman who had argued that daylight bombing was the only way to win the war.

"This girl's brother was a ball-turret gunner," Harriman said, choosing another letter. "He was hit between the legs with a piece of flak. It took him three and a half hours to die."

Bruce didn't want to read the letter. He wanted to return to the mess hall, continue planning the party, and forget all about these horrible deaths. All his life he had protected himself from this kind of thing. He didn't like the ugly side of life. That's why he went into advertising—it was clean.

The letter was written on the back of an invoice for nails and rivets.

Dear Sir,

I'm sorry it has taken me so many months to respond to your letter about my brother's death, Lieutenant Robert P. Bailey. I've been working double shifts at the shipyard and I'm too tired to do anything else.

It's good to know that Robert didn't suffer and was not alone when he died. I didn't want him to enlist because he is all I have in the world, but he loved his country and wanted to fight. He especially wanted to fly.

Although nothing can ever bring him back, I'm proud that he died serving as a soldier in the United States Armed Services.

Sincerely,
Susan Bailey

Bruce had barely finished the letter when Craig took another one from the pile. "This one . . . well, this one doesn't need any explanation." He gave it to Bruce. It was printed in big block letters on a piece of brown tablet paper.

Dear Mr. Harriman,

My brother was Terry DeSanto. He was a bombardier. He died, I guess. My mom said to write you a letter.

What should I do with his stuff? He had a lot of stuff and maybe somebody needs it.

I can't wait till I get to be a bombardier too. Will the war be on that long? I am eleven.

Your friend,
Tim

Bruce's eyes stung. It wasn't so much the words of the child's letter that affected him; it was that big block printing. How the boy must have struggled over every word, to spell everything right, to make this a letter fit for a colonel to read.

Bruce wondered how often Craig Harriman sat in this office and pored over these letters. Did he come here in the middle of the night when he couldn't sleep, read them, and agonize over each loss? There must be four hundred letters in the pile on the table. Bruce glanced at the filing cabinet beside the desk. Was it filled with more letters?

He realized that he had misjudged Craig Harriman. He thought that Harriman didn't care about his men. He believed Harriman was only interested in impressing his superiors; that statistics interested him more than human lives.

Now Bruce realized that Harriman felt each man's death so deeply, took each loss so personally, that he forced himself to write to each family about its loss. The impersonal telegram that the Army automatically sent was not enough. Harriman composed a letter that made it seem as if he knew the dead man, and in each letter he reassured the family that the soldier had not suffered when he died.

Harriman could not personally know every man on the base, and surely most men suffered when they died.

How did he write the letters? Bruce wondered. Did he interview the dead man's friends, pick some personal trait to mention so that his family would think the boy was not just another boy but someone special? However Harriman did it, it must take a great deal of time and energy. No wonder Harriman was so drawn and thin. He was being eaten away inside by sorrow.

Bruce felt a sudden impulse to reach out and put his hand on top of Harriman's. He wanted to tell him that the war would be over someday and he would no longer have to write letter after letter, day after day. One day he wouldn't have to send young men off to die in the skies over France and Germany.

Bruce didn't do it. He knew that the war might not be over for a very long time. In the meantime the killing would go on and on.

Bruce suddenly realized that Harriman must be more anxious than anyone for the *Belle* to return from today's mission. It would be a tangible sign of hope, a glimmer of hope that someday it would come to an end. At the same time Harriman could not pin all his hopes on one plane. Whether or not the *Belle* returned from Bremen, Craig Harriman would have to stay and write the letters until the war was over or until he cracked.

"This girl's husband bailed out over Bremen a month ago," Craig said, handing Bruce another letter. "Before he could open his parachute, he got caught in the slipstream and was pushed into the propeller."

There was nothing Bruce could do to comfort or reassure Harriman, and no apology that would make up for the trouble Bruce had caused. All he could do was read the letters Craig handed him.

This one was written on yellow stationery with morning glories on the border.

Dear Colonel Harriman,

What a surprise it was to receive your letter. It meant so much.

A month ago I had a dream that Ken died in his sleep. I tried to wake him, but he was gone. He looked very peaceful and at rest.

I forgot about the dream until I received the telegram from the Army. A week later I got your lovely letter.

I hope Ken's death served some purpose and was as peaceful as it was in my dream.

Warm regards,
Mrs. Kenneth T. Adamski

Danny's eyes were tearing from staring for so long at the bright sky, watching for fighters. He quickly wiped away a tear with the heel of his glove. He felt tired. He had gotten to sleep so late last night because of the dance and woken up so early this morning. He wondered if he should eat his candy bar now or save it for later.

He had been thinking about the poem. It was called "An Irish Airman Foresees His Death" and was written by the Irish poet W. B. Yeats. Danny felt terrible for pretending that he wrote it. *Even if I live a hundred years,* he thought, *I won't write anything that beautiful.*

Danny knew that he had to tell the truth, even if the crew was disappointed or made fun of him. It wasn't right to pretend to have written something he didn't write. Pretty soon he'd be claiming he'd written all of Shakespeare's plays.

Danny was just about to confess when Clay's lazy drawl came over the interphone.

"Bandit, five o'clock low."

"Four o'clock high too!" Eugene cried out a moment later.

"Don't yell on the interphone," Dennis said.

"Pair at two high," Virge said.

Danny squinted into the sharp blue sky. High above and a little to his left was one of those deadly black specks. His confession would have to wait. It was fighting time again. Danny swung his gun over to the four-o'clock position and got ready to fire.

Then fighters were all over the sky again. "See this guy at eight level?" Rascal said, spotting an ME out of the corner of his eye. "Left waist, see him?"

"I see him!" said Jack, sighting in an M-109. "Come to Daddy," he coaxed. "Daddy's got a surprise for you." Twinkling lights appeared on the Messerschmitt's wings. As soon as the fighter was in range, Jack opened up.

It was as if the fighter had a big bow on it and a tag reading FOR JACK. It was coming right at him. Jack started picturing another little yellow swastika painted on the *Belle*'s nose, his second. The bandit turned on its side, exposing its tender belly to Jack's gun. "He's mine! He's mine!" Jack shouted as he hammered his gun at the little fighter.

Then all of a sudden Jack was blind. Something flew in his face and covered his eyes just at the critical moment when he was going to bag the Messerschmitt. He couldn't see a damn thing.

"What the fuck?" he screamed. He ripped the piece of paper off his face and looked desperately around for the fighter, but the Nazi was gone.

"I had him! He was right there! Goddammit!" Jack swore in frustration. He looked at the piece of paper in his hand. It was a flimsy, a thick piece of rice paper. Written on the back in big block letters was the message, COULDN'T GET LAID LAST NIGHT!

As the Messerschmitt came into range, a corner of the sign Eugene had taped to the back of Jack's jacket had come unstuck. The wind had blown the flimsy up into Jack's face just when he was going to make his kill.

It took Jack a few seconds to realize where the sign had come from. It was another of Geenie the Weenie's stupid practical jokes. But this was no joke. The sign had caused him to miss the Nazi fighter.

There was no way around it: He was going to have to murder Eugene. *I'll smash his ugly face in,* Jack thought in a rage, *knock out those buck teeth of his, then push him out the window and laugh my fool head off as he falls.*

Jack looked at Eugene. Eugene was firing furiously at a fighter that was, as usual, much too far away to waste ammunition on. Jack thought, *Just let me get my hands around that pencil neck of his. I'll squeeze until his eyes pop right out of his head.*

Just as Jack started to reach for Eugene, Rascal's excited voice came over the interphone: "Here he comes around again, left waist! Jack, get the greedy bastard! Get him!"

Jack turned around and looked for the M-109. Sure enough, it was making a second pass. *First I'll get my fighter,* Jack told himself, *then I'll get Genie the Weenie.* He started to fire.

There must have been two hundred fighters in the sky. They were so fast that a gunner barely had time to sight one in and fire before the fighter was gone. The crew kept calling them out—"Three o'clock low!" "Nine level!" "Two high!"—but there wasn't time to call them all.

Most of the fighters were concentrating on the remaining two planes in the first element. *C Cup* and *Mama's Boys* were getting hit pretty hard. Then *Mama's Boys* tipped on its side and started sliding out of formation.

"B-17 going down. Watch it!" Luke cried as the huge plane sliced across the sky right in front of them. Nothing seemed to be wrong with *Mama's Boys*. It didn't look hit, but it was falling just the same.

"They're bailing out," he said as he saw two men jump from the nose hatch. Two more came out of the waist, and a man crawled out of the opening in the radio-room roof. The plane wasn't going into a spin; it was simply sliding out of the sky. When a B-17 started spinning on its way to the ground, the crew became trapped inside, pinned to the fuselage walls by centrifugal force.

Now only one plane remained in the first element. If anything happened to *C Cup*, and the Nazis would do their best to make something happen to it, *Memphis Belle* would become the lead plane. Dennis had led several bombing raids before, but never one to Germany.

"Navigator, give me a position," Dennis asked.

"We're about seven minutes from IP, Captain," Phil reported from the nose.

IP meant initial point, the start of the bomb run. The bomb run itself was four minutes long—the four most dangerous minutes of the mission. That's when the Nazis opened up their antiaircraft batteries. As bad as the fighters were, the flak guns were worse. There was nothing you could do about them; you just had to hope you didn't get hit.

"They're starting in on *C Cup*," Luke said. Sure enough, fighters were swarming around the remaining plane in the first element.

Dennis was thirsty. He had been on oxygen for almost two hours and his mouth was dry. He glanced down at the floor to where he had stowed his thermos. He wondered if he should let Luke take the wheel so he could have some tomato soup. But the copilot was so jumpy that Dennis thought it best not to relinquish control right now. He simply would have to try to forget his thirst.

For the first time in fifteen minutes there were no fighters on the right side of the plane. As always, when he had a chance, Eugene reached down to his chest to touch his lucky St. Anthony medal.

Eugene came from a strict Catholic family and had never missed Sunday mass until he'd come to England. He never ate meat on Fridays, even sausage or bacon at breakfast.

He said his prayers every night before he went to bed. The crew kidded him about this at first but got used to it.

Eugene patted his chest. When he didn't immediately feel the medal, he looked down. He couldn't believe his eyes. His St. Anthony medal wasn't there. It was always hanging outside his flight jacket on the nickel chain he'd bought at Woolworth's.

He tore open his jacket to see if it was inside. It wasn't. He felt the back of his neck in case the chain had gotten turned around and was hanging down his back. It wasn't there, either. He searched his jacket pockets. They were empty. His medal was gone.

Eugene had never felt so scared. The medal was the only reason he had survived twenty-four missions. It was his lifeline; if it was lost, he was lost.

He ripped off his oxygen mask, turned around, and grabbed Jack. Eugene was so worried that he didn't notice that the COULDN'T GET LAID LAST NIGHT! sign was no longer taped to Jack's back.

"My medal!" he shouted. "Have you seen it? It's gone!"

Jack's first thought was, *It serves the little bastard right. He ruined my chance to get that Nazi fighter. He's lucky I don't kill him with my bare hands, but he's probably going to die of a heart attack without me laying a finger on him.* Eugene's eyes were bugging out of his head and his face was light blue.

Jack shook his head and started to turn back to the left window. As he did, he saw something silver glinting on the floor. Eugene's St. Anthony medal was lying in a sea of spent shells. Jack reached down, grabbed it, and held it up in front of Eugene's worried face.

The Woolworth's chain had broken. It must have caught on Eugene's gun and snapped. He'd meant to buy a stronger chain in London but kept forgetting.

Eugene had never been so grateful to any human being

in his life. He knew he could always count on Jack. Eugene immediately felt his pulse returning to normal.

"Thanks, Jack," Eugene said, and reached for the medal.

With a flick of his wrist Jack threw the medal out the open waist window.

"No!" Eugene screamed.

He leaned out the window in the futile hope that he could catch the medal, but of course it was gone. It was already falling thirty thousand feet down to Germany.

"Why'd you do that?" he screamed at Jack. "How could you do that?"

"Now we're even!" Jack shouted back, then he turned to his gun. Jack smiled, a little proud of himself. He thought: *It serves the Weenie right. That's what he gets for putting that stupid sign on my back and screwing up my chances of getting that ME-109. This ought to teach him a lesson he'll never forget.*

"Right waist? Right waist, call in!" Dennis was saying over the interphone. He heard Eugene's panicked scream and thought the right waist gunner might be wounded.

"Radio operator, get back there and see what's happening!" Dennis said when Eugene didn't respond.

Danny yanked out his interphone and oxygen cords. He ran through the aft bulkhead door, through the ball-turret compartment and into waist. Eugene grabbed him in the doorway. Danny had never seen anybody so terrified.

"My medal, it's gone!" he said. "I'm finished, Danny, I'm finished!"

"Stop it, Gene!" Eugene was trembling so badly, Danny thought he was going to fall down. Danny was trained in first aid, but he didn't know what to do when someone was hysterical.

"I've gotta get out of here, I've got to get out!" Eugene said, looking around for an escape hatch. Danny had to do something fast or Eugene was going to bail out of the plane.

146

"Gene, wait!" Danny pulled off his right glove, took the big rubber band off his wrist, and held it out to Eugene. "Take my lucky rubber band."

Eugene calmed down a little. He looked at the rubber band as if he'd never seen one in his life.

"It really works," Danny said, and slipped the rubber band over Eugene's glove.

"You're okay now. Go get 'em," Danny said. He patted Eugene on the back, then ducked through the door and headed back to the radio room.

Eugene was skeptical. How could a simple rubber band save his life? His St. Anthony medal made him feel that God was looking out for him. Who would be looking out for him now, the rubber-band manufacturer?

On the other hand, it was better than nothing. It had kept Danny safe through twenty-four missions, so maybe it wasn't an ordinary rubber band. Maybe it really was lucky. It was worth a try.

Eugene looked over at Jack. Jack's fat butt was right there, just asking for it. Eugene obliged, planting the toe of his boot into Jack's right cheek. Then he grabbed his gun, spotted a fighter coming in at five high, and started firing.

"M-190, twelve o'clock high!" shouted Val when he saw the Focke-Wulf descending at a fantastic speed. It flew straight at *C Cup*, all four machine barrels blazing.

"He's going for *C Cup*!" Luke cried. "Look out, look out!"

Suddenly *C Cup*'s Plexiglas nose cone shattered, and a man was blown out of the plane. He tumbled over and over as he fell to the ground.

"Jesus, he doesn't have a parachute," Phil said. The man, either a bombardier or a navigator, was quickly becoming a little dot below. "How long would it take to fall?"

"Too long," Val answered.

Phil wondered what the sky diver was thinking about as he fell. Was his life flashing before his eyes? Was he saying his prayers or simply shitting his pants? A moment later the man was invisible, gone.

"Everybody, make sure you've got your parachutes on," said Dennis over the intercom. Phil grabbed the chute from under his desk and struggled into it. He didn't like to wear his parachute—it was awkward and bulky—but now he put it on without complaint. Val was doing the same.

"Rascal, have you got a parachute in the ball turret?" Dennis asked.

"Are you kidding?" Rascal replied. "There isn't room for a hard-on in here!"

"Okay, but put your safety strap on."

"It hurts," Rascal whined.

"Put it on!" Dennis ordered.

Following orders, Rascal threaded the thin strip of canvas between his legs and hooked it to the top of the turret. The strap was tight and cut into his crotch. He squirmed around, trying to get comfortable, but the safety strap kept squishing his poor little balls.

"Captain, I just got word from *C Cup*," Danny reported. "They're dropping out of formation. We're in the lead now."

"Okay, Danny," Dennis replied. "Connect me to group."

C Cup looked like a ghost ship. Jagged aluminum was twisted and curled around the edges of the shattered nose. It looked like a can that someone had tried to open without a can opener. The plane was lagging, losing speed and altitude. The *Belle* started to pass it.

Dropping out of formation was a death sentence. As soon as *C Cup* was alone, Nazi fighters would descend like vultures. They would keep hitting *C Cup* until she fell from the sky.

"Poor bastards."

"They're dead meat."

"The bogeyman will get them."

"Bye, bye, *C Cup*," Eugene called out softly.

"Sir, you're on to Group," Danny said, connecting Dennis to all of them.

Dennis spoke in his usual quiet, precise manner. He was in charge now, and he showed no hesitation or trace of fear. But his light, high voice reminded you that he was only twenty-six years old.

"This is the *Memphis Belle*," he said. "We're in the lead now. I'll try my best to put those bombs right in the pickle barrel and get us out of here safe. I'm going to need all the help you can give me. Let's fly as tight to each other as we can. That's our best defense. Let's look alive and be on our toes. We're three minutes, thirty seconds from the bomb run."

There was silence in the plane after Dennis finished his transmission. They were approaching Bremen, a hellhole full of flak batteries and fighter squadrons. It had been tough so far, a lot of planes had gone down, but everyone knew that was the easy part. In three and a half minutes they would be on the bomb run. That's when it would really get tough.

The crew also knew what it meant to be lead plane. They had seen it happen to *Windy City, Mama's Boys,* and *C Cup*. Each one of those planes had been in the lead, and each one had been destroyed. From now to the target, the Gerries would have one single agenda: to knock the *Memphis Belle* out of the sky.

11

"Bloodsucker, one o'clock level! Ball Turret, watch out!"

The second Rascal twisted the hand control of the ball turret he knew something was wrong. His turret always responded immediately to the slightest touch of the controls, but now it didn't move. It was frozen. He turned the handgrip again and again, but it still didn't budge. The fighter was coming straight at his back and he couldn't do anything about it. He was a dead man.

"I'm jammed! He's coming right at me! Virge, help!" Rascal shouted.

Virge heard the panic in Rascal's voice. Rascal was always complaining about something, but this time he really sounded scared. Virge yanked out his intercom and oxygen cords, jumped down from the top turret, and ran toward the back of the plane. He wasn't supposed to leave his post without orders from Dennis, but Rascal was in trouble. He had to do something.

There wasn't time. The Nazi bastard was coming. Those damn twinkling lights appeared on his wings. Rascal had only seconds to get the turret working. He pounded on the handgrip. He twisted it as hard as he could.

Suddenly it unjammed. The ball turret whirled around to face the fighter; Rascal aimed and fired. His first bullet hit the Nazi's right auxiliary fuel tank. It exploded, tearing the right wing off and sending it spinning through the air. Before the Messerschmitt could even start to fall, a second explosion blew it to hell.

"And your mother too!" Rascal screamed at the fighter.

Virge was coming through the radio room when he heard the explosion. He immediately thought the worst, that the ball turret had been hit. He burst through the radio room's aft bulkhead door, afraid he was going to see a hole in the deck where the ball turret was supposed to be.

But the ball turret was spinning and clanking in the floor like normal. Virge felt like kicking it. Rascal had taken him away from his station for nothing. *I should have known the little rat was joking*, Virge thought angrily. He hurried back to the top turret, reminding himself not to fall for Rascal's line again.

A moment later bullets ripped through the left fuselage wall and Jack Bocci was blown to the floor.

"Jack's hit!" Eugene shouted, looking down at his partner. Jack was screaming and swearing and clutching his bloody thigh. He had a wild, terrified look on his face. It was scary to see Jack so helpless.

"Val, run back and look at Jack," Dennis said to the bombardier over the intercom.

Until now none of the crew had ever been wounded, and Val had never had to treat anything more serious than a sprained ankle or a splinter in someone's finger. But now Jack was hit, and Val was terrified by the idea of having to administer first aid to the gunner. Desperately Val tried to find a way out.

"Captain, I'm two minutes from the bomb run!" he

said. This wasn't a lie. He had already made some preliminary adjustments to the bombsight.

"Okay," Dennis said after a pause that seemed to last forever. When Val heard Dennis say, "Gene, you're going to have to take care of Jack yourself," he knew he was off the hook.

In the waist, Eugene knelt down beside Jack. Jack was writhing around and swearing at the top of his lungs. "Jack, hold still! Let me look!" Eugene said, but it didn't do any good. He grabbed Jack's thigh and looked at the wound.

Eugene fully expected to see a gory hole with part of a severed bone sticking out of it, so he was astonished when the wound turned out to be nothing more than a superficial scrape. There was a gash in Jack's leg about two inches long and half an inch deep. That was all. It had even stopped bleeding. Eugene was so surprised, he started to laugh.

"Would you help?" Jack screamed.

"It's a scratch!" Eugene pointed at the little cut. "Look! It's nothing, and you're screaming like a stuck pig!"

Jack pushed himself up to look at his leg. He was sure that his leg was severed and that this was another one of Eugene's stupid practical jokes. Very reluctantly Jack looked at his poor leg.

He had to admit that Eugene was right. There was a little dent in his leg, a rather handsome wound. If he'd ordered a wound from a catalog, he would have ordered this exact one. There probably wouldn't even be a scar. *I've got myself a Purple Heart,* Jack thought proudly.

Then Jack saw something that made him scream in fury. "My harmonica!" he shouted, pulling it out of his ripped bunny-suit pocket. The harmonica was bent in half. It must have deflected the Nazi bullet.

"Goddammit, my favorite harmonica!" He showed it

153

to Eugene, but Eugene just laughed more. He couldn't get over Jack, who was crying over his wrecked harmonica when it probably saved his leg. Eugene removed his flight scarf and tied it around Jack's thigh.

Then Eugene helped his partner to his feet, turned back to the right waist window, and started to look for fighters. At the moment the skies were clear and, as he always did when there was a break in the action, Eugene reached for his St. Anthony medal. But it wasn't there. He remembered with sadness that it was gone for good. Jack had thrown it out the window. He touched Danny's rubber band for good luck, which made him feel a little better.

Eugene felt a tap on his shoulder. It was Jack. Jack did a strange thing. He reached behind Eugene's left ear. Eugene couldn't figure out what Jack was doing.

Eugene's eyes practically popped out of his head when Jack pulled his precious St. Anthony medal from behind his ear. It wasn't lost, after all. The silver medal turned on the chain and shone in the bright sunlight like a promise that it would always keep him safe.

"How'd you do that?" Eugene asked Jack in amazement.

Jack grinned a foolish, sheepish grin. "Magic" was all he said.

Eugene took the medal and kissed it. He had his lucky charm back. Now he knew he would make it. He would survive his twenty-fifth mission. He would go back home to his family. Maybe he'd return to the pharmacy, after all. He'd get married, have children, grow old, and have a good life. He was one of the lucky ones. He was certainly lucky to have Jack as his partner. They smiled at each other, then they both went back to work.

The fighters vanished. The sky had been filled with them a moment earlier.

"Keep calling them out," Dennis ordered.

"They're gone," Virge reported from the top turret after checking the sky above.

"Christ, you know what that means," Rascal said. As if on cue, there was a small explosion in the sky on the left side of the plane. It made a soft *poof* sound. A red flash was seen for a moment, then disappeared, leaving a fluffy little cloud of black smoke in the air.

"Flak, nine o'clock level."

"That's what I was afraid of," said Rascal.

Everyone hated flak. Although the German antiaircraft gunners on the ground rarely made a direct hit on a plane, the shells exploded in midair and filled the sky with sharp, sizzling pieces of iron.

A piece of shrapnel in an engine could cause the engine to shut down or catch on fire. A piece of red-hot flak could slice through your flesh as easily as a warm knife cuts through butter. There was nothing you could do about flak. You couldn't shoot back at it. You just had to sit it out.

"They've got something like five hundred flak batteries around Bremen," Luke announced.

"I could live without knowing that, Lieutenant," Virge replied.

A pattering began on the outside of the plane. Little pieces of flak were hitting the fuselage. At any moment a piece of flak could burst through the thin aluminum shell of the plane and slice off a man's hand or his arm or his head. The Army provided flak jackets and helmets, but they were so heavy that nobody liked to wear them.

Clay Busby looked out the tail window at a sky full of black puffs. The Germans were really sending up a barrage today. Bremen boasted some of the Nazis' most accurate antiaircraft gunners, and it looked like they were out in full force.

"Clay, what are the odds of us getting out of here alive?" Jack asked.

"I was just figuring that out," Clay replied. He

scratched *3 to 1* in the frost on the window and hummed a little of "How's Chances?"

There was a sudden loud bang on the right side of the ball turret. The turret wobbled violently, and for a second Rascal thought it would fall out of the plane.

"Jesus!"

"Ball turret, what's wrong?" Dennis asked.

"A big piece of ass-fucking Nazi flak just hit my turret!"

"Are you okay?"

"I guess." Rascal seemed uncertain.

"You guess or you are?"

"I am." As if it weren't cold enough, flak had knocked out one of the little side windows and a frigid wind began blowing on Rascal's neck. He pulled off his flight scarf and stuffed it into the hole. That helped, but it didn't completely stop the draft.

"I hope we're all wearing our flak jackets," Dennis said in a voice that reminded everyone of his father.

Danny was struggling into his weighty flak jacket when he heard the rookie radio operator from *Mother and Country* calling him on the radio.

"Danny, quick question. This flak, it's not like I expected. It's worse." The rookie gave a nervous little laugh. "Can't the captain do something about it? Avoid it or something?"

"Not this close to the bomb run," Danny answered. "We have to fly straight through it or we'll be off target. It's just four minutes."

"Just," the rookie said, as if the next four minutes were going to be the longest of his life.

Just then there was a bang like a gunshot. A hole opened in the left wall of the radio room and a small piece of scalding flak skated across Danny's wooden desk. It scratched the wooden desktop and landed on Danny's open logbook. Danny quickly brushed the piece of flak away, but it had already burned a hole in his neat log of today's mission.

"Captain, this is the bomb run," Phil reported after studying his maps and making a visual check of the ground. He was lead navigator now, so he didn't want to make any mistakes. "We're exactly four minutes from target, sir."

"Okay," Dennis replied, then he addressed Val. "Bombardier, I'm turning on the auto pilot. You're flying the plane from here to delivery."

"Roger."

"Seventy thousand pounds of bombs are going to drop on your command," Dennis told him. "I want pinpoint bombing."

"Yes, sir."

"Pinpoint," Dennis repeated, then flipped the autopilot switch. A light blinked on the instrument panel.

During the four minutes from IP to MPI, main point of impact, the pilot abandoned control of the plane to the bombardier, and the bombardier steered the plane through the Norden bombsight. The bombsight's internal computer helped the bombardier determine the exact moment and location to make the delivery, taking into account airplane speed, altitude, and drift. It anything was going to win the war against the Nazis, it was the Norden bombsight.

Val was sitting on his little cracked seat behind the bombsight in the top of the nose. Directly ahead, the sky was filled with black blossoms of flak. No sooner did one inky puff disappear than two new ones took its place. Val ignored them. He also ignored the continual patter of shrapnel, like metal rain, on the outside of the plane. It seemed it would never stop.

"Christ, I've never seen it this thick before," Luke said. The words were barely out of his mouth when there was a loud bang and blood sprayed all over the cockpit. It covered the windshield, the instrument panel, and the two men. Both Dennis and Luke were drenched. They were so shocked that for an instant neither man said a thing.

"What was that?" Virge asked in alarm, then jumped down from the top turret and looked into the blood-splattered cockpit. He felt his stomach turn over. "Jesus!" he exclaimed.

"Luke's hit!" Dennis said.

"Dennis is hit!" Luke said almost simultaneously.

"Who's hit?" Virge asked.

Dennis checked himself quickly to see if he was wounded. He didn't appear injured, so he turned to Luke. "It's not me. It must be you," he said.

"It isn't me!" Luke said, just as certain. "It must be you!"

"I think he's in shock," Dennis said to Virge.

"*I'm* not in shock! *You're* in shock!" Luke screamed.

"Val, you better get up here fast," Virge told the bombardier over the interphone.

"I'm on the fucking bomb run!" Val shouted back.

Dennis quickly checked himself again. He tore open his flight jacket and looked at his chest. He felt his face and head. He was in one piece.

"It's not me," Dennis said.

"Me, either," said Luke, looking at both of his arms and legs, then opening his jacket to examine his chest.

"It's got to be one of you," Virge said anxiously. "There's blood all over."

Then he saw it. It was lying on the floor of the cockpit, cut in two. Virge leaned down and picked it up. Dennis's thermos was destroyed. A piece of flak had come through the floor, hit the thermos, and it had exploded. He held up the thermos for Dennis and Luke to see.

"Tomato soup," Virge said, and started to laugh.

The expressions on Dennis's and Luke's faces made Virge laugh even harder. He wished he had Danny's camera to take a picture of them. He'd never seen two men look so relieved.

And then there was a bang louder than any they had heard before. The plane rocked wildly back and forth. Virge was almost thrown off his feet. He caught himself on the back of Dennis's seat.

"What was that?" Dennis shouted.

"There's a hole as big as my dick in the left wing!" Rascal reported from the ball turret.

Dennis, Luke, and Virge looked out the left window. There was a hole, all right. It was about two feet in diameter, directly between Engines One and Two. Flak had sliced right through the wing. Gas was pouring out of one of the wing tanks. It was a miracle the plane hadn't exploded.

"We're losing fuel!" Luke said, watching as the needle on the left fuel gauge rapidly sank.

"Virge, fuel transfer valves," Dennis said, but Virge had already spun around and crouched down to work the transfer switches. With these controls Virge could siphon gas from the damaged tank into one of the intact tanks. The trip to Bremen was eight hours long. They couldn't afford to lose a drop of fuel.

But nothing happened when Virge flicked the left transfer valve switch. "The electrics must be out on the left side," he said. "The pumps aren't responding. I'll have to do it by hand." Virge ducked into the bomb bay, where the emergency hand pumps were located.

"Luke, work with him," Dennis said. "We've got to save as much fuel as we can."

"Two minutes to target," Val reported from the nose.

"Let's drop those bombs and get outa here!" Clay said. The flak was flying thick and fast. Black puffs littered the sky. The rattling on the outside of the plane never stopped.

"Bomb-bay doors open," Val said, pulling the control handle on the left side of the nose.

Virge was working the manual fuel transfer pump at the forward end of the bomb bay when the bomb-bay doors started to open under him. He couldn't help himself—he looked down at the ground, thirty thousand feet below. For a panicky moment he couldn't remember whether he was wearing his parachute or not. Yes, he had it on; he could feel the straps hugging his chest.

A flak shell burst right below the open bomb-bay doors. Virge saw a red flash in the center of the burst, and there was a frantic clicking and tinging as shrapnel bounced off the eight bombs. Virge tensed and waited for the bombs to explode. More than one plane had disintegrated when flak made a direct hit on the open bomb bay. But the clicking and pinging went away. Virge shivered and got back to work.

"Bombardier to captain," Val said from the nose. "The target's covered. Looks like a smoke screen."

This was Bremen: green land and a snaky river, just as the target photographs in the briefing had shown. But the square, gray Focke-Wulf factory could not be seen. Nor could the railroad tracks; the long, rectangular hospital building; or the playground that were the identifying landmarks surrounding the factory. Where there should be a target was only white, low-lying smoke.

It was a smoke screen. The Germans had guessed that the formation was headed for the FW factory and ordered smoke pots to be lit to cover the target and foil the bombing.

"Bombardier, how's that target?" Dennis asked.

"Target totally obscured," Val reported as he made delicate adjustments to the directional knobs on either side of the bombsight. When the two intersecting cross hairs met at right angles directly in the center of the sight, Val would press the bomb-release button.

Although Val couldn't see the target building or the identifying landmarks, the bombsights didn't need a visual point of reference. The information that Val had fed into the Norden was enough for it to compute the approximate location of the factory. The bombs might not be right in the pickle barrel, but they would be damn close. That was as good as Val could do.

"Thirty seconds to delivery." Keeping his eye to the sight, he reached out to the control panel on his left, flipped up the safety catch on the bomb-release switch, and put his finger on the button.

"Bombardier, I need those bombs on target," Dennis said. "The whole group is bombing with us."

"If I can't see, I can't see. I'll be as accurate as possible." Val's finger trembled a little on the button. Easy, easy, he told himself. Wait for the cross hairs to meet in the exact center of the sight.

In the cockpit, Dennis put his finger on the autopilot switch. If he flicked the autopilot off, he would stop the bombing and regain control of the plane. He didn't press it yet; he waited. Perhaps the smoke screen would clear. Perhaps a miracle would happen and he wouldn't have to take the plane back to IP to make another run at the target.

"What do you think you're doing?" Luke saw Dennis's finger on the autopilot switch and knew immediately what Dennis had in mind. Even so, he couldn't believe it was true.

"We came here to bomb a factory," Dennis said. "We're going to bomb a factory even if it means going around again."

"Are you crazy?" Luke said. "Going around on the bomb run is like sending out an engraved invitation to the Nazis to blow us out of the sky!"

"Luke, I'm in command!" Dennis said, cutting Luke off.

"Captain, what do you want me to do?" Val asked from the nose. In a moment the cross hairs would be at perfect right angles. At the most Val would have a few seconds to press the bomb-release button.

"Bombardier, give me a report," Dennis ordered.

"Visibility zero." Val could see nothing down below. The smoke screen was thicker than ever. With his left index finger he increased the pressure on the bomb-release switch.

In the cockpit, Dennis's finger hovered over the auto-pilot switch.

"You do it and we're dead," Luke said.

Dennis didn't disagree. It was suicide to go around on a bomb run. That was asking for trouble. The *Belle* already had a two-foot hole in the left wing. They lost a lot of fuel. Jack was wounded. They had a bad scare when the thermos exploded tomato soup all over the cockpit. The next time it might be someone's blood.

By going around again, Dennis would be risking not only the lives of his own crew but also the lives of all of the crews in the twenty remaining planes in the group.

We've made it this far, Dennis told himself. *We've done a good job through twenty-four missions. No one would blame me if I drop the bombs right now and get the hell out of here. I have a responsibility to bring my men back safe. We're close to the target. Some of the bombs will land on the fighter factory. We can only do our best. No one expects any more.*

But then Dennis remembered the school and school yard right next door to the Focke-Wulf plant. Children might be hiding in the basement, terrified at the sound of the bombers above. There was also a hospital nearby as well as houses. Being close to the target wasn't good enough. Dropping some of the bombs on the factory wasn't acceptable. Every single bomb had to fall on the FW plant. It was all or nothing.

Dennis knew they could do it. They could hit the target right on the money. This was their last chance. After today Dennis and his crew would be out of it. If they dropped the bombs now and there was even a possibility of hitting the school or the hospital, they would have to live with it the rest of their lives. That was not the legacy Dennis wanted for his men. He wanted them to be proud of their service and to know they had done everything in their power to end the war.

The war won't be won, Dennis thought in that split second of decision, *until each one of us gives a hundred percent and then just a little bit more. This is our moment to give that little bit more.*

He flipped the autopilot switch to off. A light went out on the instrument panel. He put his hands on the control wheel. The plane was hit again. He tightened his grip and spoke to the crew over the interphone.

"Men, we're going around again."

12

Phil had been so busy that he'd completely forgotten he was going to die.

When he wasn't poring over his maps to make sure they were on target, he was covering both the right and left guns in the nose. During the bomb run the navigator was responsible for the bombardier's gun, as well as his own. Although the Nazi fighters were staying away because of the flak barrage, they could reappear at any moment.

But when Phil heard the captain say they were going around again, the old fear came back stronger than ever. He tried to fight it down, but panic welled up inside Phil until he thought he was going to die of fright.

That's when he decided to push the bomb-release button himself. If the bombs dropped, there would be no reason to go around again on the bomb run. They could head for home and maybe, just maybe, Phil would survive. It was an act of desperation, but he had to do something. He couldn't die without putting up a fight.

Val took his finger off the button to make a delicate adjustment to the Norden bombsight. The button was two and a half feet away. Val's back was turned. All Phil had to do was lean forward, place his finger on the button, and push. Val wouldn't even know what was happening until it was too late. Phil knew he could be court-martialed, but even that was better than death.

He went for the button. Out of the corner of his eye he saw Val turning toward him. Phil put his finger on the button and was just about to push when Val's strong hand clamped down on top of his. Val tried to rip Phil's hand off the button while Phil desperately tried to press it. Sometimes Phil and Val arm-wrestled for money, but this arm-wrestling match was life and death.

Phil threw himself against Val's shoulder to throw him off-balance, but Val didn't budge and Phil himself was off-balance. Val grabbed Phil's right index finger and bent it as far as he could. Phil gasped with pain. In a second it would snap.

Phil hit his head against Val's. There was a sickening crack, and Val staggered back, stunned. He let go of Phil's hand. The button was free. Phil reached for it again, but before he could push it, Val socked him in the jaw. Val was strong—he was always exercising—and he had quite a punch.

Phil reeled toward his desk, his head ringing like a gong. Quickly Val snapped the safety back on the bomb release and pulled the bomb-bay doors shut.

Breathing hard, Val sat on his cracked seat behind the bombsight. A second later the plane banked into a turn. They were going around again.

Phil leaned on his desk, shaking. He had failed. If there was any doubt in his mind that he was going to die, that doubt was gone. Phil knew he had only one choice left: to accept his death and try to do the best job he could for as long as he had left. He sat down. His headache was back.

A moment after the plane went into the turn Dennis's voice came over the interphone. "It'll take us five minutes to get back to the start of IP. Navigator, give me a position."

Phil was having trouble breathing. His heart was beating very fast and there was a frightening tightness in his chest. *Maybe I'm dying now,* he thought. *Good, let's get it over with.*

"Navigator, did you hear me?" Dennis asked sharply. Val turned and looked at Phil. Phil was sitting at his desk, shoulders slumped and hands clenched. Val blamed himself; he never should have protected Phil. He should have told Dennis that Phil was incompetent, and Dennis would have applied to have a new navigator assigned to the plane. Phil had no business being in the air, Val thought. He had cracked.

"Navigator!" Dennis said for a third time, and Phil seemed to come out of his trance.

"Yes, sir. I'm working on it," he said, turning around and looking at his maps. At first the lines and figures were blurry and far away. He couldn't even remember what city they were bombing. Then he saw a circle drawn around Bremen and everything started to come back to him. His vision began to clear. He got to work.

"Everybody listen," Dennis said over the interphone. "I know you all want to drop the bombs and get the hell out of here. But there are civilians down there, there's a school right next door, and if we don't get these bombs right in the pickle barrel, a lot of innocent people are going to be killed."

"They're all Nazis," Luke said, breaking in. "What difference does it make?"

"Luke, shut up!"

The crew had never heard Dennis speak so sharply to the copilot before. It was a moment before Dennis spoke again. He continued quietly but firmly. No one interrupted.

"I don't want to go around again any more than you do. But we were sent here to bomb a factory, and if we don't do it, somebody's going to have to come back here again and do it for us. Nobody promised us this would be fun and games. It's our job. Ours, nobody else's."

In the tail, Clay noticed the odds he had written on the frosty side window. *3 to 1.* Uh-uh, Clay thought, not anymore. He scratched out the figures. All bets were off now. The casino was closed.

"If we do this right," Dennis said in his light, boyish voice, "it's something we can be proud of our whole lives. That's all I want, believe me."

Horseshit, Luke thought. *Dennis loves this. If he had his way, we'd go around and around on the bomb run like it was a goddamn merry-go-round. He's having the time of his life and he doesn't want it to end.*

"Now let's get back to work. Stay alert and call out those fighters as soon as you see them."

There was silence when Dennis concluded his speech. The only sound was the constant pattering of flak on the outside of the plane. Every man knew what was ahead: a nightmare of flak and fighters. Going around on the bomb run was like winning a game of Russian roulette and then playing again to see if your luck held. It was madness, plain and simple.

But Dennis was captain, and if he thought they could do it, maybe they could. They had no choice. The plane had already banked out of the turn and was headed back to initial point. A moment later a squadron of fighters appeared overhead on the right side of the plane.

"Bandits, three o'clock high!"

Virge spun his turret around to face them. Eugene swung his gun to the three o'clock position. The Nazis were so determined to shoot down the *Belle* that they were flying through their own flak, risking being blown out of the sky by their own antiaircraft gunners. No duck in a shooting gallery ever felt as vulnerable as the crew of the *Memphis Belle* at that very moment.

"Bogie, ten high!"

"Two 109s coming in at eight."

"I don't like being in the lead," Rascal whined.

"Yep, we're the piece of shit the flies are headin' for," said Clay.

It was the attack they had dreaded from the moment they took over the lead. Fighters were everywhere they looked; where there weren't fighters there were those deadly black puffs. The awful pattering of shrapnel on the outside of the plane never stopped.

"Here they come, here they come!" shouted Virge, not knowing whether to fire at the squadron at three high or the bogie at eight. He chose the squadron, but as he opened up his twin .50-calibers, he could feel the bogie swooping down toward the back of his head. There was nothing he could do about it.

In the cockpit, Luke watched the battle impatiently. *If only I had a gun,* he thought, *I'd show those Nazi bastards. I'd send them scattering.* His hand clutched at an imaginary weapon.

"Bandit, twelve o'clock high!" Virge cried out, his voice rising with excitement. "Cockpit, look out! He's heading straight for you!"

Luke saw the fighter headed toward him. It was aiming right at his face.

"What am I supposed to do, spit at him?" he shouted in frustration, then ducked down. The fighter streaked by overhead. Virge pounded his guns at the bandit, but it passed by unscathed. The throbbing of the twin .50s rattled the cockpit. Dennis kept his hands gripped tightly on the control wheel, flying the plane straight and steady. He never batted an eye.

Luke bobbed up as soon as the 190 was gone. He was sick of waiting for Clay to keep his promise to let him take over the tail guns. It was now or never.

"Tail gunner, how are you doing back there?" he asked.

"Jus' fine, Lieutenant," Clay replied in a relaxed drawl, despite the fact that he was fighting off Germans so fast, he didn't have time to sing.

"Let me know if you need help," Luke said.

"Sure will," Clay replied, not taking the hint. "But I'm doing just—"

Clay stopped in mid-sentence. *Damn, I completely forgot about our deal,* he thought. This was a hell of a time, with fighters as thick as mosquitoes in a Louisiana bayou. But Clay's legs were cramped and his back was aching from the reverberation of the guns, so maybe a little breather wasn't such a bad idea after all.

"Oh, right, Lieutenant," Clay said, trying to sound spontaneous. "I *do* need some help back here."

Jesus, Luke thought, does he have to be so obvious? The guy needs acting lessons.

"Tail gunner, what's wrong?" Dennis asked.

"I'm runnin' out of ammo," Clay replied, and Luke immediately unlocked his seat belt, unplugged his oxygen tube and interphone cord.

"I'll take care of it," he said.

"Can't somebody else do it? Right waist, left waist? Can you help Clay?" Dennis asked.

"Captain, we got fighters all over us back here," Jack said.

"I'm the only one not doing anything," Luke said quickly, anxious to get back to the tail before the fighters disappeared again.

"Well, okay," Dennis said reluctantly, "but make it fast. I need you up here."

Luke didn't need Dennis to tell him to make it fast. He jumped out of his seat; squeezed past Virge, who was thundering his guns at the bandits above; and headed into the bomb bay on his way back to the tail.

In the nose, Val was preparing the bombsight for the

170

second run at the target. IP was approaching and he wanted to be prepared. He was worried about the smoke screen. If it was no better than before, he wondered if Dennis would insist on going around for a third try.

Val felt a hand on his shoulder. He turned to see Phil looking at him like a forlorn puppy dog. *What now?* Val wondered. *Does he want me to change his diaper?*

"Val, I'm sorry for that," Phil said, stammering. "You know, for trying to drop the bombs. I just . . ." He shook his head as if bewildered by his own behavior. "I guess I just went a little crazy. I don't know what's wrong with me."

"You're a coward, that's what's wrong with you," Val said, looking straight into his friend's eyes. Phil's eyes were pale blue. They seemed to have become paler during the mission. "A big fucking coward, and you're in big trouble when we get back down on the ground. Now leave me alone and let me do my job!"

Val turned back around and put his eye to the bomb-sight. He did it so angrily that he bumped himself on the eyepiece and probably gave himself a black eye. That moved Phil up one more notch on Val's shit list.

Phil was stung. He didn't blame Val for being mad at him for trying to hit the bomb-release button, but he wished Val would try to understand what he was going through. Val just didn't believe Phil was going to die, no matter how many times Phil tried to tell him.

Maybe he'll believe me when I've got a hole through my head, Phil thought bitterly, *or when I'm falling thirty thousand feet to the ground with my parachute on fire*. Phil wondered if Val would feel bad for calling him a "fucking coward" or if he'd shout "Serves you right!" as he fell.

Phil looked into the sky. A quartet of fighters was poised up above, just ready to come in. *Maybe they're coming to get me*, Phil thought. Now that he'd accepted his death, he felt calm and almost curious about it, as if it were hap-

171

pening to somebody else. The fighters came into range. Phil grabbed his gun. He might as well go down fighting. He opened up.

Guns were pounding in the nose, top turret, radio room, waist and ball turrets. If the Gerries kept up the attack long enough, the *Belle* would go the way of *Windy City, Mama's Boys, and C Cup*. It was only a matter of time.

The voices of the crew tumbled over one another on the intercom.

"Jack, careful! M-190 breaking to nine o'clock."

"I'm going to break him."

"Another one, high at three. Radio operator, hear me?"

"Gotcha. Thanks, Virge."

There was room for only one man in the narrow tail gunner's position, so when Luke reached the back of the plane, he tapped Clay on the shoulder and the two men changed places. Clay eagerly dropped to his knees in front of the big, twin .50-caliber machine guns. Clay watched over Luke's shoulder.

The moment Luke put his hands on the hot guns, he felt an excitement he had never known before. It was as if he'd been impotent for nine months and now had his manhood back. *Just send those fighters to me*, he told the plane-filled sky. *One of them has my name on it*.

Two summers ago Luke had taken his girl to a carnival in Del Mar. He had won so many stuffed animals at the shooting gallery that she let him lay her in the backseat of his car while they were still in the parking lot. Based on this experience, Luke had no doubt that he would get a kill. The problem was, fighters were attacking every gun position except the tail.

"Gerry breaking at three. Getting ready to roll under, Rascal."

"Thanks, Gene."

172

"I think I hit this guy at ten, the one that's smoking. Can anyone confirm? Virge?"

"I wasn't looking. Sorry, Jack."

The other gunners were so busy, they barely had time to make their calls, but Luke didn't even have one Nazi fighter in range.

"Come on, come on . . ." he said anxiously. He had to make this quick. If he stayed away from the cockpit too long, Dennis would become suspicious.

"Tail gunner, see that bandit at seven low? He's too far out for me. He's all yours, Clay." This was Rascal, and it was just what Luke was waiting to hear.

A little speck had appeared down below, dodging fast through the formation. Flying Fortresses were firing at it, trying to knock it down, but it kept coming. Luke hadn't been this excited even when he'd lost his virginity. He aimed the twin .50 at the little fighter and waited.

Don't fire too soon, he coached himself. *Fake him out. Let the pilot think your guns are frozen. He'll come in extra close and you'll get a better shot at him*. Luke had learned all the tricks from listening to the gunners for the past nine months.

The fighter kept climbing. Luke saw himself on the beach at Laguna, telling two wide-eyed girls the story of the day he got his Nazi fighter.

The Gerry was four hundred yards out when Luke started firing. The vibration of the guns shook his bones, and long tongues of fire leapt from the barrels. It felt great. It had been worth waiting for.

Luke didn't let up for an instant as the fighter climbed up past the tail, moving from right to left. He could see his bullets ripping through the black cross on its side and cutting across the swastika on its tail. He had hit it, but the fighter kept climbing.

Luke continued to hammer at the bandit until the Messerschmitt was peppered with his bullets, but it was still in the air. Luke couldn't believe it. He fired off one more

173

round, but it looked like the fighter had escaped. It wasn't fair. By all rights the Nazi bastard should be his, but it was getting away. Luke felt the curses already forming on his lips.

Then it stopped. The Messer simply stopped in midair, as if the pilot had slammed on the brakes. For a moment it hung suspended above the *Belle*'s tail. A brown-black stream of smoke started to pour from the fighter's belly. Luke had never seen anything so beautiful. The fighter's nose tipped downward and started a slow dive to Luke's left.

"I got him!" Luke shouted. "I got him! Did you see?" he asked Clay. "Clay, confirm it! Confirm it!"

The fighter was very graceful as it fell into *Mother and Country*. Its left wind sliced off *Mother and Country*'s tail as cleanly as a pocketknife cuts through an apple. The tail section was completely severed. Luke could see the tail gunner trying to get out. A second later the fighter started tumbling down toward the ground, and *Mother and Country*'s tail section went with it. The tail gunner was still inside.

"No!" Luke screamed.

"It's the rookies!" Rascal shouted. "They got the rookies!"

With the tail gone, the back end of *Mother and Country* dropped down and two men rolled out. Their parachutes opened. They must be the waist gunners. Luke looked desperately for other parachutes, but those were the only two he saw.

The huge plane hung suspended in the air for an instant, like a giant cross. Then it began to plunge toward the ground.

Luke watched with horror. This couldn't be happening to him. Perhaps the pilot would be able to pull out of the dive, Luke desperately thought. Without the tail, of course, this was impossible. The plane started to spin. It spun its way down to Germany below.

174

The second Danny heard Rascal say, "They got the rookies," he let go of his gun, swung around to his desk, and tried to contact the crippled plane.

"*Mother and Country*, come in!" he shouted. He wanted to tell the rookies to bail out. If the plane started spiraling, they would be trapped inside by centrifugal force, pinned to the fuselage walls.

But it was too late. *Mother and Country* was already corkscrewing down to the ground. It went fast. It was a huge green arrow aimed for its target and wasting no time in getting there.

"*Mother and Country*, come in!" Danny shouted again. He flipped a switch and listened, hoping he could pick up the rookie radio operator's voice.

The first thing he heard was a prayer being said, almost shouted: "Our father who art in heaven hallowed be thy name . . ." The young man's voice was very high and shrill; it penetrated the radio static. "Thy kingdom come, thy will be done . . ."

Then Danny heard someone calling for his mother. "Mama, mama!" he called over and over. "Mama, help me!"

They were trapped inside the huge plane. They had seconds left to live. "Get me out! Get me out of here!" someone else was shouting. Danny heard another voice say something about the flaps. It must be the handsome rookie pilot he saw Dennis speaking to last night at the dance. The rookie pilot was trying to control the plane. Even though it was hopeless, he kept giving instructions to his copilot. He was doing his job.

Then Danny heard another voice, a familiar one, calling, "Mayday! Mayday!" It was his friend, the rookie radio operator, making his distress call.

Danny shouted, "Get out! Bail out!" But the rookie didn't hear him.

"S.O.S. Mayday!" he kept saying. "Mayday! Mayday!'' Danny remembered with a pang how he had reprimanded the rookie for calling him on the radio.

Suddenly, silence. No prayers, no shouts or screams or distress calls. Complete silence. It was over.

Luke saw *Mother and Country* when it hit the ground. It was very small by then, and it happened very fast. There was a quick flash and a little plume of smoke and that was all.

Luke tried to imagine what it looked like on the ground: the mangled plane and the bodies of the rookies—what was left of them—scattered. He imagined, after the smoke cleared and the fire was out, that curious people would gather around the wreckage. He saw them taking the rookies' boots and going through their pockets.

"How many chutes from *Mother and Country*?" Dennis asked over the interphone.

"I saw two," said Eugene.

"Yeah, two," said Rascal.

Luke couldn't move. His legs were numb. His body was numb. His brain was numb. He wanted to die. He wanted to be away from everyone, in a quiet room where he could think and try to understand what had happened. He didn't want to be in the plane a moment longer.

Clay saw that Luke wasn't moving, so he grabbed the copilot by the collar of his jacket and yanked him to his feet. He shoved Luke out of the way, fell to his knees in front of the guns, and started firing. The fight was still on. It couldn't stop because of the loss of one plane.

Luke started to stumble back toward the front of the plane, knowing that by now Dennis would be missing him. He only got as far as the tail wheel area, where the fat tire was retracted up into the plane, when he had to stop. He felt faint. He put his hand on the fuselage wall to steady himself. He thought he would vomit.

He had seen the rookies at the dance last night. Most of them couldn't have been more than nineteen or twenty. He'd seen Danny talking to an angle-jawed boy who barely looked old enough to shave. The rookie pilot must have been only in his early twenties. It had been their first mission. They hadn't even gotten to the target.

Luke hadn't meant to kill them. All he wanted was to knock down a Nazi fighter. It wasn't his fault that the fighter fell into *Mother and Country*. It was an accident that could have happened to any gunner. It had happened before and would happen again. It was fate. A gunner didn't control fate.

But Luke *wasn't* a gunner. He was a copilot, and a copilot had duties and responsibilities that didn't include shooting a gun. There was a reason the copilot didn't have a weapon; he had to be ready at any second to take over for the pilot. It was a vitally important job that took experience and maturity, but it wasn't enough for Luke.

I wanted to have a notch on my belt, he thought. *I wanted to have something to brag about. Now I have something I'll have to live with for the rest of my life. I murdered eight men.*

He couldn't remember the last time he'd cried; now he felt tears stinging his eyes. He held them back. No matter how terrible he felt, no matter how much he wanted to die, he knew he couldn't fall apart. If he fell apart, he wouldn't be any good to anyone.

He had made a terrible mistake, but there was nothing he could do about it now. There were still nine men aboard the *Belle* who were depending on him to do his job. If he did it well, maybe their lives would be spared and that would make up for a fraction of the damage he had caused.

Luke forced himself to make his way back to the cockpit. He was determined to stop contradicting Dennis, to obey orders, and to help the captain get the plane back home safe.

"Captain, this is the bomb run," Val said from the nose shortly after Luke took his seat and plugged in his oxygen and interphone cords.

"Okay," Dennis replied. "Bombardier, I'm turning it over to you."

"Roger."

Dennis flipped the autopilot switch. The red light flickered on the instrument panel.

"Luke, right after delivery," Dennis said, "on our way to the rally point, I'm going to take some evasive action and try to avoid this flak. Be ready on rudder."

"Whatever you say, Dennis," Luke replied, then added, "You know what you're doing."

Dennis was surprised. For the past nine months, whenever Dennis gave an order, Luke complained or rolled his eyes or replied in a childish, petulant manner. Luke was a frustrated pilot and made no secret of it. To have him suddenly be so cooperative was a shock; to have Luke compliment him was an even bigger shock. Dennis was touched.

Sometime I'm going to have to thank him for being my copilot, Dennis told himself. *He's not the easiest guy to get along with, but he's a good right-hand man and I'm lucky to have him in the seat beside me. I've never really told him what a good job he has done. He probably doesn't even know how highly I regard him.* Dennis reminded himself to return Luke's compliment when they were out of action and on the way home.

In the nose, Val was looking through the bombsight at the target area. The smoke screen was just as thick as before, if not thicker. He could see a building or two and the bend of the river, but that was all. The rest was covered.

"Bombardier, how does the target look?"

"Like shit."

Val flipped up the safety latch on the bomb release and put his finger on the button. He glanced over his shoulder at Phil, to see if the navigator was going to try for the button again, but Phil was busily firing his gun. He didn't

178

even seem to notice that they were back on the bomb run.

"Captain, I still can't see a thing," Val reported after checking the target once more.

Dennis put his finger on the autopilot switch. He expected an outcry from Luke, but the copilot was silent. Dennis didn't know what he was going to do if the target didn't clear. If he insisted on going around a third time, he might have a mutiny on his hands.

Dennis wondered, *At what point do you decide that you have done your best and that's enough? Are the lives of strangers on the ground more important than the lives of my own men? I won't be able to live with myself if we bomb a school or hospital, but will I be able to live with myself any better if I lose one of my men?*

Outside, fighters were still buzzing the plane. The voices on the interphone never stopped. The gunners were working as a team, fast and efficiently.

"Bandit coming in twelve level. Coming right at the nose."

"I'm on him."

"What about that guy at two?"

"Got him covered."

"Okay, Phil. Just checking."

"Bogie at five low, Clay."

" 'Come to me, my melancholy baby,' " Clay sang.

"Captain," Val said, his voice tense and tight, "we're over the target. I've got to do something. What do you want me to do?"

Dennis's finger trembled on the autopilot switch. Should he tell Val to push the button or should he take the group around again? Dennis was used to making quick decisions and never regretting them, but this one had him almost paralyzed. He increased his pressure on the autopilot switch but still didn't press it. The light on the instrument panel blinked at him.

Val waited for word from Dennis. The cross hairs were

at exact right angles. According to the Norden sight, this was the target. In another few seconds they would be past it. The smoke screen was as thick as ever. Val couldn't see a thing.

Then he could. Val blinked. He had been staring at the target for so long that his eye was dry and strained. He wondered if he was seeing things. He blinked again.

The target was clear. The smoke had thinned a little. The tops of buildings were beginning to show through, as well as a few trees. The top of a square, gray building was directly at the center of the cross hairs.

A photograph flashed before Val's eyes, the target photo that had been projected at the briefing that morning. The S-2 was tapping a gray, flat-topped building with his pointer and saying, "This is our target right here. It's a square building, the only square one in the area, so you can't miss it."

It was the Focke-Wulf factory. It was so perfectly centered in Val's bombsight that he almost didn't want to press the bomb-release button. He wanted to save this moment; savor it a little longer. It was the best bombing of his tour, one for the books, and Val didn't want to let it go. This was the highlight of his entire twenty-three years, and he wanted it to last just one moment longer.

"That's it! That's it!" he shouted. "Bombs away! Right in the pickle barrel!" Much as he didn't want to, he hit the bomb-release button.

The bombs started falling from the bomb bay. Val leaned over the sight and watched them go. They drifted down to the target, as if they were in no hurry. They seemed confident. The little pinwheels on their tails started to unwind. When the pinwheels dropped off, the bombs were fully armed.

As soon as the first five-hundred-pounder came out of the *Belle*'s belly, bombardiers in the remaining twenty planes in the group pushed their bomb-release buttons.

Soon big, olive-drab eggs were being hatched all over the sky.

It seemed to take forever, but when the first few bombs finally hit the target, Val saw the square, flat-topped factory explode. Val didn't shout with joy. He was quiet. He felt strangely sad. He wasn't sure why, but it was something about how men shouldn't spend their time bombing each other. There must be something better the world could do with its time.

He thought of the lives being lost and the energy being wasted in this war. It left him feeling empty and anxious. Val was glad he hit the factory right on the money, but he was also glad that he wouldn't have to do this anymore. He was tired of destroying things. It was time to do something constructive.

The target was a mass of heat and flame and towering gray clouds of smoke, and still the bombs kept falling. The bombing pattern was so tight, the bombs appeared to be dropping on top of one another.

It was Danny's responsibility to see that all the bombs were out of the plane. He left his gun position and ducked into the bomb bay. Occasionally a bomb would get hung up on the racks. That happened two months ago on a mission to Brest. Danny had to kick the bomb out with his foot. He slipped and almost fell out himself.

All of the bombs were gone. A camera in the bomb bay was clicking, automatically taking pictures of the target.

Danny looked down. Bremen was an inferno. As each bomb hit, he could see a bright little flash, like a match flaring up. It was strangely beautiful, but he shivered. He wondered what it was like to have your city attacked. He tried to picture Philadelphia being bombed, but he couldn't imagine it.

With the bombs gone, the plane felt lighter. In the cockpit, Dennis felt lighter. The factory was destroyed, the school and hospital spared. That was his first goal. Now he was determined to achieve his second goal, to get the hell out of here, get back to base safely and have a cold beer.

He banked the plane into a right turn, leaving the fiery city behind. Now he would fly to the rally point where the rest of the group would join him and form up for the flight home.

"Okay, boys," he told the crew over the interphone, "we've done our job for Uncle Sam. Now we're flying for ourselves."

13

But it wasn't over yet. They still had to get home, and the trip back home was always the toughest part of a mission. The Luftwaffe was a little wary of the B-17s when they were filled with bombs, but now that the bombs were dropped, the Nazis would come after the formation with a fury. They were no longer defending their country; now they were avenging it.

So the sky was suddenly crowded with fighters and the fight was on again. They came out of nowhere, twice as many as before, and they were flying in closer than ever. Machine guns opened up all around the *Belle*. Tracers streaked the air. The gunners' voices overlapped on the interphone.

"Two little bastards at four low."

"And two at three low."

"Those are the ones I mean."

"There's two at three *and* two at four."

"Jeeze, it's a goddamn Gerry convention!"

"Another one breaking low to nine!" Jack shouted. "Ball turret, watch it!"

The moment Rascal heard Jack's warning, he twisted the handgrips to whirl the turret into the nine o'clock position. Nothing happened. The turret didn't move. He twisted the handgrips again. It still didn't move. It was frozen.

Rascal thought he must be having a nightmare. He'd had nightmares like this when he first came to England. The bad dreams were so real, he would wake up screaming. But this was no dream; this was scarier than any dream. That bandit was right at his back.

"I'm stuck! Virge! Help!" Rascal screamed. Rascal looked over his shoulder. There it was. It was coming fast and firing. "He's coming right at me! Virge! Virge!"

He pounded on the hand controls. That had worked before—it had caused the turret to unjam—but it didn't work now. He threw his body from side to side. That didn't work, either. He knew the fighter pilot could see that the turret was stuck and he would come in extra close, with four machine guns blasting.

"Do something, Virge! Do something!"

Goddammit, I told that Virgin bastard there was something wrong with the turret, Rascal thought. *That limp wiener didn't believe me. Now I'm a dead man and it's his fault.* One phrase kept repeating over and over in Rascal's head: It isn't fair, it isn't fair, it isn't fair.

When the ball turret exploded, the explosion rocked the ship so badly that Eugene was thrown off his feet and Clay forgot the lyrics to his song.

"What the fuck was that?" Luke asked, not sure he wanted to know.

"Call in!" Dennis ordered, and immediately the men started sounding off.

"Tail."

"Right waist."

"Left waist."

184

Then there was a pause. Rascal was next, but Rascal didn't call in. Rascal might be a snot-nosed brat and a dirty-mouthed braggart, but he always answered a call. A moment later Danny's voice continued the roll call. Danny's voice quavered a little as he spoke his position.

"Radio operator."

"Top turret," Virge shouted, then he yanked out his interphone and oxygen cords, jumped into the bomb bay, and started running toward the rear of the plane as fast as he could.

"Ball turret! Ball turret, call in!" Dennis kept repeating, but Rascal still didn't answer.

Virge charged through the radio room past Danny, who was firing his gun into the sky, and burst into the ball-turret compartment. At first, when he saw that the turret was still in the plane, he thought that everything was all right; that Rascal was playing a joke when he didn't answer the call.

But then, what was that loud bang on the bottom of the plane and why wasn't the turret moving? Rascal always kept the turret going—around and around, up and down—but now it was still. Still and silent.

Virge fell to his knees beside the turret and tried to open the little hatch on top of the turret. It was jammed. Virge swore for practically the first time in his life. "Damn!" he said.

He remembered Rascal telling him that something was wrong with the turret. Virge had checked it thoroughly and was sure that it was in order, but as he tried to pry the hatch open, he was afraid something was defective in the turret mechanism that both he and the ground-crew chief had missed. *Please let him be okay,* Virge prayed. *I never meant anything bad to happen to Rascal.*

The hatch came loose. Virge yanked it open and looked down into the turret. He was sure Rascal wouldn't be there.

Rascal was there. His face was black with soot, he was

bleeding from cuts on his forehead and cheek, but he was there. What wasn't there was the bottom of the ball turret.

The bottom had been shot out, and Rascal was dangling thirty thousand feet above the ground, held to the plane only by the thin canvas safety strap between his legs. His legs were being blown violently up against the plane's belly by the frigid slipstream as he desperately tried to hold on to the top of the turret. Rascal had a helpless, terrified look on his face. Virge hoped he would never have to see that look on anyone's face ever again.

Rascal thought he was dead. The chances of the ball turret being blown apart and the gunner surviving the blast were one in a million. Rascal didn't consider himself the one-in-a-million type. And he was so cold. He had never been this cold in his life.

When Virge's pale face appeared above, framed in the turret hatch, Rascal thought that Virge must be dead, too, and had become an angel. It made sense. Virge the Virgin would make a good angel.

Then Virge reached down, grabbed Rascal's arm, and pulled him roughly through the little hatch. Rascal bumped his head on the way and realized he wasn't dead, after all. The guy he had spent the past nine months tormenting and torturing for not getting himself laid had just saved his life.

As soon as Rascal was back up in the plane, Virge quickly looked him over. Virge expected to see at least a leg missing off the little ball-turret gunner, but he seemed to be okay. Rascal was trembling so bad that Virge thought he was going to fall over. He was also crying. Tears were rolling out of his eyes and freezing on the side of his face. It was interesting to see Rascal cry. He looked just like a little kid.

"You're okay, Rascal. You're safe," Virge said, trying to calm Rascal down. He put his hand on the ball-turret gunner's shoulder. "You're fine. It's okay now."

Rascal grabbed Virge and hugged him. That was the

only thing he could think to do, and anyway, he didn't think about it. He just did it. He wanted to tell Virge how grateful he was for saving his life, but he was too cold to talk. Virge seemed to understand. He kept patting Rascal on the back and saying "That's okay. You're okay" over and over.

If Rascal could have spoken, he would have told Virge the truth: that he was a virgin too. All the stories he told about girls who had done this or that to him were just stories. Girls simply didn't find him attractive. They always said he reminded them of their little brothers. This was not a romantic situation. And Rascal had been too scared to go to a prostitute. Every time he went to London on leave, he promised himself that he would go to a prostitute, and every time he chickened out. He was afraid he would remind the prostitutes of their little brothers too.

The funny thing was, Rascal now realized, it didn't matter if he was a virgin or not. All this time he had fretted and agonized about it, and it really was such a little thing. He had survived. He knew if he could survive having the ball turret shot out from under him, he could survive anything, even sex. And he knew that Virge would survive it too. Meanwhile Virge kept patting him and saying, "You're fine. You're okay. Don't worry."

A second later there was a second explosion, which blew Rascal and Virge off their feet. They fell hard to the deck, not knowing what had hit them.

"Now what?" Luke cried out.

"Call in!" Dennis ordered, and once again the roll call began.

"Tail."

"Right waist."

"Left waist."

There was no answer from the ball turret, but that was because it had been destroyed. There was a pause, and then it was Danny's turn to call in. But Danny didn't call in, and there was no explanation for that.

Thirty seconds before the explosion, Danny was aiming his .50-caliber at a fighter in the six o'clock high position. It was a little far out and he was waiting for it to come into range.

Out of the corner of his eye he saw his camera. He had stowed it safely in the corner of his desk, but the vibration of the plane had caused it to drift across the desktop. Now it was poised on the edge of the desk; in another second it would fall and smash on the floor.

Danny had a full roll of film inside: pictures of the dance last night, the crew in the barracks, and the locker room that morning, snapshots he had taken during the mission that day, including a picture of the rookie. If the camera fell, all of his pictures would be lost. He would never have a chance to take them again.

So Danny didn't think, he just reached for the camera. It dropped into his hands just as easily as the football had fallen into his hands the day before. Danny couldn't believe his good luck. His camera was safe.

He put it in the far corner of his desk. Then he remembered the fighter. The last time he had seen it, it was about six hundred yards out. A Messerschmitt flew at almost four hundred miles per hour. He'd better get on his gun right away. But before Danny had a chance to turn around to his gun, there was a bright flash, like the flash of a photographer's camera, and a white heat.

At first Danny couldn't figure out who was taking a picture of him. He was the photographer. He didn't think anybody else on board had a camera. The flash blinded him. He looked for the fighter but couldn't see a thing. He couldn't feel much of anything, either. *I forgot the fighter,* he said to himself. *That was stupid of me. I forgot the fighter.* A moment later the flash faded and everything was dark.

Virge and Rascal picked themselves off the deck in the ball-turret compartment and ran through the bulkhead door into the radio room. The room was on fire. Radio equipment was smoking and throwing sparks. There was a hole in the roof where the cannon shell had come through. Danny was lying facedown on the floor. Flames were licking at his left boot.

Virge grabbed Danny's arm and pulled him away from the fire. Rascal had already yanked a fire extinguisher off the wall and was turning it on the fire, so Virge ran up the bomb-bay catwalk, ducked through the top turret, and crouched behind the control box in the cockpit.

"Danny's hurt!"

Dennis remained calm. "Val, Danny's hurt," he said over the interphone. "Get back there right away and see what you can do."

"How bad is it?" Val asked.

"I don't know. Just get back there."

Now that the bombing was over, Val was back on his gun. He covered the sky from twelve to three o'clock. "I can't," he said, firing at a Messerschmitt banking down from three high. "There's fighters all over."

"I'll cover your gun," Phil said, crossing the nose and coming up behind Val on the right.

"Maybe somebody in the back of the plane could look at Danny," Val suggested. Phil looked at his partner as if he were mad.

"What's wrong with you? It's Danny!" he shouted. It didn't make sense to Phil. Somebody was seriously hurt, and Val wasn't doing a thing. "You're the fucking doctor!" he added. Every second lost was a second off Danny's life.

Val turned around and looked at Phil. Phil saw something in Val's eyes he had never seen anywhere except in the mirror: pure, distilled fear. It was the kind of fear you could smell. It smelled like sulfur. It left a metallic taste in your mouth. Phil knew it like an old friend.

"That's just it," Val stammered, pulling off his oxygen mask so that only Phil could hear him. "I'm not. Phil, I

189

lied about it. I'm not a doctor. I only had two weeks of medical school before I enlisted. I don't know anything."

At first Phil didn't understand. He thought Val was babbling incoherently. Then it began to clear up. For whatever reason, Val had let the crew believe he was a doctor, when in fact he was barely a student. He hadn't been found out because no one had ever been seriously wounded.

Seeing Val so scared made Phil scared all over again. *No, we both can't panic,* he told himself. *Somebody has to hold on.* Phil took a few quick steps to the rear of the nose and grabbed the first-aid kit off the wall. He held it out to Val. When Val didn't take it, he shoved it into Val's hands.

"Just do it! Help Danny! Do what you can!" he said. He tried not to be angry. He knew Val could help Danny if he just gave himself the chance. But when Val still hesitated, Phil grabbed him and pushed him toward the back of the nose.

It was the thing Val had feared all along, ever since he'd cured Eugene of his twisted ankle way back at the beginning. Val wanted to feel important, to be the big man on campus, so he let everyone believe that he'd finished medical school and only had his internship to complete. He didn't want them to know that he came from a poor family that couldn't afford to put him through school. Now the lie had come back to haunt him. Maybe he'd always known it would.

As Val slowly made his way up the hatch to the cockpit, through the top turret and down the bomb-bay catwalk, he felt sick and faint. He felt like *he* needed a doctor. He wished the walk to the radio room would last forever.

He didn't know what to expect, so when Val first saw Danny, he was relieved. The radio operator was lying facedown on the floor, but there was very little blood. Danny was unconscious and the side of his face was scarred, but the wounds appeared superficial. Perhaps it wasn't as bad as he feared.

Together, Val, Virge, and Rascal turned Danny over on his back. There was a jagged hole on the upper right side of his chest. Danny was hit, all right, but it wasn't necessarily serious. There still wasn't much blood. As long as shrapnel hadn't hit any organs, he would be fine. He was breathing regularly. But his face was pale. He was so pale, his freckles had disappeared.

When Val opened Danny's jacket, he felt sick. Danny's chest was ripped open below his right shoulder. It was a big, fleshy wound. Blood was freezing and crusting around the edges. *He's going to die,* Val thought. *I can't help him.* Shrapnel could have ricocheted inside his chest and torn him all to hell. He needed a real doctor, not a fake.

Val felt Danny's pulse. At first he couldn't even find it. He lifted one of Danny's eyelids. The eye was staring blankly.

Val's hands were shaking so badly, he couldn't even open the first-aid kit. The latch wouldn't work. His fingers felt thick and stiff. Rascal and Virge were watching. *Calm down,* Val told himself. *First give Danny a shot. Then stop the bleeding. Take it one step at a time.* The latch opened.

Val took a syringe from the kit. He had never given an injection before, but he had seen it done enough. As a kid, he always watched the doctors when they gave him a shot. He didn't turn away. He thought it was interesting.

The needle shook as he tried to insert it into the vial of morphine. *Don't rush,* he told himself. *Take it slowly. The most important thing is not to let Danny die in pain. You can't do much, but you can do that.* As soon as he told himself this, the needle went in.

Luke wasn't himself. Usually in action he was jumpy and skittish, always trying to get a view of the fight. Bandits were still out there. Gunners in the front and rear of the ship were firing at them, but Luke seemed to take no notice. He was silent. He kept his head turned away so Dennis couldn't see his face.

"Luke, don't worry about Danny. Val will take care of him," Dennis said, guessing that this was the reason Luke was so low. Luke didn't reply at first. He continued looking out the right cockpit window. When he finally spoke, it was in a quiet, sad voice.

"It's such a waste," he said. "The whole fucking war. There's got to be a better way." Luke was thinking about the rookies but also about all the men who had lost their lives this day. The dying started with the crew of *Windy City*, and now it might end with Danny.

Danny was a kid who wouldn't hurt a fly. He liked to write poetry. He didn't belong in a war; neither did Eugene or Virge or any of them. They all should be back home going to school or falling in love or just having fun. They were kids, mostly. After this they would never be kids again.

"Luke, don't take the world on your shoulders," Dennis said. The phrase seemed familiar; then Dennis remembered who'd said it before—his father.

"Luke, you didn't start the war. Neither did I. We're stuck here and all we can do is try our best. Nobody expects us to be perfect. Only as good as we can be."

Dennis knew this was the moment to tell Luke how much he appreciated him. Luke was down, and maybe the compliment would cheer him up. It would be sincerely meant. Dennis wasn't good at compliments, he rarely gave them; but the copilot looked like he needed a good word.

Dennis opened his mouth to speak, but at that moment Luke shouted, "Fire on Number Three!" Dennis looked out the right window. The first engine on the right side of the plane was blazing. Neither Dennis nor Luke had to be reminded of the seriousness of an engine fire; they remembered what had happened to *Windy City*.

"Cut fuel, feather prop. Fire extinguisher," Dennis said, but Luke was already reaching for the Number Three feathering switch. Closing down the engine would prevent the fire from spreading. The engine fire extinguisher would put out the flames.

But just as Luke was reaching for the fire-extinguisher

192

switch, a fighter materialized right overhead and bullets suddenly raked across the instrument panel, spraying glass and sparks all over the two men.

"Christ Almighty!" Luke shouted in surprise. It was a miracle his hand hadn't been shot off.

"Call out those fighters!" Dennis reminded the crew.

It was too late. Half of the instruments, dials, and gauges on the panel were destroyed. What used to be the fire-extinguisher switch was now a bullet hole. Luke looked out his window. The Engine Three propeller had reversed directions and stopped, prop edges facing into the wind, but the fire was burning hotter than before. At any moment it could spread to the fuel line.

"Prop feathered," Luke told Dennis, "but the fire's still burning. If we don't do something quick, we're going to lose the wing. You're going to have to dive."

Dennis hesitated. Luke was right, diving the plane could blow out the fire, but it created other serious problems. The B-17 was so heavy that Dennis might not be able to pull out of the dive. Or the *Belle* could break apart when he did pull her up. The risk was great but, Dennis decided, the risk from the burning engine was greater.

"Okay, Luke, but I'm going to need you to help me pull out of it."

"I'm not going anywhere," Luke said, tightening his seat belt.

"I'm going to dive and try to blow this fire out," Dennis warned the crew over the interphone. "Everybody hang on!"

Without another moment's hesitation Dennis pushed on the control wheel and the plane began to plunge.

In the waist, Jack and Eugene became weightless. Their feet lifted off the deck and they started to fall up to the ceiling. Eugene grabbed his gun and held on for dear life, but Jack was slammed against the roof. He uttered a string of obscenities.

In the nose, Phil was lifted into the air, along with everything that wasn't nailed or gummed down: Phil's log-book, pencils, compass, maps, and hundreds of spent shells. As he hovered three feet above the deck Phil looked out the Plexiglas nose and saw the ground coming up fast.

The *Belle* quickly picked up speed: two hundred miles per hour, two twenty-five, two fifty. The plane was vibrating so violently, it felt like the rivets would shake loose and it would come apart. The fire on Engine Three still burned.

In the radio room, Val was trying to inject Danny with morphine. It had taken time to find a strong vein on Danny's arm. The radio operator's pulse was weak and his blood vessels had disappeared. As soon as Val inserted the needle, the plane began to shake.

He tried to hold his hand steady, but it was impossible. He was afraid the needle would rip Danny's arm open. Instead it broke. Val had injected only half of the morphine when the plane jerked so roughly that the needle simply snapped in half. He pulled the broken needle out of Danny's arm and reached in the first-aid kit for another.

"Two seventy-five," Dennis said, glancing at the airspeed indicator, one of the few instruments still working on the panel. "We're exceeding maximum diving speed. We better level her."

"The fire's not out." Luke was monitoring the burning engine. "Just a little more."

"A little more and the windshield could crack," Dennis warned him.

"Trust me," Luke said, not taking his eyes off Engine Three. "A few seconds more."

The needle on the airspeed indicator crept past three hundred miles per hour. The control wheel was shuddering so badly, Dennis could hardly hang on to it. The plane groaned and shivered. If he pulled out of the dive right now, the fire would still be burning. If he didn't pull her up right now, he might never be able to.

For the first time Dennis wondered if he was going to lose the plane. If the fire didn't creep up the fuel line to the gas tank and blow the plane apart, Dennis might bury her headfirst in the brown-and-green farmland of northern Germany just below.

"Fire's out!" Luke shouted, then grabbed his control wheel. Without a word the two men pulled back on their wheels. The plane moaned in protest. It trembled. It didn't want to level.

It took every ounce of Dennis's and Luke's combined strengths to hold on to the plane. It was as if they were physically pulling up the thirty-ton machine. Their biceps ached. The ground was approaching fast. The plane still plummeted.

"Come on, come on, come on . . ." Luke sweet-talked the plane. "You can do it. I know you can do it."

That's when the plane started to come up. The nose rose a little, sniffing the air. Then, straining every bolt and rivet in her seventy-four-foot long body, the *Belle* sat back on the wind and leveled as if it were the easiest thing in the world.

In the waist, Jack was slammed back down to the deck. He uttered another string of obscenities. In the nose, Phil was pelted with empty shell cartridges.

The moment the plane was level, Dennis pulled off his oxygen mask. "Crew, we're at ten thousand feet. We can come off oxygen," he told his men over the interphone.

Luke unhooked his mask and rubbed his face. It was rubbed raw. He took a deep breath. He could smell the sea. It smelled good.

"Thanks, Luke," Dennis said.

"Yeah, well, once in a while I do something right," Luke answered.

They had done it. They put out the fire and pulled the plane out of the dive. They had done it together, working as a team. Luke knew that didn't make up for what he had done to *Mother and Country*, but it was a start. You had to start somewhere.

Val quickly filled another syringe with morphine and injected it into Danny's arm. He stopped the bleeding by emptying a sulfur packet into the open wound, then he bandaged Danny's chest as best as he could. Danny was still unconscious. Even the desperate plunge and the shuddering of the plane hadn't awakened him.

"I don't know what else to do," Val said. "He's lost a lost of blood." Rascal, Virge, and Eugene were gathered in the radio room. Phil, Jack, and Clay were at their stations, fighting off the few fighters that were still buzzing around the plane.

"How far is it to base?" Eugene asked.

"On three engines? Two hours, maybe two and a half," Virge answered, quickly calculating.

Val shook his head. "Two and a half hours? He'll never make it."

"Val, help him!" Rascal pleaded, looking down at Danny. His breathing was very shallow. His lips were tinged with blue. His red hair made his pale face even paler.

"What do you want from me?" Val shouted. "He needs a hospital! I've got a stupid first-aid kit!" he said, kicking the metal kit. It skidded across the deck and hit the wall.

After that there was silence. Eugene knelt down beside Danny. He touched his St. Anthony medal and started to say a quick prayer. But the prayer froze on his lips. He remembered something, something he didn't want to remember. His eyes darted down to his wrist. There it was. He was still wearing Danny's lucky rubber band.

He had been so overjoyed when Jack gave him back his St. Anthony medal that he never even thought to return the rubber band. There had been fighters all over, and Eugene had been busy. It was no excuse. *If Danny dies, it's my fault,* Eugene thought, tears stinging his eyes. *I should have just shot him in the back. That would have been kinder.*

Eugene pulled the rubber band off his wrist and slipped it around Danny's wrist. Danny's hand was so cold. Please, God, don't let him die, Eugene prayed. Please help Val think of a way to save him.

A moment later Val spoke. "There's one more thing we can do."

"What? Let's do it!" Rascal said before he even heard the idea. Rascal, Virge, and Eugene all waited for Val to tell them what they could do to save Danny, but he didn't tell them right away.

A week ago Val had heard a story in the officers' club. A gunner had been hit and his arm severed at the shoulder. The crew had managed to stop the bleeding, but the gunner had no chance of surviving the long ride back to England. The plane was over northern Germany. There was only one way to save the gunner's life.

Val knew what he was about to suggest was going to make the enlisted men hate him. He knew they were going to put up a fight, and he was going to have to convince them it was the only way. It was Danny's best, his only chance.

Val took a breath. The enlisted men were looking at him. They had such hope in their eyes. With all his heart Val wished he didn't have to say what he was going to say.

"We can put a parachute on him . . . and push him out."

14

Virge, Rascal, and Eugene couldn't believe their ears. Val was actually talking about throwing Danny out of the plane.

"It's crawling with Germans down there. He'll get picked up and they'll take him to a hospital," Val explained.

"If they don't kill him for fun first!" Rascal said. Rascal didn't understand how Val could make a suggestion like that. With all of Val's medical training there had to be something he could do to help Danny.

"Rascal, it's his only chance," Val said. "Another crew did it. This gunner lost an arm—"

"Yeah, but that guy was conscious," Virge interrupted.

"Danny couldn't even pull the cord," Eugene added.

"We can pull it first and put the chute under his arm."

"He could fall in a lake and drown!" Rascal shouted.

"Val, can't we wait?" Eugene asked.

199

Virge looked at his watch. "We'll be over the North Sea in ten minutes. Then it'll be too late."

"If we're going to do it, we've got to do it now," Val said.

Rascal was looking at Val with such an angry expression that Val almost expected the ball-turret gunner to come at him with both fists. Eugene was fingering his St. Anthony medal and looking down at the still figure of Danny. Virge's broad forehead was creased and his arms were folded tight across his chest—he was thinking. Val knew that any one of them would have willingly changed places with Danny.

Val didn't want to throw Danny out of the plane any more than they did, but it was the only solution. Danny's pulse was weak and he'd lost a lot of blood. He could die at any moment. He needed a real doctor, not a onetime medical student with Boy Scout first-aid training.

Rascal was right, there was no telling where Danny would land. He could land in a tree. He could break both of his legs in the fall. Val had heard stories that the German peasants captured parachutists and killed them with pitchforks. Val didn't want to think about that.

But if Danny survived the landing and was picked up by the Gestapo, he would be taken to a hospital and would receive proper care. It was a slim chance, but if Danny stayed on board, he had no chance at all.

"Look, I'll talk to Dennis about it," Val said to the three enlisted men. "He's the one who should decide."

Val made his way forward to the cockpit. He met Phil at the end of the bomb bay. Phil was the only man aboard who knew Val's secret; at any moment he could tell the crew that Val had lied, that he wasn't a doctor, that he was a fake. Val avoided Phil's look and brushed past him

200

as quickly as he could. Phil followed him into the cockpit.

"Dennis, I've done everything I can for Danny," Val said as he crouched behind the control box in the cockpit. Luke was flying the plane. The coastline of Germany was ahead. "He's not going to make it all the way back to base. My suggestion is we put a parachute on him and drop him out. With luck he'll get picked up and taken to a hospital. I hate the idea, too, but it's his best shot. I told the enlisted men. They're against it."

Dennis didn't answer right away. Abandoning one of his men, no matter what his condition, was unthinkable. It was a violation of his command. Dennis remembered Danny shyly reading his poem right before takeoff. The poem was good. Now he was dying in the radio room and no one could do anything about it. This was the hardest decision Dennis had ever made.

Dennis thought: *Val is a trained physician and I have to rely on his judgment. He wouldn't suggest bailing Danny out unless it was absolutely necessary. As hard as it is to return home without one of my men, I have to do what's best for Danny. His life is more important than my pride.*

Bursts of gunfire came from the rear of the plane. Gerry fighters were still worrying the *Belle*, but only Clay and Jack were at their stations. A decision had to be made; Danny's condition was paralyzing the plane.

Finally Dennis spoke. "I'll go along with anything you say, Val. You're the doctor."

Val almost flinched when he heard the words "You're the doctor." Phil was right behind him. He felt Phil's breath on his neck. Val expected Phil to speak up, to tell what he knew, but he remained silent.

"We just don't have a choice, Dennis," Val said.

"We've got to do it." The words sounded hollow.

"Okay. Tell the men that's my decision, and I don't want any argument," Dennis said in a resigned, quiet voice.

Val started back toward the radio room. He had just stepped into the bomb bay when Phil grabbed him. His hand was tight on Val's arm. Val knew what was coming.

"Please don't do it, Val."

"It's his only chance," Val answered right away, but he didn't look at Phil. He looked through the bomb bay into the radio room. Virge, Rascal, and Eugene were holding Danny in a sitting position and reluctantly strapping a parachute on him.

"No, *you're* his only chance," Phil whispered, "but you're too goddamn chicken to help him."

"Phil, if he stays on board, he'll die." Val's throat hurt when he said it. His mouth was dry; his head ached. *It's not my fault,* he thought. *I've done all I can for Danny. It's not my fault.* The phrase kept echoing in his head.

"He's going to die if you throw him out," Phil said, tightening his grip on Val's arm. "And you know that!"

Val did not deny it. Danny would most likely never survive the fall. But if they dropped him out of the plane, at least Val wouldn't have to see him die. He would be gone. If Danny stayed on board, Val would have to watch him die, and that would be worse. Val couldn't stand to see Danny die.

"Val, you can save him!" Phil said, forcing Val to look at him. "You're not a doctor, so what? You can help Danny, I know you can! Don't give up!"

Val didn't even think, he just said it. The words felt strange in his mouth. He didn't know when he'd said those words last. Maybe when he was a little kid.

"Phil, I'm scared."

Phil didn't hesitate. He knew the answer to that, the only answer that made any sense. Val had given him the answer last night. Now it was Phil's turn to give it back.

"No you're not. You're not scared. You're Val."

Val didn't know why, but he felt a little calmer. If Phil believed in him so much, maybe he could do it. It was worth a try. Val knew that if he walked away from Danny right now, he would never become a doctor. He wouldn't go back to medical school, no matter how much he loved it. If he lost his nerve now, he lost it forever.

If I try to help Danny and he dies, Val told himself, *at least I will have done my best. But if Danny dies and I didn't do everything in my power to save him, I'll go through the rest of my life half alive. Just keep repeating: I'm not scared, I'm Val. I'm not scared, I'm Val.*

"Now go help Danny," Phil said, squeezing Val's arm one more time, then releasing his grip. Val took a breath, nodded, walked into the radio room, knelt down by his patient, and started to remove Danny's parachute.

Men started gathering on the lawn in front of the control tower around 1630 hours. They drifted across the base; some bicycled in. There was no rush. The planes hadn't come back yet, but the first ones would appear soon. It was overcast but warm. The flag fluttered in the breeze. Occasionally it made a sharp snap.

Some young men were wrestling in front of Hangar C. Their laughter was just about the only loud noise; their laughter and the snap of the flag. Most men were whispering or not talking at all. This was sweating it out at its worst.

A softball game was in progress. The score was three to two. It had been three to two for the past twenty minutes. The players were playing so desperately and competitively that you knew they didn't care about the game at all. They were burning up energy. Killing time. Keeping busy.

The top turret gunner's name was Mick. He had hit in the only two runs his team had scored. He shadow-swung a few times and then stepped up to the plate. The plate was an old parachute. The softball was big and sluggish, but Mick intended to knock it halfway across the field. Mick's arms looked like they could do just that.

The pitcher had a hairline that came down almost to his eyebrows, and it made him look mean and determined to strike out the batter. He threw. The pitch was intended to be high and inside, but it curved a little and came in straight over the plate. If Mick could have ordered a pitch from a menu, it would have been this very pitch. He cocked his bat and got ready to punch that melon of a ball right out of the park.

That's when he saw them. They were right over the pitcher's shoulder. The ball sailed right over home plate and into the catcher's mitt. Mick didn't even try to swing, and he didn't hear the curses of his teammates when he let that honey of a pitch go right by.

"There they are!" he shouted, pointing to the horizon.

Everyone turned. Three planes, in perfect formation, were flying right below the clouds. It was a beautiful sight. The drone of their engines was sweeter than music. If three planes could return from Bremen, so could the remaining twenty-one.

The sleepy base woke up. More men gathered on the

control-tower lawn. Those already there stood up, shaded their eyes, and started counting the planes. The softball game broke up. The wrestlers stopped wrestling. The windows of the infirmary opened and men leaned out. The control-tower balcony started to fill.

Bruce Derringer tossed away his cigarette and looked around for the *Life* magazine photographer. Bruce had seen him a few hours before when the photographer had shown Bruce some shots he had taken of takeoff. They were good. The guy knew his business.

"What I want is a picture of them running toward the camera," Bruce said after he located the photographer and the two men were striding quickly toward the field. The photographer, loaded down with a heavy camera bag and tripod, struggled to keep up with long-legged Colonel Derringer.

"I want to see them throwing their hats in the air, going crazy, the plane in the background. We might have to do it a few times to get it right," Bruce added. A plane roared overhead. It was so low, he ducked.

Les Enright awoke. Les always boasted that he could sleep through anything, but the sound of a B-17 always woke him. He looked at his watch: 1705 hours. They were right on time. He wondered if the *Belle* had appeared yet. He didn't want to miss the landing. Les jumped into his boots and headed for the barracks door, the laces flapping at his feet.

Les, with his pear-shaped figure, was the last person who should ride a bicycle, but it was the best way to get around the sprawling base. When he arrived at the control tower, the first plane had landed. It wasn't the *Belle*, but more planes were appearing in the distance. The men on the lawn were shouting the count.

"Seven!"

"Eight, nine!"

"Didja get that one?"

"That's nine!"

"There's ten right there!"

Colonel Craig Harriman joined Comstock on the control-tower balcony. The S-2 was identifying the planes by the numbers painted on their broad tails and checking them off on his master list.

"How many so far?" Craig asked.

"Nine, sir. There's another one. Ten." He checked off *Baby Ruth*.

"The *Belle*?"

"Not yet, sir."

Craig raised his binoculars and looked at *Baby Ruth*. It had no damage, not even a flak hole. It could have been out on a Sunday pleasure cruise. Craig was reassured. Maybe today's mission hadn't been as bad as he'd expected.

But then he remembered that *Baby Ruth* had been the *Memphis Belle*'s left wingman. The two planes should have returned together. They would not have separated unless they were forced to. And where was the *Belle*'s right wingman, *Mother and Country*?

"Another plane, sir," the S-2 reported. Craig Harriman looked far out at the horizon where a little horizontal line had appeared in the sky. He strained his eyes trying to read the identifying numbers on its tail. Craig knew the *Belle*'s number by heart: 124485. *I bet it's the* Belle, Craig guessed. *It has to be the* Belle.

At that moment the *Belle* was over the cold North Sea, flying low at eight thousand feet. The plane had been steadily losing altitude for the past hour. Forty-five minutes after Engine Three caught on fire and they had to dive, black smoke began twisting out of the second engine on the left side of the plane. Dennis ordered Luke to close it down before they had another fire on their hands.

206

The propeller reversed direction, slowed, then came to a halt, its edges facing into the wind. The loss of a second engine meant that it would take twice as long to reach England; it might be another hour and a half before Danny could receive medical help. The icy white-caps of the North Sea were not far below and were getting closer.

"We're running on two engines now," Dennis told the crew over the interphone. "Let's lighten up. Throw out everything you can. We're close enough to home that you can lose your guns."

The men started to toss out anything that wasn't bolted to the ship—flak jackets, flak helmets, ammo, and ammo boxes. The Norden bombsight had done its duty, so the Norden bombsight went. The radio equipment was destroyed, so the radio equipment went.

In the waist, Jack stroked the long barrel of his gun one last time. "Well, Mona . . . we didn't get a fighter, after all," he said a little wistfully.

Eugene always made fun of Jack when he talked to his gun. It seemed like something an insane person would do. A gun was a gun, not a person. And Eugene never understood why Jack had named his gun Mona. A .50-caliber machine gun was the most unfeminine thing in the world. But Eugene didn't make fun of Jack now. Even Eugene was a little sad to throw out his gun, although he never named it.

It was the end of the road. Eugene and Jack could not have said what they were feeling. They had fought their last fight, fired at their last Messerschmitt, called out "Bandit, three o'clock high" for the last time. There would be other battles in the life to come, but nothing to match these battles in the sky.

Eugene threw his gun out the window. He watched it fall toward the water. He expected a big splash—the gun weighed sixty pounds—but it disappeared into the sea with barely a ripple.

Then Jack decided to hell with it and threw Mona out the left waist window. A man can't be in love with his gun. He didn't even watch it fall into the sea, but the thought occurred to him that Mona would be there for a very long time, maybe even hundreds of years.

A gun leads a hell of a life, Jack thought. Then he chuckled, though he didn't know why. He caught Eugene's eye. Eugene smiled back at him. Eugene had more teeth than anybody, and when he smiled, he showed every single one.

Jack remembered the first time he found out that this dunderhead was his partner. Jack had imagined that his partner would be someone like himself; they could cuss and crack dirty jokes and tear London apart on leave. Instead he was stuck with this nervous Nellie, this religious fruitcake. Well, it had worked out all right. Eugene wasn't so bad. *I'm going to have to keep in touch with the Weenie,* Jack thought. *The poor, goofy bastard can't live without me.*

Funny, Danny thought, I guess I dreamed the whole mission. Dreamed that *Mother and Country* went down, dreamed that the captain made us go around on the bomb run, dreamed that brilliant white flash that felt like somebody was taking my picture. There was something else in the dream, too, something Danny couldn't quite remember, something about him getting hit. It was very vague, the way dreams are when you wake up.

But there was nothing to worry about, because it was all just a dream. They hadn't even gone up yet. There was a cloud cover over Bremen, and Danny and the crew were still sitting on the ground, waiting for HQ to make up its mind. Phil was asleep on the wing. Everyone was a little nervous and acting up. The captain told everybody to relax and be more like Phil.

Val asked Danny to recite some of his poetry, then the

rest of the crew started in on him too. Jack played "Danny Boy" on the harmonica. Danny didn't have any poems of his own, so he recited a poem he knew. He let everyone assume he wrote it. It was called "An Irish Airman Foresees His Death."

> "I balanced all, brought all to mind,
> The years to come seemed waste of breath,
> A waste of breath the years behind,
> In balance with this life, this death."

Danny was cold. That didn't make any sense, because there was a warm breeze and he was dressed warmly too. But he was so cold, it hurt. He opened his eyes. That didn't make any sense, either, because he thought he already had his eyes open.

The second Danny opened his eyes he knew the dream wasn't a dream. It was real. They had gone to Bremen. *Windy City* had blown up and they couldn't remember the waist gunner's name. *Mother and Country* had gone down and Danny had heard the rookie radio operator calling "Mayday" over the radio. They'd gone around on the bomb run and hit the target. Danny's camera almost fell off his desk and he caught it just in time. There was a bright flash, like the flash of a photographer's camera, then Danny slept.

Danny was wounded. He knew that now. The flash had been a cannon shell coming through the roof. He didn't know where he was wounded or how badly; his whole body was numb. Val was looking down at him. He had a worried expression on his face, so Danny guessed that he must be wounded pretty badly. He felt tired and wanted to sleep. Sleep was the only way to escape from the biting cold.

The poem worried him. He had taken credit for something he didn't write, and that was wrong. He didn't care anymore if the crew was disappointed or if they made fun of him. *I have to tell the truth,* Danny realized. *I mean, what if something happens to me?* That phrase sounded familiar, but Danny couldn't remember why.

"Yeats!" he said. Val put a hand on his forehead. Danny could see Val put his hand there, but he couldn't feel it.

"It's okay, Danny," Val said. His voice sounded very far away, not close like it usually was on the interphone.

"I didn't write that," Danny said to him. "It's by W. B. Yeats. I couldn't write that."

Val nodded and smiled a little and stroked Danny's forehead. Danny could see the movement of Val's hand, but he couldn't feel it. When Danny was a kid, just the touch of the doctor's hand made him feel better. Val was a doctor, and Danny knew the touch of his hand would make him feel better if only he could feel it.

"Take it easy, Danny," Val said. Val looked tense and worried. There was nothing to worry about. Danny had confessed about the poem. He knew the crew would kid him about it, but that was okay. Everything was going to be okay.

Danny closed his eyes. He felt sleep coming fast. It lapped over him like warm bathwater. The cold started to go away. *That's better,* he told himself. *I'll stay asleep until I'm not cold anymore.*

Val didn't know what Danny was talking about. It was something about writing, but the words didn't make sense. It was bad for Danny to be so anxious. He needed rest. So Val was relieved when Danny stopped talking, closed his eyes, and slept. Val kept stroking his forehead.

Then Danny started to shiver. Val tucked Danny's flight jacket around him tighter, but he still shivered. His whole

210

body shook. Danny's face was white, blue-white, and when Val felt Danny's pulse, his skin was clammy and cold. The pulse was racing. Val pulled up Danny's eyelids. The eye was turned up into Danny's head.

"Danny!" he shouted. Danny was in convulsions. Val didn't know what to do. He was alone; Rascal, Virge, and Eugene had gone back to their stations. There was no one to call on or tell him what to do. "Danny!" he shouted again.

The convulsions stopped, just stopped on a dime, and Danny lay utterly still. His freckled face was slightly gray. The only color in his face was a little red stubble on his chin. Val ripped Danny's flight jacket away and put his head down to Danny's chest. There was no heartbeat. Not a sound. Not a beat.

"No!" Val screamed. This was what he feared. This was why he had wanted to throw Danny out of the plane. Now everybody would blame Val for killing Danny. This couldn't be happening.

"Don't do this!" he shouted at Danny. Val's hands reached for the first-aid kit, even though he knew there was nothing that could save Danny now. A bandage or a bit of antiseptic was no help now.

It wasn't fair. They were so close to home. They had made it through twenty-five missions. Why did someone have to die, and why did it have to be Danny? Danny was the nicest guy on board. He was always taking pictures. He wrote that poem.

"Goddammit, Danny! Don't do this to me!" Val wanted to slug somebody. He wanted to get drunk and get in a fight. He wanted to beat up somebody or have somebody beat him up. But there was no one around to fight with, only Danny. Well, nothing could hurt Danny now.

Val hit Danny, just hit him right in the center of the chest. Danny didn't even flinch. Danny's sternum felt thin

under Val's fist. Val pounded again. And again. He was
going to keep pounding Danny until somebody pulled him
away; then, whoever pulled him away, Val would start
pounding him.

Danny gasped. At first Val thought he had imagined it.
He stared at Danny, hoping it was true, hoping for another
breath, but Danny was as still and cold as ever. *I'm going
crazy,* Val thought. *I'm losing my mind. I want him to live
so much, I'm seeing things.*

Then Danny took another breath, this one deeper and
more solid than the first jerky one. This one came from
way down, a gulp for air, a real attempt to live. Pounding
on Danny's chest had brought him back to life. Val
pounded him again.

"One more! Come on, buddy, just one more!" and,
like he was following doctor's orders, Danny gasped
again and started to breathe regularly. The breaths were
a little shaky and congested, but they came every ten
seconds.

Val put his head to Danny's chest and heard a steady
beat. He felt Danny's pulse. It was faster than it should
be, but it was there. Maybe it was Val's imagination, but
Danny's skin seemed warmer.

Val brushed the hair back from Danny's forehead.
"You try that again and I'll kill you," he said, then put
Danny's jacket over his chest and tucked it around him
tight. Danny was going to make it, Val was sure of it. If
he could survive that, he could survive anything. The kid
would be hurting for a couple of weeks, but he would
recover.

Val didn't understand what had just happened. He didn't
know if it was a miracle or just dumb luck, but he had
saved Danny's life. Phil had been right. Maybe Val wasn't
a doctor yet, but he had the right instincts. He had the
touch.

• • •

A moment later they passed the white, rocky coastline of England. Virge jumped down from the top turret and crouched behind the control box, a happy grin spread across his boyish face.

"Ain't that a pretty sight?" he said.

As green farmland unrolled below the plane, Virge thought that he'd like to come back to England when the war was over. He would like to see more of the country. It was pretty countryside, and the English people were nice. He wondered if a hamburger restaurant would be a success in England.

Virge saw a squadron of fighters in the sky straight ahead and automatically ducked back up into the top turret. He put his hand on the gun controls and got ready to fire. It was instinct. He'd completely forgotten that his guns were gone. They were settling on the cold bottom of the North Sea.

"Fighters!" he cried out. "A whole squadron, twelve o'clock high!"

The fighters were coming right out of the sun. It was Gerry's favorite trick. The sun blinded the gunners and made it difficult to sight in the bandits. There were ten of them. In another twenty or thirty seconds they would attack.

"Look alive, men," Dennis warned. "Fighters, twelve o'clock high!"

"What do you want us to do about it, Captain?" Clay drawled in his thick Southern accent. "You told us to throw out our guns, 'member?"

For the first time as commander of the *Memphis Belle*, Dennis knew he had made a serious mistake. Dennis didn't consider himself perfect by any means, but he prided himself on his foresight and good judgment. This time it looked like his good judgment had failed.

There was legitimate reason to have the crew jettison

213

their guns. With two engines out, the plane was losing altitude and every pound mattered. They had seen their last Nazi fighter almost an hour before. The British coastline was in sight, and the Nazis never attacked so close to England. Never, that is, until now.

Now ten fighters were nosing down at the *Belle*, and there was nothing anyone could do about it. The *Belle* couldn't escape and couldn't return fire. The plane was a sitting target. Dennis wondered if he should give the order to abandon ship, to bail out. He didn't know what to do. He looked over at Luke for help.

Luke was squinting up at the fighters and grinning. A big smile was on his handsome face, and Dennis felt a familiar surge of anger at his copilot. Luke never took anything seriously, not even when their lives were in jeopardy. He wondered if Luke would ever grow up. Dennis was suddenly glad he hadn't gotten a chance to tell Luke he was a good copilot. Luke didn't deserve it.

"Relax, Dennis," Luke said, as if he could read Dennis's mind. "They're little friends."

Dennis took another look. Luke was right—the planes were Thunderbolts. Now he could see the white rings around their blunt noses. They had come to escort the *Memphis Belle* back to base. Dennis felt his face turn hot, but he was so relieved to have been wrong about the fighters that he didn't even mind that he was blushing.

With the friendly fighters by their side, everything would be fine. In less than an hour Dennis would aim his plane at the runway. He would ease her down. Her two big front wheels would touch down, there would be the smell of burning rubber as he applied the brakes, and that would be it. Their twenty-fifth and final mission would be complete. Just anticipating the landing made the strain of the past eight hours fall away.

Dennis felt relaxed. Nothing could happen to them now.

A moment later the Thunderbolts soared overhead, wiggling their wings in hello.

"I love those guys," Luke said, and no one disputed it.

15

Nineteen planes had returned to base. Five were still missing. One of them was the *Memphis Belle*. It was last seen diving down to Germany with an engine blazing.

At debriefing, the crew of *Baby Ruth* told how *Windy City* had exploded in a ball of fire. They told how *Mama's Boys* had listed to one side and slid out of the sky. They told how *C Cup* had its nose shot off and how the Nazi fighter had fallen into *Mother and Country*, slicing it in two. Those four planes would not be coming back. Only the *Memphis Belle* had a chance of returning.

Les Enright, the *Belle*'s crew chief, waited on the lawn in front of the control tower. He tinkered with his bicycle chain and planned what he would do if his ship didn't return to base. He would get as drunk as he could as fast as he could, and then get in a fight. He'd fight until the MPs arrested him and threw him into the brig. When they let him out, he would get drunk again and get into another fight. This would go on until he was either dead or court-martialed. Right now he didn't care which.

But Les wasn't giving up on the *Belle*. If Dennis put out the engine fire, the plane would be fine. The *Belle* could easily fly on three engines. His baby would come back, Les was sure of it. He tightened the bicycle chain a notch too tight and it snapped.

Bruce Derringer was also planning what he would do if the *Belle* didn't come back. He had struck up a conversation with a young pilot who had been on the mission to Bremen. His name was Tony Something—he had one of those Italian names with far too many a's and i's in it. Tony was a lanky fellow with lots of thick, unruly hair.

Tony and his crew had just completed their twenty-fourth mission. Once more and they would go home. If the *Memphis Belle* didn't make it back, Bruce reasoned, Tony's plane would have to do.

"What's your plane called?" Bruce asked, lighting a cigarette for Tony. Tony drew deeply on the cigarette. A little smoke drifted out of his nostrils when he spoke.

"Nancy's Knockers." He pointed to his plane. On the side of the nose was a painting of a voluptuous woman with breasts in the shape of bombs.

"Nancy's Knockers," Bruce said, repeating the name to see how it rolled off the tongue. "We might have to change that," he added, trying to picture the huge bomb-breasts on the cover of *Life* magazine.

Then a dog started barking, and when Les Enright realized the dog was Luke's shaggy mutt, he grabbed some binoculars and looked out at the horizon. There she was. The plane was too far away to read the ID numbers on the tail, but Les didn't need any numbers to identify his plane.

"That's my baby!" he cried out happily.

The *Belle* was flying low, just clearing the tops of the trees. Props Two and Three were feathered. There was a hole in the left wing, a bite out of the tail, and the ball turret was broken in half, but she was back.

Bruce Derringer immediately forgot the young pilot from *Nancy's Knockers* and yelled at the *Life* photographer to get ready. The photographer grabbed his camera bag and tripod and rushed to Bruce's side.

On the balcony above, Craig Harriman was also watching the *Belle* approach. He noticed the two feathered props and the damage to the tail, wing, and ball turret. He wondered if the ball-turret gunner could have survived a direct hit. Craig wanted to see ten men—not nine or eight—climb out of the plane when it landed. Craig had lost forty men today; he didn't think he could stand to lose even one more.

Phil was crouched in the very tip of the nose. The base was directly ahead. It wasn't much, just a collection of hastily built, drab green buildings, but it looked very pretty right now. When the crew first arrived at Bassingbourn, "home" meant Duluth or Rochester or New Orleans. Now it meant this cloudy little corner of England.

It had been quite a ride. Phil wouldn't forget this day for a long time. He had been both cowardly and brave, drunk and sober, ashamed of himself and proud of himself. It was all mixed up together, and Phil didn't know if he would ever sort it out. Just one thing was clear: He hadn't died.

When they were in action, every fighter attack and every flak burst seemed to have Phil's name on it. He had been terrified from the moment the plane took off until the little friends appeared to escort the plane on the last leg of its journey. He had been so sure he was going to die that even now, a few minutes from landing, he hadn't quite gotten used to the idea that he was going to live.

He had a whole life ahead of him instead of just a few hours, and he was going to have to figure out what to do with it. His father wanted him to work at Kodak; his dad had worked there twenty years. Phil might do that, or he might do something else. Everything seemed exciting to him now, even working for Kodak. Grass and trees had never looked so pretty.

In the cockpit, Dennis gave the order to lower the landing gear. Luke flipped a switch on the control panel. There was a high electric whine and the familiar groan of the wheels descending. As he had done a hundred times before, Dennis glanced out his window for a visual check.

"Left wheel down."

Luke looked out his window and started to say, "Right wheel down," as he had a hundred times before. But the right wheel *wasn't* down. It was still stuck up in the belly of the plane.

"Something's wrong. My wheel didn't come down," he said, glancing at the control box to make sure he had flipped the right switch. He had. "What'll we do?"

The wheel could be lowered by hand—a hand crank was stowed in the radio room—but it took time, and Dennis was concerned about the fuel supply. They'd lost fuel when one of the left wing tanks was hit; the fuel quantity indicators were shot out.

"Pull the landing gear back up and we'll belly-land," Dennis said. A belly landing was a drastic measure, but the B-17 was built to withstand it. A crash landing was safer than landing on one wheel.

Luke flipped the landing gear control switch again, but there was silence—no electric whine, no gears groaning.

"Nothing's happening," he said. Virge, who was crouched behind the cockpit in his landing position, reached for the switch and flicked it back and forth. Luke looked out his window at the wheels. "Nothing's coming up, nothing's going down."

"The electrics must be totally out," Virge said, getting no response from the switch.

One wheel wouldn't pull up and one wouldn't go

down. No one had to remind Dennis, Luke, or Virge of yesterday's disaster. A plane had landed on one wheel, then tipped over on its side, pivoted on its one wheel, and exploded. All ten crew members had been lost.

"All right, Virge," Dennis said, "lower the wheel by hand."

"It'll take time," Virge warned.

"Get Jack to help. Luke, you monitor the wheel and tell me when it's down." Then Dennis flipped a switch on the lower wall by his knee. A loud alarm bell rang throughout the plane.

"Take positions for crash landing," he told the crew.

Luke loaded a flare gun. A red flare would alert the emergency vehicles that there was a wounded man aboard. He opened his side window to fire the gun and saw black smoke pouring out of Engine Four. It sputtered and backfired, then the prop started to slow.

"We're losing Number Four!" he said.

"Are we out of fuel?" Dennis asked. Luke looked at the instrument panel, but the fuel gauges had been shot out in the fighter attack.

"I don't know. How long can we fly on one engine?" Luke asked.

"I don't know," Dennis said. "I guess we'll find out."

At that moment Virge was just entering the radio room. Danny was lying on the floor. Virge was watching over him. Rascal, Clay, Jack, and Eugene were taking crash-landing positions, backs against the aft bulkhead.

"Jack, come on!" Virge shouted. He pulled a small hand crank from its brackets on the wall, spun around, and headed back into the bomb bay. Jack followed.

The hand crank for the manual landing gear control fit

221

into a socket at the front end of the bomb bay. Virge straddled the catwalk, attached the crank, and started to turn it.

In flight school Virge had learned about lowering the wheels by hand, but he'd never had to do it. He remembered that the crank turned slowly and took a great deal of muscle. Still, he was surprised by how difficult it was. The first revolution seemed to take all his might, and he recalled that it took one hundred and twenty turns before the wheel came down. Virge was already sweating. He wondered how many he would be able to do before he was exhausted.

Now only the outboard engine on the port side of the plane was keeping the plane aloft. Dennis increased the RPMs and hoped the engine wouldn't burn up. The plane was quickly losing altitude. Dennis would have to land soon, whether the second wheel was down or not. The runway was in view. Luke fired the flare.

On the control-tower balcony, Craig Harriman saw the red flare arc through the sky and felt his stomach tighten. Now that the *Belle* was closer, he could see the many flak holes in the fuselage. He wondered if all ten men possibly could have survived such a battering. They would have to be remarkable men.

Below, on the control-tower lawn, Les Enright was the first to notice there was a problem with the landing gear. He guessed that the electrics had gone out, leaving one wheel up and one down. He knew what an effort was required to hand-crank the wheel down. Les had done it once. It had taken him fifteen minutes. Seeing the *Belle* rapidly descending toward the landing strip, Les knew that the *Belle* didn't have fifteen minutes.

Virge was already exhausted. His arms were burning; in a moment they would cramp and become useless. His hands were sweaty and starting to slip on the handle. The landing gear wasn't even halfway down. He wanted to crank it all the way, but he knew he couldn't. He stepped aside, and Jack leapt into his place.

Virge was dizzy from the effort of cranking the handle; otherwise he wouldn't have fallen. He knew the bomb bay like the back of his hand. The catwalk was narrow and one misstep could be fatal. So when he fell, he cursed himself for being so stupid.

As he fell, Virge remembered one interesting fact about the B-17: the bomb-bay doors opened automatically when they were hit from inside. If a bomb accidentally dropped from the racks, it would trip the doors, they would open, and the bomb would fall out of the plane. So would a man.

Virge's shoulder hit the right bomb-bay door and it started to open. He desperately tried to grab hold of something, a rivet, a strut. His fingernails clawed at the door. His fingernails broke. He couldn't get a grip. His left foot slipped out of the opening. Jack was too busy cranking the handle to notice. Virge's whole left leg fell out of the plane. The ground was a thousand feet below and he was falling toward it.

Virge found himself thinking about the restaurant. It was his one big dream, and now it would never come true. It was a great idea. He could have had fame and fortune.

He would never see his family again. He would never make love again, just when he was starting to get the hang of it. *I don't even have a will,* he thought. *They'll divide up my stuff just like we divided up Becker's things. I wonder who'll get what.*

Then he caught the end of a bomb rack with his right hand, and he was hanging like a monkey, both feet dangling out of the bottom of the plane. The rack cut into his hand and hurt like hell, but Virge was not about to let go.

Goddammit, he swore for the second time in his life, *I want my restaurant.*

He pulled himself up on the catwalk and tried to catch his breath. That was close, he thought. But he wondered if he had saved himself, only to be killed in a few minutes. The wheel was only half down. The ground was getting closer. Jack was turning the crank, grunting and cursing with every turn. His back looked like it was breaking.

Dennis nosed the *Belle* toward the runway. With only one engine turning, the plane was descending by itself. At the most he could keep her in the air another minute and a half. Dennis didn't know if that would be enough time for Virge and Jack to crank down the wheel, but it was all the time they had.

Suddenly, silence. After almost nine hours of the continual pounding of the engines, the silence was startling. Dennis and Luke knew instantly what had happened. It was what they had feared ever since the left wing tank was hit. They were out of fuel. The last drop was gone. Their last engine had quit.

"We lost Number One!" Luke shouted, and immediately the nose of the plane dropped and pointed straight at the runway.

"Flaps!" Dennis shouted, but Luke's hand was already on the flap controls. Together the men struggled to elevate the nose of the plane. Their only chance was to come in evenly. They knew that the second landing gear was only half extended, but there was nothing they could do about it. They were coming down.

In the bomb bay, Virge heard the sudden silence and knew the plane had lost all power. Jack was still cranking the manual landing-gear control, but he was winded and drenched in sweat.

"Hurry!" Virge shouted, although he knew Jack was cranking as fast as he could. They had only a

224

matter of seconds, and both he and Jack were exhausted.

When Phil Lowenthal saw that the right wheel wouldn't come down, he knew he should laugh. It was fate's practical joke—just when he was getting used to the idea of living, the plane was going to land on one wheel, explode, and kill them all.

What had scared Phil before was the unknown. He knew he was going to die, but he didn't know how or when it was going to happen. The fear paralyzed him. Now that he knew what was going to happen, he wasn't afraid anymore. It made him want to fight. He was facing death square in the face, and death didn't seem like such a tough customer, after all.

So Phil ran into the bomb bay, pushed Jack aside, grabbed the crank, and started turning. It did not turn easily, but Phil didn't worry about that. He knew he was stronger than any crank. It was a cold metal object with no feelings or dreams. He had a little of both, and he was damned if he was going to give them up at age twenty-four.

"We're not going to die, we're not going to die!" he kept repeating as he turned the crank. "We're not going to die!" His biceps ached but it felt good. As long as he ached, he was alive.

In the radio room, Val was cradling Danny to protect him from the crash. Danny was still unconscious, but his breathing was steady and his pulse regular.

In the corner, Eugene was saying his prayers as fast as he could. Rascal was sitting beside him. Rascal always made fun of Eugene's praying, but now he prayed along with Gene.

On the balcony of the control tower, Craig Harriman was gripping the railing so tightly, his knuckles threatened to split the skin on the back of his hand.

On the lawn below, Les Enright was talking to the plane,

trying to coax her down. "Come on, baby, come on . . ." he said.

Bruce Derringer watched with horror as the plane dived straight at the runway. The *Life* photographer snapped pictures.

In the cockpit, Dennis pulled back on the control column as far as he could, and Luke worked the flaps, but the plane continued to plunge.

"We're not going to die, we're not going to die," Phil kept saying as he turned the crank. Maybe it was his imagination, but the crank seemed to be turning faster. *It's going to be close,* he thought. *It's going to be a photo finish, but we're going to win.*

Maybe the nose hit a pocket of air, or maybe Dennis found one more fraction of an inch in the control column, but twenty feet above the hard tarmac, the plane lifted. It lifted right up, and half a second later the right landing gear clicked into place. Then the plane came down. The wheels hit hard on the runway and the plane bounced back into the air.

Danny woke. He had felt the ground under him for an instant and wondered if he had dreamed it, just as he'd dreamed they hadn't taken off yet. He was in a little pain, but that didn't scare him. What had scared him so badly was the cold, and he wasn't so cold anymore.

For a moment the *Belle* looked like it was going to come down on its right wing. The tip of the wing brushed the tall grass on the side of the runway. But the plane straightened, hovered in the air for a moment, then settled down as lightly as a bird. It was a beautiful landing.

"Brakes!" Dennis shouted, but Luke was already on them. The tires skidded. The two men smelled burning rubber. It smelled as good as French perfume. The plane began to slow. The runway was coming to an end, so Dennis pulled into the grass. The plane stopped.

An ambulance streaked across the field. "Come on!" Bruce Derringer shouted to the *Life* photographer, and the two men ran toward the plane. It seemed like the whole base was running with them.

In the bomb bay, Virge and Jack were pounding on Phil's back and wringing his hand. He'd done it; he had saved their lives. They called him a hero.

Phil remembered Val's words: "You're a big fucking coward, and you're in a lot of trouble when we get back down to the ground." Val was right—going for the bomb-release button had been an act of cowardice. But maybe being called a coward was just what Phil needed to get off his butt and do something. Well, there would be a lot of years ahead when he could think about the mission, replay it in his head and figure out what he would have done differently. For the moment, though, it felt good to have Virge and Jack pounding on him and thanking him for saving their lives.

The ambulance came to a halt beside the plane. A moment later two medics were setting up a transfusion for Danny.

In the cockpit, Dennis and Luke quickly turned off the controls.

"Wing flaps."

"Up."

"Tail wheel."

"Unlocked."

"Batteries."

"Off.

"Generators."

"Off."

That was it. It was over. They were finished.

Luke had never felt so tired. He didn't think he even had the energy to unhook his seat belt. He did it, anyway, then heaved himself up out of his seat and left the cockpit.

Dennis just sat there. He didn't know what he felt. He was numb. He couldn't believe it was over so soon.

The medics carried Danny out of the plane on a stretcher. Rascal and Jack helped. Danny had his camera. There was one picture left. He asked Val if he could pose for a shot with the whole crew before he was put into the ambulance.

"One picture, Danny, then straight to the hospital," Val said.

"You're the doc." *Well*, Val thought, *maybe someday*.

Bruce wanted a group shot of the triumphant heroes, the golden boys, but when he saw Danny being carried around to the front of the plane on a stretcher, he was annoyed. This was going to ruin his picture, especially since the *Life* photographer was so eager to get a close-up of the bloody radio operator.

"Okay, set him down in front," Bruce said, pretty sure that Danny would be out of the shot. "Let's have the officers in the center. Come on, Phil. Luke, I want you down front."

"Bruce, just take the picture," Luke said. Luke couldn't understand why Bruce had suddenly turned into a callous, pompous ass. He used to be such a nice guy. Luke tossed Danny's camera to Bruce.

Then Danny noticed that everyone was in front of the plane except Dennis. "Where's Dennis?" he asked. "Yeah, we've got to have Dennis in the picture," Rascal said.

A moment later Dennis dropped out of the forward hatch. He was holding the bottle of champagne. He had discovered it in a corner of the radio room, wrapped in a pair of long johns.

Danny had forgotten all about the bottle. He'd bought it in Cambridge a couple of weeks before. It had cost him two months' flight pay. He wanted to surprise everyone by popping it open on the last mission.

It was against regulations to have liquor on the plane. Dennis looked pretty angry. He looked like he was really going to chew Danny out.

He didn't. Instead he whooped and hollered and opened the champagne, and it spurted out.

Dennis never smiled. He was so serious, the crew kept forgetting he was twenty-six. Some of them called him Pop. Seeing him now, laughing and dousing his men with champagne, Dennis didn't seem much more than a kid.

The whole crew started whooping and pounding on each other and jumping up and down. Men crowded around and pumped their hands and ruffled their hair. They were really back. They were really safe. They'd made history. The first crew in the Eighth Air Force to complete their tour of duty.

On the control-tower balcony, Craig Harriman saw the crew cheering and popping the champagne and he relaxed his grip on the iron railing. Everyone had survived, even the wounded man. Craig's stomach unclenched, and he realized he was hungry. He couldn't remember when he'd eaten last. He turned to go back into the control tower.

The war wasn't won, not by a long shot. This was just one small victory. But now Craig knew that it would be won someday. One day everyone, not just the crew of the *Memphis Belle*, could go home. Craig hoped he would be around to see it happen.

Before Colonel Craig Harriman had even gone through the door into the control tower, he was already thinking of the thousand things that needed to be done before tomorrow's mission.

The medics put Danny in the ambulance and it started across the field toward the infirmary.

It was Rascal, of course, who started the running. He

took off after the ambulance and jumped on the running board. This looked like fun, so Virge jumped on the other running board, and pretty soon Dennis and Luke and Phil and Clay and all the others were running after the ambulance and climbing aboard.

The men of the base started running, too, but the ambulance soon left them behind. The sun was just breaking through the clouds. It had been dull and overcast all day, but now the late-afternoon sun appeared and turned the olive-drab buildings a leafy green. The bright cross on the side of the ambulance was the only trace of red.

For the men of the Ninety-first Bomb Group, Bassingbourn, England, this was a day they would remember all their lives. Ten young men had done the impossible. They had beaten the odds. Something was in the air that had never been there before: hope. You could smell it. It smelled like new-mown grass.

In a war where nothing was certain and life was short, every man on that field that day, May 17, 1943, had one thing he could be absolutely certain of: There was going to be a hell of a party that night.

Author's Note

The *Memphis Belle* completed its tour of duty on May 17, 1943. The crew returned to the United States and began a coast-to-coast tour, raising money for war bonds.

The author would like to acknowledge the generosity of the original crew members of the *Memphis Belle*, who allowed me to take liberties with their names and their story.

Many events of the events depicted in *Memphis Belle* were drawn from accounts of other crews in the Eighth Air Force. In writing the screenplay upon which this novel is based, I attempted to portray the experiences of not just a single crew, but also of the experiences of the many men who fought, lived, and died in air battles over Europe during World War II.